Exposure

Kelly Moran

This is a work of fiction. Names, characters, places, and incidents either are the product of the author's imagination or are used fictitiously, and any resemblance to actual persons living or dead, business establishments, events, or locales, is entirely coincidental.
© COPYRIGHT 2016 by Kelly Moran
All rights reserved. No part of this book may be used or reproduced in any manner whatsoever without written permission of the author except in the case of brief quotations embodied in critical articles or reviews.
Content Warning: Not intended for persons under the age of 18.
This book contains graphic love scenes between two consenting people, mild language, and some instances of violence.
ISBN-13: 978-1518803710
ISBN-10: 1518803717
Cover Art by: Kelly Moran
Photo Credit: Dollar Photo Club
Createspace Paperback Edition
First Edition
Published in the United States of America

I wholeheartedly dedicate this book to the two best critique partners in the world: AJ Nuest and Mackenzie Crowne. Fabulous authors who I could not have done this without. Love you guys! xo

Acknowledgements:
Writing is a solitary profession, but authors can't do this crazy gig without help. I'd like to thank authors Alison Bliss and Theresa DaLayne, along with readers Kathy Branfield and Annita Harton, who gave me the inside peek at Alaska and helped so much with making the setting accurate. You were such a big help! Any errors are my own. And I'd like to give a big shout out to my street team, Moran's Moxies, who tirelessly listen to me, offer advice, help promote, and support me without bounds. You guys are the best!

Praise for Kelly Moran

The Dysfunctional Test
"Great escape reading." ~Library Journal
"Sexy, snarky, heart-tugging fun!" ~*USA Today* HEA

***Covington Cove* Series**
"I read in one sitting. A rollercoaster ride."
~*New York Times* bestselling author Carly Phillips on *Return to Me*
"Touching and gratifying." ~Kirkus Reviews on *Return to Me*
"Impossible not to root for this couple."
~Romantic Times on *Return to Me*
"Fun, emotional, and totally engaging."
~*New York Times* bestselling author Carla Neggers on *All of Me*
"Breathes life into an appealing story!"
~Publishers Weekly on *All of Me*

***Phantoms* Trilogy**
"A gem of a writer."
~*New York Times* bestselling author Sharon Sala
"I was completely captivated." ~Bitten by Books
"A thrilling, chilling, compelling, heartrending story."
~The Reading Café
"Absolutely adored it!" ~RhiReading

Chapter One

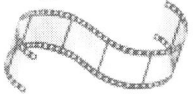

To Want

February 14th:
I have never been anyone of great significance. I was raised in an Anchorage shack of a house to a woman who collected more men than things, and through the years her heart had been broken so many times I had to wonder why she bothered. To her, love was an eternal hope, a way to make this bitter life shine like the many little trinkets she collected. To me, love was something a person gave up a piece of themselves for and never walked away from.

I quickly learned that if I wanted anything, I had to work for it. Where my mother fruitlessly dreamed, I preferred reality. That's not to say my mother doesn't love me. She does, with every fiber of her flighty, spirited being. Our family dynamic left me more the parental figure than her, but I never lacked for anything and my need for control didn't mind.

I worked my ass off to get a scholarship to college and earned a Fine Arts degree so I could move us out of nowhere to somewhere. And I did. In a beautiful location pocketed between Anchorage and Prince William Sound, I bought my own gallery in a postage stamp of a town called Tartok Crest. Not for my own art. I have no artistic talent other than being able to recognize it. I showcase brilliant Alaskan photographs and once a year publish those pictures in a book collection. The tourists eat it up. It was a step up from the little girl who got picked on constantly by classmates or ignored throughout high school as if nothing more than dandelion fluff caught on a breeze.

Since opening the gallery six years ago, my clientele has soared from local artists to some international while still maintaining the intimate charm. Showings at Elements Gallery are in high demand. And though all this seems well and good—a rise from poor upbringings—I remain someone of little consequence. I linger in the shadows, letting the artists shine. That is their place, not mine. I merely give them the means. I much prefer it this way, for reasons I dare not pull from memory or I'll sink back into the dark.

So when my assistant strolled into my office on the second floor of Elements and set her palms flat on my desk one idle Tuesday morning, I had no way of knowing this would be the moment everything changed. A series of dominoes tipping with a clack, all leading to an unexpected and crazy end. One I fear I won't ever recover from.

Raven Crowne took in her assistant's strawberry blonde hair, loosely flowing over her shoulders in soft waves, and sat back in her office chair. Nicole's green eyes were a mix of excitement and shock, framed by the palest, longest eyelashes known to mankind. Her willowy body had caught the attention of more than one artist they'd showcased, and was now wearing an emerald green wrap-around dress that would make Raven look frumpy.

Because Nicole was one of the closest things Raven had to a friend, she never minded her interruptions during the workday, often and pointless as they were sometimes. Besides, Nicole was a work horse and Raven could appreciate that. A smile tugged at her mouth. "Yes?"

"You'll never believe who's downstairs." Nicole's words came out in a rush, as if keeping them inside would cause a rupture.

Raven's gaze darted over Nicole's shoulder to the gallery below. She'd designed her office with a glass wall facing the show floor, partly to be able to see the comings and goings, and mostly to not feel closed in. Standing just outside Nicole's small office was a man in a gray suit. She didn't recognize him, but she'd dealt with a lot of people through the years. Still, she was good with faces, and his she didn't know. He was lean and tall, with dark hair cut too short to compliment his face and hands deep in the pockets of his pants.

"Who is he?" She didn't have any appointments today. They'd just finished a week-long showing for a Washington artist who liked working with black and white. They were two weeks from another show.

"He says he's Hoan Dwell's agent." Nicole squealed and slapped a hand over her mouth.

Raven sucked in a shallow breath, hiding her own excitement. Hoan Dwell, originally rumored to be from the San Diego area, was a photographer unlike anyone they'd ever worked with. He captured women, in various stages of undress, in nature settings. He wasn't particular with his models either. Some were full figured, others thin as a rail. He made them all beautiful. Desired.

She owned one of his photographs from very early in his career, of a blonde in a white sheet, laying over a boulder near a waterfall in Argentina. What was he doing in Alaska?

"What does he want?"

Because, in honesty, Hoan Dwell was out of her league. Though they did work with established artists, none were of his caliber. He'd had shows in New York, Milan and Paris. Most of Elements' bookings were new, upcoming artists and very small market. They'd launched quite a few careers, but…wow.

"He wants to see you." Nicole bounced on her toes.

Raven closed the program she was working on and put her PC into sleep mode. "All right. Send him in."

As Nicole sashayed away, Raven blew out a calming breath and steeled her face to pleasantly neutral. He nodded once to Nicole and ate the distance over the bamboo floors to the open staircase. Smoothing her hands down her plain black dress, she rose when he reached the doorway.

"I'm Raven Crowne, and you are?"

He accepted her handshake with a firm, brief grasp and sat in one of the brown leather chairs across from her desk. "Michael Hawthorn. Agent for Hoan Dwell."

She nodded, as if this were an everyday occurrence. "What can I do for you today, Mr. Hawthorn?"

His eyes were a cold gray, but his smile was assuredly amused. "My client would like to discuss having an exhibit at your gallery."

She leveled him with a stare, raising her brows. "No offense, Mr. Hawthorn, but why would Mr. Dwell be interested in such a small gallery in Tartok Crest?"

"Can you not handle a showing for him?"

Her hackles rose, but she didn't take his bait. "Of course, we can. Elements has every means to accommodate his work. My question is why would he want to?"

"Mr. Dwell's quite enamored with your gallery."

He looked around her office, taking in the burnt sienna-colored walls and small prints she'd collected from new artists. Her tastes ran wide from surrealism to impressionist. If it struck a chord with her, it stayed. She designed the gallery below her second floor loft with clean, simple lines and naturist elements. Glass and wood. Wide open floor plans. Beams carved from indigenous birch. A frosted glass ceiling made to look like branches weaving out, as if standing on a forest floor with sunlight spilling down. She knew what she'd created was a work of art in itself, utilizing both the vast region that surrounded the location and new touches.

It had taken five years, but she'd paid off the investors. The gallery was hers now, and she was so damn proud. He seemed satisfied with what he saw, nodding his head.

And then she realized what he'd said.

She leaned forward and rested her forearms on the black walnut desk. "Mr. Dwell has been here before?" Surely not. She wouldn't have missed that. Then again, Hoan Dwell was an elusive mystery of a man. He didn't have his own portrait taken and he avoided media. Aside from his models, who supposedly signed a confidentiality agreement before posing, no one had laid eyes on him.

"He saw the article on your gallery in Architectural Digest this past fall. He came to one of your showings last month."

The information rattled around in her brain, and she came up blank in connecting the dots. She didn't know what the man looked like, so she wouldn't know if she'd seen him. "He didn't introduce himself."

One corner of his mouth quirked, not including her in the joke. "He's a private man."

"So private he can't strike up a conversation with someone he wants to do business with?"

Slowly, he unbuttoned his suit coat and reached inside the breast pocket, pulling out a business card. He slid it across the desk with one finger. "My card, Miss Crowne. Call me if you'd like to set up a meeting. Mr. Dwell is unconventional. I'm instructed to tell you he'd like to arrange dinner with you, at a restaurant of your choosing, to discuss…things. Soon." He rose from his seat and nodded. "Good day."

Good day? That was it?

She stood. "I need more information than this, Mr. Hawthorn. I don't just meet men I don't know for dinner…"

"Consider it a business transaction, Miss Crowne. You'll be meeting in public."

His tone suggested he knew about her fear of strangers, men specifically. And why. A bead of sweat trailed down her back. Yet this could be huge for the gallery. Bringing in Hoan Dwell would not only secure Elements financially for quite some time, it would bump up their prestige, too.

"I'll meet him. With the understanding that there will be no promises."

Mr. Hawthorn turned to face her fully. "Where?"

Her gaze drifted over his shoulder, as she ran through the options in her mind. It would have to be a location close to Anchorage, with a well-lit parking lot. Italian was too messy, but Salvatore's had booths spaced pretty far apart so they'd have a semblance of privacy. Gino would let her park right out front and see her to her car if necessary. She'd used him before for catering an opening.

She looked up and gave Mr. Hawthorn the address. "I can't make it this week, not until Friday."

He nodded once. "Friday at seven. I will relay this to Mr. Dwell." He reached into his breast pocket once more. "I've been instructed to give you this if you agreed to dinner."

He held out a small pink envelope, non-threatening in nature, but her heart stopped on a dime. Cold sweat broke out on her forehead, a contradiction to the heat that churned in her gut. All pretenses of professionalism gone, she took it from him with trembling fingers and whispered a thank you.

She stood for several moments after he left, staring blankly at the envelope. She'd gotten others like it by carrier with no return address and no signature. One every year on her birthday for the past five years. On occasion, for seemingly no reason, she received three others. Eight in total, and all eight knocking her thoughts straight into orbit without gravity for anchor.

They'd been anonymous, hand-written letters. Until now. Did this mean they'd been from Hoan Dwell all along? She pressed a cool palm to her forehead. What was someone like her doing on his radar? She stared at the envelope, wanting to tear it open and read the sensual words she knew would be inside.

Nicole rushed into her office. "Well? What happened?"

Raven cleared her throat and drew in a deep lungful of air. "Mr. Dwell wants to set up a showing. We're meeting for dinner on Friday."

"Shut the front door! Seriously?"

"Yes." The envelope weighed heavy in her hands. She needed to get out of here. The letter couldn't be read where anyone could see her reaction. Besides, Noah was coming for dinner tonight and she still needed to stop by the market. "I'm going to head home early. Why don't you lock up and call it a day?"

"Will do." Nicole paused. "Why aren't you more excited?"

"I am." She laughed nervously. "Just in shock, I guess."

Nicole grinned. "I can't wait to find out what happens on Friday. Happy Birthday to you! Best present ever. Showing Dwell's work will put us in the black for years."

A smile curved her lips. "I'll see you tomorrow. Thanks again for the bracelet."

Nicole had shown up for work today with a large mocha and a small present for Raven's birthday. The two people who never forgot were Nicole and Noah. The greatest friends a gal could ask for. Her mother had yet to call but, judging by history, she'd ring at ten tonight as an afterthought, her mind too scattered to remember sooner.

Bundling into her coat and scarf, she stepped out into the biting January wind and walked the few feet to her SUV. The seemingly eternal dusk for this time of year would be pitch black in a couple of hours. After hitting the market to pick up fresh crab legs, she made her way to the edge of town and parked in her apartment complex's lot, directly under a street lamp and closest to the entry.

Once inside, she stripped out of her dress clothes and into pajamas. Noah wouldn't care. They'd been best friends since day one of college when they'd literally slammed into each other rushing to class. He'd seen her in worse getups and she'd known him before he made his millions with his tourism recreation company. There were no pretenses with him. For that, she was grateful.

After putting everything away, she started dinner and stared again at the envelope on the counter, teasing her to pick it up. When the first letter arrived six years ago, she'd been frightened at first. Even though arousing in context, it still was an unknown. Unknown sender, unknown admirer, unknown reasoning. She didn't like the unknown. Not even a little. The one surprise party Nicole threw for her birthday a few years ago created a panic attack that Noah had barely managed to calm. The rest of the party had been nice, once she got over the shock.

Noah had found the letters amusing, claiming she should be flattered. Raven wasn't so sure. But then time passed and nothing more than letters came. Except now she knew who they were from and he wanted to meet.

Unable to take the suspense anymore, she lifted the flap of the pale pink envelope and drew out the embroidered card. The stationary was always the same, a cream-colored embossed card with a lace overlay. Simple and elegant. Feminine.

Miss Crowne,

The time has come. I've watched you from afar for many years. You are beauty personified and sexual desire emblazoned. I've kept my distance, imagining the day I could claim that clever mouth in a kiss and ravage you the way you deserve. I believe we're both ready. I know you, and now you will know me.

Ever Yours.

He always signed them that way. *Ever Yours.* There was never anything threatening about the letters, other than him blatantly stating he'd watched her. The sensual quality of his words washed over her, leaving her hot and aching. And embarrassed. They were just words on paper but, for someone like her, who hated attention, it was a rare treat to know she'd been desired by a man to this degree.

He was probably eighty years old and hideously scarred. Or had bodies buried in his yard. Hoan Dwell. What could she possibly have done, or how had their paths crossed, to enlist this kind of response?

Noah knocked and strolled in, closing the door quickly behind him. He chucked his coat and shivered. In his hand was a mountain bouquet of wildflowers, his customary birthday present. Where he got them in January in Alaska was a mystery, but with as much money as he'd acquired, he could afford the luxury.

A thick grey Henley stretched across the muscles of his shoulders and chest. His jeans were faded in all the right areas and low on his hips. He kicked off his boots and offered a grin, sexy as all get out with the light stubble on his jaw.

It really was a crying shame they never slept together when they first met. Just to test the waters. After all this time, though, it would be awkward. He never seemed interested in her that way, and her curiosity had been fleeting back then. Noah was the only man in existence she trusted. It would be unwise to focus on anything other than what they had. Soul mates in best friend form. She wondered what made her think of old memories now. Perhaps the manifestation of another letter. It always threw her off-kilter.

Shoving his sandy blond hair off his forehead, he walked deeper into her apartment, blue eyes scanning her kitchen.

"Happy birthday. Whatcha cooking?"

She accepted the flowers and buried her face in them, inhaling the bit of spring she missed. "These are perfect."

He shook his head. "Most women want roses and diamonds. You want wildflowers and pajamas. You're easy to please."

She wasn't easy to please, and that was part of her problem, why she'd been stuck in this rut the past few months. Or years. Nothing ever felt...satisfying. "We're not dating. If we were, you could buy me roses and diamonds. I'm happy with these. You can drain your bank account on the revolving door of women you sleep with." Grinning for effect, she reached for a vase and filled it with water, setting the flowers inside. "Seriously, I love them."

Ignoring her jab at his dating life, he peeked at the stove. "And I love your food. I repeat, what are we having?" The last part of his sentence was spoken in a whisper as his gaze landed on the letter she'd set on the counter. "You got another one." His jaw tensed.

She leaned against the counter. "I know who's sending them, too. Remember me talking about that photographer, Hoan Dwell? I have one of his earlier prints."

His gaze didn't meet hers. "Yeah. A bigwig who snaps pictures of women rolling in grass or fondling a tree stump. They're from him?"

His lack of surprise was interesting. From the moment the first letter arrived, Noah had been as interested in her response to them as the mystery of the notes themselves. He knew her well. They'd go to hell and back for each other. She'd told him things she wouldn't dare repeat to anyone. So he knew she needed control in most things, especially her private life and who she dated. But he didn't know how dark, how deep that control brought her at times.

The conversation she wanted to have with him about the matter would need to be treaded lightly. As much as she loved Noah, no way was she going in the metaphorical bedroom with him. She wanted, *needed* his advice, though.

"He wants to meet."

Slowly, his gaze lifted to hers. Saying nothing, he picked up the letter and skimmed it before tossing it down. "What do you want to do?"

"I'm curious, I'll admit, but…"

"But what?"

She shrugged. "He could be a mass murderer."

Noah crossed his arms. "He's taken six years to initiate a meeting. Odd serial killer behavior if he was one." He took a step forward as if to touch her, but retreated quickly and braced his hands behind him on the counter.

For whatever reason, they didn't touch. They hadn't hugged or kissed on the cheek or even patted each other on the arm in all the years they'd been friends. If it was strange, she appreciated the oddity in it. Raven had the distinct impression they had this unspoken rule for her benefit, though it was never anything they'd discussed.

"What should I do?"

He studied her in that intent way she'd grown to be comfortable with. For all his banter, he'd had a serious side since his parents died shortly after sophomore year. "Are you going to do it? Meet him?"

She turned and pulled the roasted potatoes from the oven. "I said I would. I told his agent so when he came to the office today."

"Doesn't mean you won't back out."

"My word is golden, Noah. You know that." She lifted the steamer from the pan and placed the crab legs on a serving platter. When he didn't respond, she looked at him.

His jaw muscles were getting a workout. "I also know that anything that puts attention on you scares you to death. Whoever this guy is, whatever he ultimately wants, you should at least think about it." He paused a beat. "You can't keep the world at arm's length forever. Your depression is under control. You're stronger than you give yourself credit for."

She moved the buttered asparagus to the small kitchenette table, ignoring his words. He cared. She got that. But he had no idea how much every day was a struggle just to get out of bed. And all because of some long ago nightmare she didn't even remember, outside of small flashes in her memory.

With tense movements, she set the table. "As my friend, shouldn't you be scared he's going to chop me up into tiny pieces and feed me to the bears?"

He sighed. "No."

She turned to glance at him.

"My security team will drive you to and from wherever you're going."

His security team. Well, that was new. She'd never actually seen the men herself, other than Max, who'd been Noah's guard since…She scratched her head. Since forever.

Noah was an only child to a former New Jersey state senator who'd hit the wrong end of an ice patch doing eighty with his wife in the passenger seat. The family had left him money, but Noah accumulated more than he knew what to do with after college when his adventure startup took storm. His time and resources were valued. Some people took advantage of that. Plus, that much wealth brought out the crazies. Two years ago, Noah had been shot at over the watch he was wearing. As beautiful and scenic as Anchorage was, the drug abuse rate was near the highest in the country, as was the suicide rate. People were desperate.

He uncorked the wine and poured two glasses, handing one to her. "I'd never encourage you to do something that would put you in danger. I care about you." Before she could respond, he sucked in a breath and drained half his glass. "And as someone who cares, one of these days you need to let me take you out to dinner. It's really crappy you're cooking on your own birthday."

She smiled, moved by him. "Says the man who has his own cook."

"I do not. I have a housekeeper who occasionally cooks for me. And she's not as good as you."

She laughed as he tried to shrug it off. He could do that for her every time. Knock her from *freaked out* to *that's better* in three seconds flat. "Seven days a week is hardly occasional."

"Six days a week." He sipped his wine. "Every night but Friday."

"Which reminds me, I'll have to rain check our typical dinner this week. I'm meeting…him that night." She swirled the wine in her glass. "I like cooking, especially for you because you appreciate it." Plus, she was much more comfortable at home with him in her PJs. She started to regret her decision to meet Mr. Dwell. Again. Why venture out of the normal when she had perfection in her best friend right here? "I care about you, too."

Downing the rest of his wine, he quickly refilled the glass. What was up with him tonight? He was broody and, if she didn't know any better, she'd swear he was nervous, too. Perhaps it was just a bad day at work. Being the owner of Gallivanting Adventure, he didn't get out on the trails or boats or up in the planes as much as he wanted. He hated being stuck behind a desk.

She took a sip of wine. "Everything okay?"

He tore his gaze away from the pink envelope on the counter and focused on her. After a beat, he grinned. "You bet. Let's eat."

After they'd cleaned up the kitchen and Noah had gone home, she went into her bedroom and pulled down the shoebox from the top shelf of her closet. Not one to collect memories, she wondered why she kept the items inside. Nonetheless, she set the box on her bed and scrolled through the other letters Hoan Dwell had sent previously. Each of them were short and sultry, teasing her with a craving she'd skillfully banked until it was appropriate and safe to bring it out.

What did he see in her? And what were his expectations?

His letters spoke of desire. Wanting her. Savoring her until they were both spent. She didn't take lovers lightly. Research and observation went into each decision until she made contact. What if she was attracted to him, wanted to go the distance and be with him?

Would he be disappointed when he learned her likes in the bedroom? They weren't exactly traditional and most men didn't take well to what she needed. Sex, any form of intimacy, had to be on her terms. Hoan Dwell didn't seem like the type of man to submit control. Not that she knew him, or anything about him, but someone who obviously knew women as well as he did and was able to capture them on film with stark clarity, as if peeking into their souls, couldn't possibly be willing.

She shook her head. There had to be something really wrong with him if it took him this long to initiate. All this wondering was moot. All that would happen come Friday night was a dinner, a business discussion about a showing for his work, and then she'd head home.

Alone.

Setting the letters back inside the box, her knuckles brushed over something cool. Her fingers closed around the polished stone and removed it. No larger than a thimble, it fit into her palm. It had fit into her hand when she was just a girl, too. The only thing she had from her life before her mother adopted her was this. Just a rock and some vague memories.

She sighed and put the lid back on the box, replacing it on the shelf. Then she took a hot bath until her mind was blank and her body lax. Except when she crawled between the sheets, sleep eluded her.

Chapter Two

Noah Caldwell stood facing the rear window of Salvatore's and resisted the urge to run his fingers through his hair again. Instead, he smoothed his tie down and shoved his hands in the pockets of his Armani suit. He despised suits. A privileged upbringing and a lucrative business meant they were required, but he didn't have to like it. He'd much rather be in Raven's apartment in his jeans but, for what was going down tonight, it was vital he use class and distance from their usual routine. He'd had Gino set up their table in the private room and threw enough money at the man when he'd booked the reservation to close the restaurant tonight just for them.

He blew out a breath. Raven was going to flip out. She hated surprises, hated anything that didn't fit into her perfect order. And wasn't this the biggest whopper of them all? *Yes, best friend of mine. I am the famous photographer you've admired for years, and the man who's admired you.* For going on ten fucking years. Six of which he'd been secretly writing to her.

He'd had his reasons for not stepping up. Damn good reasons. He still wasn't sure this was a good move. There was more than the danger of losing their friendship involved, such as Raven losing her life if the wrong people caught wind. He was assured by the right people that things were finally settling down on that front. He'd never risk her, not for anything, but damn if he could do this anymore. Week in, week out. Dinners and movies and laughter. Pretending not to want her. Watching her fight the darkness and acting as if she didn't wish for more. He'd wanted to be that more for a third of his life.

"She's here." Max Gerard looked up from his phone near the doorway to the private room. "The car just pulled up."

Noah turned from his bodyguard and closed his eyes. Acid ate away at his gut while his heart shoved against his ribs. Ten years boiled down to what happened in the next ten seconds.

He glanced around the dimly lit twelve by twelve room. The only table was theirs, small and intimate, decorated with a white tablecloth and a candle. On the cream stucco walls were prints of Italy Gino's parents had brought over when they acquired citizenship. Noah knew because he'd once asked during a dinner to celebrate his and Raven's college graduation. The scent of chicken cacciatore wafted from the kitchen, rolling his stomach. How was he supposed to eat? Then again, that would require her sticking around long enough for dinner to be served.

Everything he'd rehearsed in preparation for this moment died on his tongue as she walked across the Moroccan tile floor in her black heels. His gaze traveled up her shapely legs to the slight hourglass curve of her hips, past her small, perfect breasts and briefly paused on her regal neck. He could spend hours kissing that spot right there.

She wore a red dress he'd seen her use for openings, one that fit her slender curves and stopped just above the knee. Her black hair was down—he loved it down—and trailed just to where her shoulder blades cut her back. Not for the first time, the contrast of her alabaster skin to her ebony hair stole his breath.

Snow White, she may resemble, but Big Bad Wolf was what lived inside.

Her red lips parted in shock. Her cat-like brown eyes, which had hazel flecks he couldn't see from this distance but knew were there, rounded as she froze inside the doorway. She looked around the room and swiftly back to him, clutching her black purse.

"Noah? What are you doing here?"

Keeping his hands in his pockets when he wanted to plunge them into her hair, he maintained a neutral stance and expression to not frighten her. He nodded to Max. His bodyguard left the room in silence.

He looked back at her and forced a swallow. "I think you know why. Take just a moment to think about it."

The arch of her brows drew together in thought. From across the room, he waited her out. He knew the moment the puzzle fit together in her mind by the subtle drop in her jaw. She figured out the algorithm in switching the letters of his name around. Noah Caldwell. Hoan Dwell. Had he encouraged chatter about his alter ego when she brought up the name now and again, her clever mind would've figured it out sooner. He'd deftly avoided the topic until the time came to tell her the truth.

The time was here and he still couldn't fathom it.

"No," she whispered and covered her mouth.

Was that a shocked "no" or an "oh shit" no? Cautiously, he stepped forward. "Yes."

She pressed a hand to her forehead and gazed heavenward. "I'm such an idiot."

He ground his molars. "You are not an idiot. I was careful not to—"

"Why?" she squeaked. "After all this time, how could you keep this from me? Why would you?"

Since she wasn't spitting nails or running for the hills, he walked to the table between them and pulled out a chair. "Sit and talk with me." When she made no attempt to move, he gently smiled. "I'm still the same guy you knew five minutes ago."

Several beats passed before she walked to the table and sat. Rounding her chair, he chose the one next to her instead of across. She set her purse down and avoided his gaze.

For the first time in their friendship, he touched her. More than a casual hug for a picture or shoulder bump. Just a graze of his knuckles over the back of her hand, but the impact was staggering. Her skin was as soft as it looked. Setting his hand back in his lap, he watched for her reaction. Her fingers flexed on the table, but she offered nothing else. She stared at the space between them.

He shook his head. "Still the same guy, Raven."

Her gaze lifted to his, the golden flecks swimming in warm cocoa. "Are you?"

Pouring them both a glass of wine, he leaned back in his chair, trying to find the words. "There are things about my earlier years that prevent me from being in the spotlight. Too much attention could draw out people from the past. That's why I have the pen name."

Her eyes widened. "What kind of people?"

The kind that killed his whole family.

Fiddling with the stem of the glass, he sighed. "The kind who would hurt those I love to get to me." Or get to a specific someone, but best he stick to himself for the moment. Having her undivided attention, he lifted one corner of his mouth in a smile. "It took many years, but that part of my past is being reconciled. I could no more tell you the truth before now than I could shut down my creative spark and stop taking pictures."

"You could have trusted me, Noah."

"I do trust you. It's them I don't. For your own safety, it had to be this way."

She offered a slight shake of her head, looking fearful for the first time ever in his presence. "What did you get into? What is this all about?"

"It's being handled. Which is why I'm telling you now."

"That's not an answer." She took a healthy drink of wine, her hand shaking when she set it back down. "When did this mysterious past occur? We met freshman year of college. You had to have been a teenager at the time to..." She straightened in her chair. "Was everything between us a lie?"

He took the barb and pretended it didn't rip apart his organs. "My withholding of this particular incident led to needing to lie about Hoan Dwell. Everything else was truth." For the most part.

A waiter came in and set down their salads. Noah kept his gaze on her while she politely smiled at the young man as if she wasn't about to freak out over loss of control. He waited until the plates were arranged and the waiter was about to walk off before speaking.

"Could you tell Gino to hold the main course for a little longer than we discussed?"

"Yes, sir."

Alone again, he studied her. He couldn't get a handle on how this was going. How was that for power? "Look at me."

She briefly closed her eyes before sliding him a look.

"One day I'll tell you everything. For now, just trust me that I won't hurt you. I lied so you couldn't be hurt." He should've kept the part about his past out of the equation, but to have her learn later would only make her irate. Reasonably so. He'd lose her for good. And later would come. He couldn't hide from himself, from this, anymore. He needed to see where this led.

More than that, she needed it. She lived behind control and reason, never feeling the magnitude of what could be. He hoped he was deep enough in her comfort zone for her to let go. He had his own control issues, but at least he knew why his were in place.

She took a bite of her salad, staring at the plate as she chewed. Hands down, he'd bet she wasn't even tasting the food, nor was she hungry. He picked up his own fork and ate, waiting for the next deluge of questions.

Setting down her fork a few minutes later, she was obviously done processing. He didn't think it would take her long.

"You're rich. As in millions. Plural."

Where was she going with this? "I've been a millionaire more than half our friendship." It'd never bothered her before.

Her gaze pinned him, lethal in its intensity. "From Noah Caldwell's adventure company or his inheritance. That guy likes jeans and hanging out. Noah isn't pretentious. Hoan Dwell is a whole different brand of rich. God, Noah. You could buy Texas!"

That was stretching things a margin, but she was pretty close. No sense in saying so. He didn't like the way she was using third person to distance herself from him either. "What does money have to do with anything?"

"I live in a two-bedroom apartment. You..." Her face twisted as she blushed. "I made Friday night dinners when you should've been at five-star restaurants." She glanced around the room as if just seeing it for the first time. "We're eating in Salvatore's."

"I like this place and your cooking. What's the problem?" It's not as if Salvatore's was a slum. Didn't she know him well enough by now to know he preferred fish fry to caviar?

"This is so humiliating." She rose and pushed away from the table.

He caught her hand before she could retreat, panic making him tighten his fingers. "Don't go. We're...not done." They hadn't even broached why he really brought her here.

She stopped and swallowed hard, gaze directed at the floor. This wasn't her. Raven looked shit in the eye and always came out on top. Pushed through problems like she fought her depression because she was the furthest thing from weak.

He ducked his head to look in her eyes. "I'm still the same guy." This was the third time he'd said that, but it wasn't sinking in. "Please sit back down."

After what must've been a severe internal battle, she finally nodded and reclaimed her seat. He drew air into his lungs, unaware he'd been holding his breath. Except now he had no idea how to touch upon the topic of...them. He'd had ten years to dredge up a trillion variations of this conversation, but none seemed right when faced with the moment.

Gino came out of the kitchen, wiping his pudgy hands on an apron wrapped around his girth. A wide smile split his ruddy face as he patted both their shoulders. "How are we doing, folks? Ready for my famous chicken cacciatore?"

Noah glanced at Raven for an answer, but she was frozen in her seat. He looked at Gino. "You bet. Bring it out."

Raven pinched her forehead. Noah didn't have time to say more because Gino returned and two steaming plates of food had been set down in front of them.

"You two lovebirds enjoy."

She flinched—actually flinched—and swiftly grabbed her fork as if to cover the move.

Alone again, he pushed the chicken around his plate and gave up. His stomach couldn't handle food, not with her sitting there as if he'd slapped her. He withdrew an envelope from his breast pocket and slid it across the table.

She eyed the familiar stationery. Her lips gaped open, as did her eyes.

He'd been on a shoot in Paris when he'd seen the design. Feminine, durable and unique, it reminded him of her. So he'd bought two boxes and became her secret admirer. At the time, it was the only way he could have her. He wrote about the things he wanted to do, how he ached to touch, and left it at sending one every year for her birthday.

"Open it," he said.

She hesitated, but eventually picked up the envelope. Her gaze scanned the paper. Confusion marred her forehead. "It's blank."

Was that disappointment in her tone? He'd wondered how the letters had affected her. She'd, of course, told him about them as they came, but she'd never given any indication to how they made her feel. Did they turn her on, make her want to touch herself? Did she blush when reading his words and desires?

He leaned forward. "You know everything now. What I want, what I've always wanted, and who I am. Anything else I wish to relay—or do—will be directly to you. No more cards."

Finally, her gaze whipped to his and held. Something intense and altering shifted between them. The charge hit his midsection and ramped his pulse.

Her gaze dropped to his mouth and back up. She was thinking about it. "You've never…" She tucked a strand of hair behind her ear. "We're friends. We've never crossed that line. You never gave me any indication you wanted more."

But he did. Oh, he wanted so much more. What started out as respecting her as a friend grew to admiring her as a woman, then downshifted into the fiercest need to have her. "Have you ever thought about it? You and me. More."

"No," she said quickly. Too quickly to be believed. "Well, maybe when we first met, there was attraction. But the buddy thing…" She shook her head. "I guess I just put it out of my mind. I didn't think you saw me like that."

"I want you." As if she hadn't figured that out by now, he decided to ram it home. Maybe hearing it from his lips would get her head in the game. Gel the truth.

"But…you don't do serious relationships."

Tricky point. He didn't. With reason. And she would be no different. He loved her, lusted to the nth degree for her, but he wasn't in love with her. He was pretty confident he was incapable of the emotion. If he couldn't fall in love with Raven, he was lacking the genetic makeup to do it at all.

"You don't enter into relationships either." He'd yet to see Raven with a man. He knew she'd had them, many by his calculation based on their conversations, but they were short lived and she always walked. She was only in it for the release. She'd also been extremely unsatisfied with her sex life. She'd said so herself.

Oh, the things he could do to her.

"What is all this about then, Noah?" A hard glint lit her eyes. She was bouncing back from the shock. Good. "Letters and a private dinner and rogue secrecy. What are you after?"

Now they were getting somewhere. He barely had time to register the relief. When all was said and done, he didn't want to lose what they had before she learned the truth. He took a sip of wine, holding her gaze. "What I'm after is visceral. Basic. You and me, giving each other pleasure."

Her pupils dilated as warmth hit her cheeks. There was an unmistakable hitch to her breathing as she leveled him with a look bordering on carnal. "You want to risk ten years of friendship for a short..." She waved her hand. "Fling?"

If he thought for one second that was the case, he wouldn't be here. He could count on one hand the number of people he trusted, and she was one of them. "We're a different breed of people, Raven. You and me, we're not like everyone else. We can keep the sentiments out of sex." He took in her beautiful features and grew semi-hard. "One month. That's what I'm after, what I'm proposing."

She reared back, eyes wide once more. "Is this the part where you bust out a contract? Set hard limits and give me a safe word?" Her eyes narrowed. "I'm no submissive, Noah."

Interesting how her thought train stopped at that station. No. A sub she definitely wasn't. "Are you a dom?" he toyed.

She glanced away, not answering.

He stilled.

Oh, hell no. No way. Did he have her all wrong? That certainly changed things. Even though he wasn't a submissive, would never be, his shaft responded, thickening against his inseam. "I'm not into BDSM. Handcuffs maybe. Toys definitely. But whips and flogging and collars? Not even a little." Not that there was anything wrong with that world, it just wasn't his thing.

Returning her gaze to his, she let out a breath, relief relaxing her features. Why didn't she just deny the suggestion if she wasn't a dom?

Her gaze searched his. "What then? Why one month?"

A quiet clatter came from the kitchen. His gaze darted to her plate and back to her. "I tell you what. Let's eat, and we can get into specifics after."

Her lips thinned. "You expect me to eat?"

"Yes. I wouldn't want to insult Gino after he went to all this trouble. Besides, knowing you, you haven't eaten or slept much since my agent walked into your office on Tuesday. Am I right?"

Just like that, she was back to old Raven. A twist of her lips and she picked up her fork. "Touché."

Taking a sip of wine, he dug in, suddenly hungry after all the heavy junk was out of the way. She was still here. Nothing would come between them. They were solid.

After swallowing the last bite, he wiped his mouth on a napkin and was pleased to see she ate half her meal. Raven never did have a large appetite, so it was decent work for her.

The waiter came and cleared their plates, asking about dessert. Since Noah was pretty sure Raven wasn't on the menu, they declined.

He topped off their wine and leaned back. "Back to my offer. One month, you and me, and then it's done. We go back to friendship and Friday night dinners discussing everything from our businesses to politics." In his experience, anything longer than thirty days got the heart involved. He didn't think Raven was like other females in that regard, but he wouldn't risk it.

She shook her head. "Sex changes things."

He raised his brows. "Has it ever before? For you? Have you wanted to get married and breed perfect little dark-haired children after sex with any of your partners?"

He knew the answer was no. Any other possibility and she'd be barefoot and pregnant. Every guy she set her sights on would capture the moon in a box if she desired such a thing. Her not being the other half of someone's whole was because she didn't want to be.

She sighed. "You know I haven't. But we know each other. Don't you think that makes this different?"

The most interesting fact about this conversation, this entire night up until now, was she never denied interest. Not once did *I'm not attracted to you* spring from her lips. Scooting his chair back, he grabbed the arms of hers and drew it flush, trapping her knees with his. When her breath caught, he leaned closer and inhaled her scent in the curve of her neck where her pulse beat wild.

Rain. She smelled like rain. Through the years, he wondered how she mastered that, and he'd yet to watch a storm where he didn't think about her.

Her hand landed on his forearm, warm and steady, fingers tightening. "Noah?" Her hot breath fanned his cheek, catapulting his erection from hard to painful.

"I want you. And I usually get what I want. I had to wait too long to have you already." He lifted his head, the rasp of his shadow filled the quiet as his cheek brushed hers. Her lashes fluttered to half-mast, cementing his belief she wasn't unaffected. "You live inside your head, where all the power is overruling your ability to enjoy. It's why you've been unsatisfied with your partners. I want you, and you need to learn to let go."

He leaned in to whisper against her mouth, until even a tremble couldn't come between them. "It'll be so good, Raven."

A noise trapped in her throat. Desperation? Frustration? Didn't matter. He'd made his point and she understood.

Slowly, he rose and set a stack of bills on the table. He waited for the desire to clear from her eyes while he shoved into his coat. After several beats, her questioning gaze lifted to his, her fingers tightening over the chair arms.

He buttoned his coat, hiding all traces of her affect on him. "You need time to process. When you make your decision, come to my condo on Friday night. One week. I'll cook for you for a change." He paused, shoving his hands in his pockets so he didn't touch. "Please wear that dress. It does things to me you can't begin to understand."

Grinning when her eyes widened, he nodded and walked out.

Chapter Three

Halfway through Monday, any progress in regards to work was shot. Raven couldn't get what happened with Noah out of her head.

Ten years they'd been friends, and she'd never once suspected. Never suspected his alter ego or his attraction to her. Worse, she couldn't decide what to do about Friday. Should she go to his place?

She remembered when he bought the condo, right after his company took off, around the same time she started looking into investors for hers. She hadn't been there since the first walk-through other than a handful of times. Noah knew she preferred the comfort of her apartment, and rendered her that small vice.

God. He was Hoan Dwell. Rich, mysterious, sexy Hoan Dwell. The man who captured women through his lens with innate skill. Noah had liked photography back in college. He used to carry a camera around wherever he went. It had been years since she'd seen him with one. So he could better hide what he was doing? Who he was?

The tight ball in her stomach clenched. He'd lied to her. For years. Part of her didn't think she'd ever be able to trust him again. His reasons seemed valid, but he was so vague in responding that she couldn't figure out what he was talking about. Just what or who haunted his past? And why were they so dangerous he was forced to lie to even her?

He was like two different people. The comfortable best friend who she could talk to about anything and the intense artist who'd shown up to dinner. The things he'd said, the way he'd said them…the letters!

Noah. All along. Her cheeks flamed even now. Heat pooled in her belly.

How strange that her mind didn't question the shift from *hands off* to *please touch*. She didn't even like being touched. It was illogical not to have a grace period when merging from friends to lovers. Right? Not her. He'd awakened something she thought dormant. And all he did was talk.

Typically, any kind of attention made her go into a full blown panic attack. When control was out of her hands, she couldn't function. Though she was embarrassed, Noah didn't make her afraid. He made her want. A temptation she never once risked. But for him, with him, could she let go? He'd said as much that night. He knew her hang ups. Most of them. It had been so very long since sex was enjoyable that she'd almost screamed yes when he presented the proposal.

Nicole strode into her office and set two containers on her desk. "Lunch is served." She looked up and did a double take. "What's wrong?"

Raven drew in a much needed breath and waved her hand. "Nothing. Let's eat. Thanks for picking this up. I was going over my notes for my two o'clock."

A new artist on the scene named Vincent Soreno had contacted Elements out of nowhere and wanted to set up a meeting. Raven had Googled him and came across an amateurish website where he claimed to be a photographer for hire. Weddings mostly. They didn't do that kind of thing, but she'd give him a chance to show his stuff if he had anything worth viewing. His site said he was from the east coast in the lower forty-eight and a recent Alaskan transplant. Something about him rubbed her the wrong way, but damn if she could place what.

Probably just her nerves about Noah. Last Friday night had thrown her world off its axis.

"Are you ever going to tell me how the meeting with Hoan Dwell went? Are we doing an exhibit for him?"

Raven opened and closed her mouth, pushing her Cobb salad around in the container. "We didn't get to discuss a lot of business," she hedged. Noah had created a pen name and kept that person a mystery to the world for a reason. Even if she didn't know why, she would respect that. Had to if it was a safeguard. Except Nicole was her friend and her assistant. If they did a showing for…Hoan, then Nicole was a big part of the process. "We have another meeting set up for later in the week."

Perhaps she should keep the tentative date with Noah after all, if for no other reason than to discuss the showing. They never did get to that during dinner, too wrapped up in…other matters.

Nicole swallowed and wiped her mouth with a napkin. "What was he like?"

God. Now she felt like she had to lie to Nicole to protect him. This was spiraling out of control fast. "He was…not what I was expecting." She almost laughed at the understatement.

Nicole's eyes lit. "Is he handsome? Dark and broody? Eccentric? I'll bet he's Hemmingway crazy. Am I right?"

This time Raven did laugh. "Not crazy or reclusive. He's just very private."

"And handsome? Give a girl some hope here."

Laughing again, she reached for a water bottle. "Very attractive, yes." Understatement of the century right there, since she was on a roll with them. Nicole would die if she ever found out Hoan was Noah. They ran in the same circles, often hanging out together, but Nicole harbored a secret crush on Noah.

"Sigh," she said and flipped her long hair over her shoulder. "I hope I get to meet him."

Raven bit the inside of her lip. Nicole was Noah's typical romp. Pretty, curvy, and blonde. Noah didn't bring his women around, but they talked about their trysts, and her assistant was exactly the kind of woman he attracted. Not her. So why his interest? Then again, Hoan wasn't particular with his models. Thin, voluptuous, tall, short, dark, light…he didn't discriminate. She wondered if he bedded all his models.

After lunch, she started playing with the promotional flyers for their next viewing in a week until her two o'clock arrived. Nicole sent him right up, so she closed the program and rose to shake his hand.

Vincent Soreno was easily six and a half feet tall, with a head shaved bald and muscles encasing muscles. Mr. Clean meets Hell's Angels. He was younger than she expected. Early thirties, perhaps? A sleeve of tattoos ran up and down each arm. In one hand he held a leather jacket, in the other a portfolio case. A white T-shirt molded to his massive chest like second skin and his jeans were ripped. He certainly didn't dress up for their meeting. This guy took wedding pictures?

Doubt niggled in the back of her skull but she gestured to a chair. A quick glance told her Nicole was helping customers on the show floor, so Raven was alone. Their security guard, Duane, was near Nicole's desk, eyes watching both Nicole and the second floor.

Raven sat down and forced a smile. "So, you're from the east coast. Where, exactly?"

When he spoke, she swore the earth shook his voice was so deep. "Queens, New York. My family owns a pizzeria. I do the wedding photos gig on the side."

This guy was a walking contradiction. "What brings you to Alaska?"

"I vacation here every year. Fishing and whatnot."

She nodded. "Our gallery only showcases Alaskan terrain, whether urban or scenic. If we were to do an exhibit, one of your pieces would end up in our book collection we publish yearly. It gets circulated around nationally."

He nodded.

This was like pulling teeth. "Let's see what you brought and go from there."

She took the portfolio from his monstrously large hand and skimmed through. A sense of unease washed over her again when she noticed the vast difference between the event photos and the scenic ones. For one, the clarity and lighting was stellar in the journalistic style wedding portraits, but the edge was lost in the scenery pictures. Like snapped by two different people. Still, he had an eye.

Without looking up from her study, she said, "If we were to do business, we'd need you to sign off that all work is yours for copyright purposes. Will that be a problem?"

"No."

Okay, he wasn't getting the hint. "To be clear, there would be a lawsuit if any work wasn't your own."

He tensed and her heart stopped. Ordering herself to calm down, she sent him a level gaze when everything inside exploded in fear. He made no movement, other than a chilling glare that left her bereft of warmth.

Eventually, he nodded. "I took the photos."

She let out a quiet breath. Talent or not, and that was up for debate, she didn't want to work with this guy. But she went into this business to help struggling artists, so what did it say about her if she let silly feelings get in the way? And wasn't she stereotyping him just based on appearance?

Sitting back, she chewed on her lip. "Let me be honest, Mr. Soreno. You're much more intuitive and clean when you study people. I'm going to hold my decision and give you the opportunity to bring me some fresh shots. While you're visiting our area, take some pictures and bring them back here. We'll talk some more."

His jaw ground, but he nodded. "Thank you for your time. I'll be back."

Trying to accept his words for what they were and not a threat, she rose and held out her hand. "It was a pleasure meeting you. We'll talk soon." With security in the room next time.

Unsure whether it was the uneasiness from her interview with Vincent Soreno or the bomb Noah threw at her feet, Raven was jittery the rest of the week. She had this urgent need to look over her shoulder wherever she went and she found herself triple-checking the apartment locks at night. Crazy as it sounded, she felt like she was being watched.

By the time she stood in front of her full-length mirror on Friday night to size up her appearance, she was about to crawl out of her skin. Back and forth she debated whether to head to Noah's condo or skip it. To bail would send the message she didn't want the offer of one month with him. They'd resume things how they always had been before, as close friends with mutual interests. To go meant...

She blew out a breath. "This is nuts."

She wore her skinny jeans with knee-high black leather boots and a sapphire sweater that clung to her chest and dipped low in the back. Sexy, but not blaring. Casual, not too eager. Since when did getting dressed for Noah require five wardrobe changes?

Fisting her hair, which she'd left down, she turned from the mirror and paced. Hadn't she been stuck in her routine? Sexually frustrated and climbing the walls? It had been two months since she'd stepped foot inside the bar club to study another partner for contact. Two months, no sex. No release from tension and no control.

Noah would cure that. He'd offered. They'd have to talk over logistics, but what would be the harm? He was right. The way they viewed sex was reciprocal. The friendship, as long as he held up his end of the bargain, would remain intact.

Screw this. She grabbed her purse and headed to the front door, shoving into her coat.

The drive to his condo was roughly twenty minutes. He lived in Anchorage in the wealthier area away from the ports, so she used the time to think some more. Not that arguing with herself solved much.

She sat inside her SUV for a few minutes and stared at Noah's building, wondering why she had the suspicion everything in her orderly world was about to drastically change if she entered. Shaking her head, she exited the vehicle and stopped at the security desk to check in. She recognized the attendant from previous visits and smiled.

"Well, Miss Crowne. Long time no see." The wrinkles around his eyes deepened when he grinned. Lyle, an elder black man and skinny as heck, couldn't offer much by way of security, she assumed, but guests needed a key just to enter the building, never mind to use the elevators. He was probably there for appearances.

"Okay if I go up?"

"Yes, ma'am. Good to see you again."

"And you, as well," she called over her shoulder.

She keyed the pad to access the elevator and did it again so she could hit the button for Noah's unit on the twentieth floor. The car delivered her to the very top with a swish and the doors dinged open. A short hallway stretched before her and then his door. She hadn't realized she hadn't moved until the elevator started closing on her.

"Stop being a baby," she muttered and strode forward.

Instead of using her key, she knocked. The soft strums of jazz pulsed from behind the solid oak. She preferred blaring rock herself. Just as she was about to knock again, the door swung inward and Noah's form filled the space.

His jeans were slung low on his hips. A black tee clung to his defined torso when he raised his forearms to the doorframe and leaned into them. In one fell swoop, his gaze raked her from head to toe, leaving her more exposed than if she were naked.

One corner of his mouth quirked. "I thought I said to wear the red dress."

"When have you ever known me to follow orders? Besides, I may not be here for your...offer. Maybe I came to discuss Hoan's showing for Elements." Or maybe she could add lying through her teeth to her resume on Monday.

After a short but intense study, he grunted and stepped back. "Enter."

Noah's condo was excessively large for just one person. Two bedrooms were through the living room and down a short hallway. The master bedroom was in the opposite direction. She toed off her boots, walked through the foyer and past the ginormous stainless steel kitchen on her left, where something zesty was cooking.

She set her coat and purse on a stool by the high granite counter and glanced around while stepping down into the living room. There was mahogany hardwood throughout. His sofas were gray leather, the walls a stark white. Pictures hanging in an orderly fashion were the only pop of color. All were shots of his company, Gallivanting Adventure. Two were of his float plane flying low over the mountains, one of his charter fishing boat near a glacier, and several smaller photos of his ATVs and bobsleds.

The space spoke of wealth, but didn't flaunt it. His company brought in a sizable amount without the commission from Hoan Dwell, yet he lived in a three thousand square foot condo instead of a mansion on the harbor. Maybe he was right in what he'd said at Salvatore's last week. He was still the same guy who'd befriended her on their first day of college.

Turning, she found him staring at her from the kitchen. Palms flat on the counter and his gaze burning into her, he didn't move so much as one tense muscle.

Wondering what he was thinking, she cleared her throat. "You haven't changed anything since I was here last." She was pretty sure it had been six months ago, when he'd had some of the guys over to play poker.

His expression gave nothing away as he took his time answering. Finally, he straightened and moved to the stove. "Why would I change anything? The decorator did a hell of a job."

She climbed on a stool and crossed her arms on the counter. He looked strangely at home in a kitchen. Bare feet, forearms flexing as he stirred, he was rather sexy, too. His blond hair was carelessly disheveled, as if not bothering with it other than to finger comb. Heat flared in her belly, traveling lower as she watched him.

For ten years she'd shut off the part of her mind that allowed herself to think of him as anything other than just Noah. Now, she drank him in, considering. He was right about a few things. It would be so good between them. It had been too long since she felt this punch of lust.

Dizzying.

"You keep looking at me like that, Raven, and we won't make it until dinner. I'll chuck it and take you right there on that counter." He looked at her over his shoulder. "No doubt you'd taste better."

She sucked in a ragged breath through her nose and looked away, imagining them doing just what he said. There was a problem in his scenario though, and damn if she knew how to bring it up.

Stepping away from the stove, he poured her a glass of wine and slid it across the counter. "Drink. You've gone pale."

Taking a healthy gulp, she didn't even taste the wine as it traced a warm path to her belly. "What are we having?"

"Gumbo. My mother's recipe." He dished some into two bowls and walked them to the table in an alcove, where a basket of homemade bread sat between two placemats. A couple of candles were flickering in the dim light.

He'd gone all out.

"I didn't know you could cook."

"That remains to be seen. I followed the recipe, so we'll find out." He pulled out a chair, waiting for her to accept.

Crossing the room, she took a seat and he pushed her chair in, ever the gentleman.

He sat across from her and sipped his wine. The candlelight made his turquoise eyes darker, like the cusp of twilight. Shadows played over his face, the light scruff on his jaw and the angular edges of his features, and she could see the inner artist in him as if she'd been slapped. She didn't know how she'd missed it before. His gaze took in everything at once, dissecting and analyzing, as if seeking the perfect shot.

The silence was uncomfortable, laced with everything unsaid. Nervous on how to begin, she picked up her spoon and took a bite.

Spice exploded on her tongue, both full-bodied and rich. With only a slight after bite, it warmed her from the inside out.

"This is really good. I think you need to chip in now and again on our weekly dinners."

Breathing out a laugh, he began to eat. "It's not bad. Not as good as Mom's."

She couldn't imagine his loss. They'd been together in his dorm room sophomore year when he'd gotten the call that his parents had died. He'd been understandably devastated. "Do you have a lot of her old recipes? I could make some of her dishes if you want."

The look he gave her had all that old turmoil resurfacing. He blinked it away. "That would be nice," he said roughly.

After a few more spoonfuls, she grabbed a slice of bread and shifted the conversation. "About Hoan. Did you really want to set up a show or was that just a means to…other things?"

He stilled, staring into his bowl before carefully setting down his spoon and meeting her gaze. "Those other things being me wanting you beneath me while I pound into you and having you scream my name? Those other things?"

The breath left her lungs and damn if she didn't get damp between her legs. "You don't mince words."

"I don't see the point. I told you what I wanted. I can finally be honest in my desire to have you. I don't think you understand just how frustrating the past ten years have been."

He shook his head and took a sip of wine while she focused on drawing in oxygen.

Setting his glass down, he pushed away his empty bowl. "I'm more than willing to do an exhibit at Elements any time you want, with the understanding that my agent represent me at the show. Hoan doesn't do appearances."

"You always come to my events."

"As Noah, and I'll be there on Hoan's night. As Noah."

She still couldn't grasp what was so important about the secrecy, but she nodded, trusting him. "Okay. I'll have Nicole check our schedule and see when would work for both of us. Do you have any pieces ready?"

He crossed his arms over his chest and leaned back. "Several." The pause was lengthy and she could see he wanted to say more. Glancing up at the ceiling, he sighed and then returned his blue gaze to hers. "I want you to pose for me."

"What?"

"I've imagined it in my head a thousand times. My ultimate muse. Your black hair against a snowy backdrop. I have several places in mind, several poses."

She snapped her mouth shut. "I'm not a model." She was attractive, sure. But sexy in the way he wanted from his girls? Not a chance.

"Most of my models weren't professional when they posed. Some I stumbled on in my travels and went with it."

"No, Noah. I'm not...I hate the idea." To be the focus of all those eyes when the photos went public, to be the center of all that unwanted attention made a violent shiver tear through her body.

He shrugged. "I have a month to change your mind."

And that was the other thing. But first..."Do you sleep with all your models?"

"Not all, no. The women I've been with, the ones from around here, were a one night only deal. I couldn't risk anything long term to draw suspicion to them. You're a friend and were around before..." He shook his head. "Hoan's arrangements are different. The shoots take a week or two, and he's under an undisclosed identity. I could be a little more lax with him."

Her head was spinning and it wasn't from the wine. "Lax, how?"

Frustration marred his brow, his patience waning. "They all signed confidentiality agreements and never knew me as Noah. When, *if* I took them to bed, I had the opportunity to have a week or two with them before parting."

She nodded as if this all made sense. It didn't.

He stood and collected their dishes. "Take your wine over by the fire. I'll get this cleaned up and be right in."

Manners had her wanting to argue and help him clear the table, but she wasn't sure what to make of their conversation and needed a moment. Picking up her glass, she made her way over to the balcony doors next to the stone fireplace. The flames crackled and hissed, creating warmth to contrast the drafty hardwood floors.

Unable to sit, she looked out past the balcony at Mount Spurr's range. From this distance and so high up, the appearance seemed like they were at peak level. On top of the world. Which just made it that much easier to crash down.

What in the hell was she doing here? With Noah, of all people? Solid, stable, perfect for her peace of mind, Noah. Had she ever really known him at all? Was everything they'd shared all these years just a means to sex? The kind of sex she couldn't possibly give him.

A tight band squeezed her throat, making her head pound and her vision sway. Her chest constricted. She couldn't draw air.

Then Noah was behind her, taking the wine from her hand and setting it aside. She leaned back into him, into his irresistible heat to stop the tremors. Solid hands dropped on her shoulders, kneading the tense muscles and easing the edges of panic from her body. His thumbs traced up the curve of her neck and into her hair.

He leaned closer, his breath hot against her jaw. "Breathe, baby. It's just me. Breathe."

Yes, it was just Noah. Noah was safety.

But he'd called her baby. A pet name or term of endearment he'd never used.

She sucked in a lungful of air and held it precious seconds before exhaling. He smelled like cinnamon and a trace of spicy aftershave, the scent equally a turn on and a comfort.

His hand trailed over her ribs and around her body, drawing her closer to him. The hard ridge of his erection pressed into her backside and the realization of the past week caught up to her. In a daze, everything that happened seemed like a story in a book, not her life. Reality, her reality, never unfolded like this. Handsome billionaire artists didn't sweep her off her feet, write her scorching secret admirer letters, and claim they wanted to ravage her body from top to bottom.

Not even when that person was her best friend.

Slowly, he turned her around and, with hands on her hips, backed her up against the balcony doors. The cool glass behind her and the heat in front was an electrifying contrast. He pressed in closer, trapping her with hard muscle and enough testosterone to melt her panties.

Never taking his gaze from hers, he went in for the kill. She let her lids drift shut, waiting for his kiss, heart pounding in anticipation. Her fingers clutched the soft cotton of his tee, bunching the material in her fists trapped between their bodies. She tilted her head, offering herself to him in a way she had never done for anyone else.

Seconds ticked by. When he brushed his nose with hers, she opened her eyes and knew he was patiently waiting for…something. What?

"Say yes, Raven. See that it's me and say yes."

As if there was any other option.

"Yes."

Chapter Four

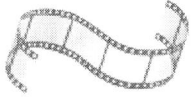

The *yes* from her lips nearly brought him to his knees, but Noah forced his body to slow down and take her mouth with the time he wanted to give the rest of her body.

Brushing his lips across hers, he smiled when her sigh mingled with his. Applying more pressure, he licked the seam of her mouth and coaxed entry. Hesitant at first, as if she'd never kissed before, she trembled against him. After a brief moment, she softened and opened. The second their tongues met, sanity was a memory.

He dove in, exploring her in ways he'd only fantasized. She met him match for match, warring for possession of the kiss. The taste of the wine she drank hit his tongue, the scent of rain floated in his head. Fuck. He knew she'd be his downfall. He pressed his hips to hers, pinning her to the balcony door and sliding his hands under her sweater, up her sides to brush his thumbs over her bra. Soft satin against his rough, callused hands.

She moaned, arching into his touch and fisting her fingers in his hair.

Much as he wanted to strip her bare and do this up against the glass, he needed her horizontal and needed it now. Or yesterday. Or, hell, for years.

Grabbing the backs of her thighs, he lifted her. Without breaking the kiss, she wrapped her legs around his hips and ground her heat into his erection through their clothing. The sensation brought new meaning to seeing stars.

Blind, he stumbled across the living room floor, debated whether to give up and lay her out right there, and climbed the step leading to his master bedroom. Feet dragging on the carpet, he pulled his mouth from hers to breathe and shoved his face into the crook of her neck.

Smells so good.

They fell sideways onto the bed, him on top, and her black as midnight hair spread over his white duvet. The sight brought a lump to his throat. He wanted his camera almost as much as he wanted her. He leaned down to kiss her again when she stilled under him, brown eyes wide in...

Fear? What could he possibly have done to put panic in her eyes?

"Raven?"

She made a sound of duress and scrambled out from under him, to the headboard and off the bed, backing herself against the wall. Though her hands trembled, she fisted them in an apparent attempt to stop. It wasn't working.

On his knees, he froze with his palms raised in the universal gesture for *I give.*

Seconds ticked by. Painful, confusing seconds. The blood roaring through his veins and his still hard erection made thought obsolete. But as time passed, his brain started clicking. Desire melded into worry and morphed into rage.

"I'm sorry," she whispered and pressed a palm to her forehead, avoiding his gaze.

"Don't be sorry. Explain." Because if she didn't start talking soon, he was going on a rampage of epic proportions. Starting with every man she ever fucked, until he found the one who'd done this to her. Women didn't go from white hot need to blinding terror without a reason.

Closing her eyes, she blew out a breath. "Wait here a minute. I'll be right back."

When his jaw dropped, she stepped from the room. He sat back on his haunches, trying but failing to process. When she came back, she clutched her purse to her chest. Shifting position, he sat on the edge of the bed and glanced around.

Yeah, everything looked the same, so why did it feel like he'd stepped in an alternate version of reality? It had to be the fact that he'd finally had his hands on her only to be yanked up short. Or just seeing her standing in his intimate space, where no other woman had ever been, could be the culprit.

"You asked if I was a dom. I'm not, but I do have to have...control. I can't have sex without it. What just happened is the result if I try."

She still wouldn't meet his gaze and her cheeks had turned molten. In embarrassment? With him? He'd known her…

A set of handcuffs landed on the bed next to him. He stared. And here he thought nothing could surprise him anymore.

She set her purse aside and bit her lip. "Now you know. I'm a freak."

She was not a—

Just to be sure he was on the same page…"You want to handcuff me?" Her gaze landed on the headboard, and he realized the depth of her depravity. "You want me handcuffed to the bed, immobile."

If it was possible, her cheeks reddened more. Her gaze darted to the floor in answer.

Shaking his head, he considered this. His furniture style was a sleigh design. There was nothing to restrain him to, even if he thought he could comply. And honestly, he didn't think he was capable. He had his own control issues. Sure, he played with toys, sometimes cuffs, but he was never the one *in them*.

With his heart pounding, he rubbed the back of his neck. This was not how this played out in his head. Not one iota. "I want to touch you." Badly. She had no fucking idea how much.

Defeat settled on her face, her shoulders sagging. Grabbing her purse, she turned.

She was halfway to the door before he called out, "Stop." A quiet command which she blessedly heeded. "You're not a freak. But I need to know who did this to you." Because he'd rip the bastard limb from limb. Twice.

Facing him once more, she lifted her brows in question. "What do you mean? No one did anything to me."

He swallowed hard and barely reined in his temper. "Something had to make you need this. We're talking you and me here, Raven. You can't trust even me not to hurt you. I want to know. Now."

"I don't…" She rubbed her forehead and tossed her purse on a nearby ottoman. "When I lost my virginity, I panicked during. At the time, I thought it was because of the pain and it just being my first time."

She bit her lip and stared over his shoulder, not seeing the balcony or the view, he was sure, but that time long ago which made her face twist in discomfort.

Sighing, she met his gaze. "The next guy played out the same way. Instead of bailing, he tied himself to the headboard and let me…take over. When we were done, he took me to this bar on the other side of Anchorage. It has a small private clientele list that caters to BDSM."

She waved her hand when he stood. "It wasn't the lifestyle he was showing me. He wanted me to know I wasn't alone in my needs. It was easier to find partners there that were willing to be restrained than in the real world."

He tried to picture beautiful, fragile Raven in such a place, and nausea swirled in his gut. No. Fragile wasn't the right word. She was stronger than anyone he knew, but her stature, though average in height, was thinner than most. She could've been hurt. One of those pricks could've mistaken her for a sub and…

"Fuck." He raked a hand through his hair.

"When I need release, I go back. I watch in the shadows to find the right person and we have sex in one of the private rooms upstairs."

Fuck again. She still went? He looked at her, torn between emotions he couldn't begin to put a name to. "Something had to trigger the first episode."

She shook her head. "I'm not a rape victim. I've never been abused. I'm just…a freak."

"Enough," he ground through clenched teeth. "Don't make me repeat myself. You are not a freak." But there was something else there, something she wasn't saying or possibly didn't even understand herself.

He wanted her. Always had. If it were possible, he wanted her more than ever. Understanding now why she'd been dissatisfied with her partners, the need grew to claim her and prove she was better than she envisioned. A fierce beast inside of him. More, he wanted her to experience every pleasure possible, which she couldn't do if he was immobile.

One step at a time. That was all. It would require him go at their fulfillment in stages until she trusted herself, trusted him. And to do that, he needed to relinquish control.

His shoulders knotted when he looked at the handcuffs. For her, only for her, would he even try. Because above everything else, she had his trust. He just hoped he didn't have a panic attack in the process.

Grabbing the hem of his T-shirt, he yanked it over his head. Her gaze took in his shoulders, his abs, until the mortification in her eyes disappeared and heat took its place. Unbuttoning his fly, he shoved his jeans and boxers down, kicking them away. His shaft swelled under her gaze.

She licked her bottom lip. "What are you doing?"

Never taking his eyes from her, he snapped the handcuffs around his wrists, leaving a small amount of wiggle room. "I'm giving you what you need."

∙∙

Raven tried to swallow and couldn't. It was one thing to be pressed against all that hard muscle and another to have it displayed before her eyes.

Wide shoulders and defined biceps made her salivate, with veins that protruded as he flexed his fingers around the handcuffs. He had a light dusting of blond hair on his chest that thinned over rippled abs. A six pack that was more of a full case. His hips were narrow, his thighs muscular. And his erection…was a beautiful thing. Thick and long, he was above average but not so large he'd cause pain when inside of her. The tip jutted up, brushing his navel.

The years melted away and her need ramped. She wanted him more than she could remember wanting anything. And he had been there all along, waiting until they could crash together. So much time wasted.

With only the light filtering in from the living room, the navy colored walls appeared darker. Night all around them. He had a large bedroom, open square floor plan. Plush, white carpet squished under her socks. A large flat screen was mounted to a wall above the fireplace and caught their reflection. Modern, sleek furniture and one helluva view. And not just the mountains.

He stroked himself and she almost swallowed her tongue. "I'll concede the cuffs and position, baby, but you need to understand this isn't in my nature. Give me some measure of control."

Baby. Was it crazy she loved hearing him say the endearment in his rough timbre? "What do you need?" Right about now she'd give him anything. Moisture pooled between her legs. Desire cut her breath short, heating in her belly and spreading.

He sat on the edge of the bed and scooted back, hands on his chest as he leaned against the headboard. "Take off your clothes so I can look at you."

All nervousness fled as she walked to the footboard. Seduction, nothing but sex, she could do. His gaze tracked her every step. Slowly, she reached down and slid one sock off, then the other. Straightening, she dipped her fingers under the hem of her sweater and lifted it over her head, leaving her top half bared to him in nothing but a blue satin bra.

He sucked in a breath and groaned. "More."

His voice alone had her throbbing. Unbuttoning her jeans, she shimmied out of them and tossed them on top of her sweater. His gaze raked over her body, creating a trail of heat in its wake.

"Now what?" She kind of liked this game, liked the effect she was having on him. He was still restrained, but calling all the shots. A bit of a win-win for both sides.

His breathing grew ragged, his eyes narrowing. "Off. All of it off."

Smiling, she reached behind her back and unclasped her bra, letting it slide down her arms and to the floor. Not very well endowed, she watched his response to check for disappointment and found none. His gaze trained on her nipples, erect under his scrutiny. When she hooked her thumbs in the waist of her panties, she swore he stopped breathing.

"Come over here." His voice was tight. Her body clenched in response. As if knowing what she needed, he scooted down so he reclined at an angle instead of sitting.

It wasn't the prone position she was used to, but she felt no hesitation in crawling across the bed to him. She gripped his ankles and ran her hands up his calves to his thighs, loving that the hard muscles tensed. He watched her face, jaw tight. Bypassing his good parts, she let her fingers brush his abdomen. His stomach caved at the touch as he emitted a feral groan.

He made a move to sit, but caught himself and lay back, cuffed hands behind his head. "I want to touch you." As if to punctuate the statement, his biceps bulged, fighting the restraint. "Straddle me. Please."

The primal need in his voice empowered her. This was hard for him, to shove aside his instincts so they could be together. She wanted it to be good for him, too. The blaze in his eyes was unlike the way anyone else had ever looked at her before.

Bringing her leg over, she straddled him and caged his hips with her thighs. Leaning forward, she braced her hands on his chest, her hair a curtain just for them. Cinnamon and spice hit her nose, the scent of him making her want to lick every inch of his skin. "Now what would you like me to do?"

His jaw clenched. "Kiss me."

A smile threatened to tug her mouth when she closed the distance and brought her lips to his. The charge was potent. His firm lips met hers and parted, tongue sweeping inside and claiming. Sliding her hands up his chest, she cupped his jaw.

He tensed and reared, but never removed his hands from behind his head. Tearing his mouth from hers, he closed his eyes and pressed his face into her neck. His tongue licked her pulse, hitting her nerve endings. He bucked his hips, sliding his shaft between her drenched folds and rubbing her clit.

She threw her head back and moaned, the sensation too good. "Noah."

He growled and bucked harder. "You're so wet for me."

"Yes," she breathed, ready to come apart at the seams. Knots bunched along her spine, tensing. "Tell me what's next."

"Pill?"

"What?"

"Are you on the pill? I'm safe." He groaned, rumbling her breasts with the vibration from his chest. "Need inside you now."

Her gaze met his. "I'm safe, too." Without breaking eye contact, she rose up and fisted the base of his shaft, aligning him to her opening. Slowly, she came down around him, the glide tight and hot and hard. Completely full, she leaned back and took him even deeper.

With his eyes shut tight, he slammed his head into the pillow. "Fuck me, fuck me, fuck me. Never done this without a condom." He panted, his eyes scrunching tighter. His abs clenched beneath her fingers.

Raking her nails lightly down his body, she stopped where their bodies joined. "Me either."

He sucked in a ragged breath. "Raven."

"I think I got it from here."

She rose until just the tip of him remained inside, and then came back down. The pressure was delicious. She quivered around his shaft, taking him again. "Noah."

He thrust up when she crashed down, setting a natural rhythm. Their bodies slapped together as she rode him hard, fast, because there was no stopping this insane need. Heat coiled in her core, pulsing, throbbing. Again and again he hit her deep, nailing her spot and stealing her breath. Over and over she chanted his name, each time it pulled a guttural groan from him and he thrust harder. Sweat beaded between them, creating a slick sheen.

"Fuck, Raven. So tight. You feel so goddamn good."

"Yes," she breathed as a spasm ripped through her center, striking out until she had nothing to ground her. She screamed his name, milking him.

He roared, driving twice more before stilling. Jerking. His release shot hot inside her as she collapsed on his chest.

They remained like that, breathing soughed, until she was confident they were on earth and she considered getting off him to clean up.

"Can I move my arms?" His voice had lost all tension, but the raspy lull was just as sexy.

She considered her answer, taking stock of her body, and nodded against his chest.

The handcuffs clinked as he pulled them from behind his head. He pushed the mechanism on the underside to release both clasps and tossed the cuffs to the floor.

"You knew how to get out of them?"

"I have a similar pair."

She touched the reddened areas around his wrists where the metal had rubbed his skin raw. He had fought the restraints harder than she thought. "They left marks."

He shrugged under her cheek. "It'll go away. It was worth it." His hands settled low on her back, tentative at first. When she didn't protest, he splayed his fingers and ran his hands up to thread them in her hair, forcing her to lift her head and look at him.

He studied her face before clearing his throat. "We need to talk."

Dread churned in her stomach, but she returned her cheek to his chest to avoid him seeing all the emotions she couldn't get a grip on. "It was a letdown from what you imagined, wasn't it? I didn't know how to tell you my preferences before now. I thought…"

His hands skimmed up and down her spine, warming her cooling skin. "Thought what, baby?"

She closed her eyes, butterflies dancing in her belly for the pet name. "I thought maybe with you I could handle normal. But panic tightened my chest and I just couldn't. I'm sorry."

He was silent for a beat. "I'm not sorry, and it wasn't a letdown. Look at me."

Resisting the urge to hide, she lifted her head and looked into his turquoise eyes. Kind, often mischievous, and always intense eyes.

"There are so many things I want to do with you. You built up this wall to protect yourself, and no one can fault you for that. But this is me, and you don't need to protect yourself from me." His gaze dropped to her mouth, over her hair and back to her eyes. "When we walk away from this after a month, don't you want it to be with everything I can give you?"

Her heart started to pound, in fear, but also excitement. Wondering if she was capable of doing more, she bit her lip.

His thumb traced over the spot, releasing her teeth from the hold. Lifting his head, he gave her a brief kiss. "I would never hurt you."

"I know that." She did, with every fiber of her pathetic being, she knew. Frustrated, she sighed, wishing she could understand why she was this way in the first place. "I want those things, too, Noah. I just don't know if I can."

"Do you trust me?"

"Of course." She cupped his jaw, no doubt whatsoever.

He nodded, even though he seemed doubtful. "Then let's do this, Raven. We'll go slow. But you need to meet me halfway and relinquish some control. Not all. This isn't a power play. It's me giving you pleasure."

She shivered, wanting that more than anything. If what they just shared was an indicator for what he had in store, she'd agree to anything. Plus, he promised to go slow. With anyone else, there was no chance she'd even try. With him, possibilities opened. God, she just wanted to be normal.

Her throat closed, but she forced words past the tightness. "Okay."

His grin was slow-coming, but it hit full watt in no time. "Good. First order of business is your living arrangements. You need to temporarily move in here with me."

Chapter Five

Raven shot up so fast his head spun. "What?"

Noah was a little shocked himself by the proposal. He'd never had a woman in his apartment, never mind asking one to move in, albeit temporarily. But after what they'd just done together, and everything they'd left on the table, no way was he letting her go until he got all of her.

She made a move to climb off of him.

He grabbed her hips to still her. "Stop. Hear me out."

She tensed, but ceased her escape.

"We live twenty minutes apart. Between your work schedule and mine, travel would waste time. One month, Raven." It would build trust on her end if she stayed. Falling asleep with her, waking up, it would push his typical boundaries, but she'd relax with him, put them in more intimate capacity. It would speed progress.

She shook her head. "That goes beyond the agreement. You don't share well with others. We'd kill each other."

Something else was going on in that pretty head of hers. "Right back at you. But what aren't you telling me?" She hedged. He pressed. "Honesty, Raven. I need you to talk to me or we're not going to get anywhere."

Her teeth sank into her bottom lip. "I've never slept with a man before."

It was damn frightening how alike they were. "Me either. Man or woman," he teased. She didn't see the humor. "We'll figure it out. Worse case scenario, I take the guest room."

He wondered if she realized he was touching her now. With a firm grip on her hips, his thumbs stroked her skin while she argued with herself. She had no problem with him touching her in the living room, so he tried to gauge her triggers as they went along.

She drew in a breath, and his gaze dropped to her nipples with the movement. She had perfect breasts. Small, perky, and they'd fit in his hands. If she let him touch. Rose-pink in color, they begged to be sucked. Bit.

This wasn't helping. He was growing hard again. Already. They needed a shower, but he wanted her again desperately. An idea bloomed.

"Stay tonight. We can test things out over the weekend."

Her gaze met his, more mocha than cocoa in the dim light of his room. Slowly, she nodded.

Fighting a grin, he failed. "Come on. I have an…exercise for us."

Her brows lifted. "I draw the line at exercise."

There she was. There was his Raven.

"You'll like this one." Gently urging her off the bed, he took her hand and led her into his adjoining master bath. He started the water in the tub and turned to her.

She was really something, standing there naked in full glory and not an ounce of embarrassment or insecurity. He hated it when women hid their beauty. She was taking in the room with curious eyes and, for the first time, he wondered about the design. It wasn't as if anyone ever got to see the room.

The bathtub was big enough to seat six, complete with jets, but he typically used the shower just on the other side of the counter. The heated stone benches and three-dimensional sprays were worth the small fortune. Not that money was an issue. There was a his and hers vanity in slate, even though he never had a "her." The floors and walls a sage tile.

"Do you like it?"

She looked at him, pink tingeing her cheeks. "Yes. It's like a spa. I love the colors."

Seeing the tub was nearly full, he gestured for her to get in.

"You want me to take a bath?"

"Us. I want *us* to bathe together." He waited for her argument, but she didn't offer one.

Stepping in, she went to the farthest corner and moaned as she sank under the hot water, neck deep. He turned the dimmer lights on over the tub and clicked off the harsh vanity lighting. Fully aroused, he climbed in and took the spot opposite her. She watched his movements, gaze dipping to his shaft and exploring his body.

"You're comfortable with this?"

She shrugged. "Oddly, yes. In most aspects of intimacy, I'm fine, until it gets down to the actual deed. I've never been big on touch, though. That's what initiates panic."

He nodded, wondering how she got to hate touch so much. He loved using his hands, so the restraint was immeasurably difficult. His hand dragged over his shaft, wanting inside her again. She watched the movement, teeth sunk into her bottom lip.

"It drives me insane when you do that."

She tilted her head, the tips of her black hair floating on the water. "Do what?"

"Bite your lip. I want to follow the same path and lick the ache away." He studied her. "You do it a lot, but never so much as you have the past week."

She offered a slight shake of her head. "What is this exercise you wanted us to do?"

His shaft thickened just imagining. "Touch yourself. Make yourself come for me. I want to see how you like to be touched and where, want to know what makes you mindless."

Her red lips parted and a ragged breath escaped. The blush from the water's heat added to the arousal in her cheeks. Her nipples pebbled. She wasn't unaffected, wanted to do what he asked. "Why?" she breathed.

"Call it a trust exercise." And one day soon, she was going to let him do the same with his fingers that she'd do with hers. "Dip your fingers under the water, Raven. Show me what pleases you."

After a moment, she swallowed and moved her hands to her breasts, cupping them. Her eyes closed and her head fell back as she arched into them. So fucking beautiful. He wanted his camera.

"Open your eyes. Watch me as you pleasure yourself."

Moaning, her lashes fell to half mast and her gaze locked on his, dark with arousal. One hand slid lower, over her taught belly to the small patch of dark hair. She shaved or waxed he'd noticed earlier, leaving only a small triangle.

"Spread your legs. Let me watch."

Responding to his low voice on command, her knees fell open, exposing her to him through the clear water. Her fingers spread her folds, her thumb flicking her swollen clit. Even through the water he could see she was slick, wanting. She moaned, her head drifting back.

"No. Eyes on me." He fisted his shaft, stroking harder, faster. "Does that feel good, baby?"

"Yes."

"How good?"

She moaned. "So good."

His balls tightened. "Imagine they're my fingers touching you. Dip a finger inside, baby. Are you hot and tight?"

"Yes. And wet. So wet for you."

Fuck. He could come right now and still be hard. "Pinch your nipple with your other hand. Yes," he hissed. Two strokes and he'd be done. He wanted them to come together. "Massage your clit. I want you to come for me."

Her breathing grew shallow, breasts rising and falling in the water, sending ripples across the space toward him. Her eyes went black with lust, lost in her pleasure, and it took more restraint than he had to wait her out. Faster, her fingers worked. Over her clit, in and out of her channel.

"Come, baby."

She cried out, throwing her head back and tensing, jerking against her fingers. Her lips parted, and he came unglued. He groaned, seed hitting his chest in spurts, his body taut with spasm. He stroked twice more through the aftershocks and watched her go limp.

"Fuck, Raven. That was…amazing."

With her eyes still closed, one corner of her mouth quirked. "Not so bad yourself, Noah. Watching you stroke yourself is fantasy material."

Death of him. No doubt, she'd be the death of him.

"Scoot a little closer."

She opened her eyes in question, but shoved off the tub and complied.

When their knees brushed, he tentatively put his hands on her waist. She didn't shy away, so he slid them down her hips and to her thighs, parting them to wrap her legs around his waist. He grabbed a small pitcher from the ledge and dumped the potpourri his maid refreshed weekly onto the floor.

"Tilt your head back." With a raised brow, she did, and he filled the pitcher with water, pouring it over her hair. So many fantasies involved her hair. Adding shampoo, he lathered the soft strands and massaged her scalp when she didn't show signs of duress.

"That feels good."

"Yeah? Never done this before."

She moaned deep in her throat. "You have great hands."

He paused for just a moment. "You have no idea." Refilling the pitcher, he rinsed the suds out.

She blinked at him through wet lashes, dark as midnight. The honey flecks were back in her irises, a sultry mix with the warm chocolate. Reaching for a bar of soap, she held it up in question.

His jaw clenched, but he nodded.

Running her hands over his neck, she worked the bar into a lather. She stroked his shoulders, down his chest. Her gaze followed the movement, appreciation in her eyes.

"What sets off the panic?"

She avoided his gaze, rinsing her hands. "I don't know." She used the pitcher to rinse the suds from him and then poured water over his head. Silent, she washed his hair. She had pretty damn amazing hands, too. The tips of her fingers massaged his scalp, the nails lightly raking.

Once she'd rinsed his hair, he laid his hands on her forearms. "You let me touch you in the living room. You're letting me do it now."

Drawing in a deep breath, she looked at his chest. "Some contact from Nicole or my mother doesn't bother me. Hugging or pats on the arm. It's more of an aversion than a dislike. Before your proposal, you and I didn't touch often. Maybe because we've known each other so long it failed to make me uncomfortable." She shrugged. "I liked it. Until…"

"Until I laid on top of you."

She met his gaze. "Yeah."

Without taking his eyes from hers, he reached for the soap and lathered his hands. He held them up before going forward. "Just tell me if it's too much."

She nodded and worked a swallow.

Starting with her shoulders, he slid his hands down her arms, careful to avoid any intimate area. Her lips parted on a sigh.

Encouraged, he traced her throat and collarbone, moving south and keenly watching for panic. To his surprise, her eyes went hazy with lust, her breathing shallow. How could she be so receptive one moment and freak out the next? It was driving him insane, not just the need to have her, but the need to release her from the fear. He traced around her nipples. She arched into him.

"Like that?"

Nodding, she closed her eyes.

Cupping her breasts in his palms, he closed his eyes. She was nothing like he'd imagined. She was softer, responsive, and there was no way he could've possibly gauged just how much she'd affect him. Part of it was their deep friendship, the way he cared about her, but having her like this…There was nothing comparable. His own heart started to pound.

He opened his eyes to find her staring at him. Something flickered in her gaze, part alarm, part…hope. Sucking in a breath, he shook his head.

He rinsed his hands and then her body. "Time to get out."

She stared at him another beat and then nodded. He let her towel off before climbing out and drying himself. Having her go to bed aroused could only help break the ice, so leaving them both unsatisfied after round two in the bath seemed like a good plan. She'd ache and want and perhaps make her own move toward more.

Making their way into the bedroom, he picked up the remote to turn on the fireplace and close the drapes.

When they'd swished shut, she touched her throat. "Can we leave them open?"

That's right. She had a thing for enclosed rooms. Without a word, he pushed the button to reopen them and shut off the light. He tugged the sheets down and held them up for her. She climbed in, taking one side of the bed and laying stiffly on her back. Swear to God, he was getting a picture of her in his bed before the month was through. The contrast of her dark hair against white sheets, her red lips and pink nipples…

He wondered if his dick would ever go back to normal.

Sliding between the sheets, he lay on his side, facing her. Firelight flickered over her profile, her wide eyes as she stared at the ceiling. If it was the last thing he did, if it took every hour of their thirty days together, he was going to wipe the hesitancy from her features. A sexual creature by nature, she was fantasy wrapped in daydream. Time she opened herself to all she was capable of being.

Unsure of proper bed-sharing etiquette, he sighed. He wasn't the cuddle type. Smothering in any form stole his breath. But this was different. This was..."Raven."

She turned her head.

"Come over here."

When she hesitated, he rolled to his back in the hopes that the position was non-threatening. After a moment, she scooted closer and rested her cheek in the crook of his arm. There was an awkward shuffle of arms and legs before they finally settled with her hand on his chest and leg covering his thigh, with his hand low on her back.

Silence stretched while he took stock of the situation. Her soft, warm body fit against the hard edges of his, as if made to be there. The scent of him clung to her, instead of her usual rain, and he found himself oddly liking it. His chest didn't restrict and he didn't want to back away for a semblance of space.

"This isn't so bad."

She laughed, pressing her face into his arm. "Goodnight."

■ ■

Raven opened her eyes and blinked at the dusky light streaming in through the balcony doors. She stilled and forced air into her lungs. She was at Noah's and everything was fine. And wow. She'd slept through the night. While sharing a bed. With Noah.

The night before sped through her mind and an ache began between her thighs as she smiled. Raising onto her elbows, she noted his side of the bed was empty. The scent of coffee filled the room and a clatter sounded from the kitchen. Rolling onto her back, she ran her hands through her tangled hair. She probably looked like a mess.

Stepping out of bed, she padded into the bathroom to relieve herself and looked in the mirror. Well, someone looked properly screwed. Red cheeks, swollen lips, whisker burn on her neck. She grinned. Finding some toothpaste, she brushed her teeth with her finger and splashed water on her face before going in search of her purse. She brushed the knots from her hair and tied it up in a loose ponytail with a band.

Then, wondering what to wear, she grabbed his T-shirt from the floor and shrugged into it. Pressing the fabric to her nose, she inhaled the spicy scent of him before realizing that was silly and…girly. She loved the smell of him, though. Like Christmas or warm baked goodies.

Pausing on the spot, she questioned what was happening to her. She didn't spend the night with her lovers or wear their clothing or get all soft when smelling them. She'd certainly never let them to touch her or allowed herself to drop her barriers to do something as intimate as bathe with them.

And hell. She'd promised to stay the weekend, maybe even the whole month…

Striding out of the room, she made her way through the living room and to the kitchen, where the sight of him stopped her dead. Wearing nothing but a loose pair of flannel pajama bottoms, he sat at the counter on a stool, phone to his ear and back to her. A cup of coffee was cradled in his large hand, perched halfway to his mouth.

Seeing the soft light skin over the hard muscles of his back and shoulders made her ache to touch him. Run her hands down his sinfully yummy body. Watch him come undone beneath her like he'd done last night.

His forearms flexed as he took a sip of coffee and set it down. "I'm sorry," he said into the phone, his voice low. "I can't make it for a few weeks. I know. I miss you, too."

The hairs on her arms stood erect. Dread coiled in her gut.

He had someone else.

She placed a palm to her forehead. Of course he did. They never said anything about exclusivity and neither of them did commitment. This temporary thing between them was no different. So why did her stomach clench at the thought of him doing these things with someone else? She wasn't the jealous type.

He turned suddenly on the stool, eyes widening a fraction. His gaze leveled on her, devoid of any recognizable expression. "I have to go," he said into the phone, still watching her.

Making her feet move, she walked deeper into the kitchen and poured herself a cup of coffee. Turning, she forced herself to face him and leaned her butt on the counter.

With his jaw tight, his gaze traveled the length of her. "Damn, Raven. The only thing better than the sight of you naked is you in nothing but my shirt." His voice, sleep-roughened and low, caused heat to replace the anxiety in her belly.

She took a sip of coffee, staring at him over the rim. "If you need to go, I understand."

"What are you talking about?"

Pushing off the counter, she rounded the island. "We never said anything about not seeing other people in this arrangement." Shame filled her knowing she probably hadn't satisfied him last night, hadn't allowed him to do half the things he'd wanted.

He grabbed her arm when she went to pass him. "I'm not seeing anyone else. That call was…regarding something else."

She'd never known him to lie, not up until last week anyway when she'd found out the past ten years had been false. According to him, it was one lie, just about his alter ego, but how could she be sure? "You don't need to make excuses. I won't break. If you need to get it somewhere else—"

He took the coffee from her hand, set it down, grabbed her hips and pinned her to the counter in one swift blur. Her breasts and hands trapped between their bodies. He shoved his face close, breath heavy across her cheek. His gaze bore into hers—a searing arctic blue seething with anger.

"I'm not seeing anyone else and I don't share. I may not be the forever guy, but I have never cheated when I'm with a woman. Not until it's run its course and I've ended it do I move on. Understand? There is no one else."

Remembering to breathe, she nodded. Her heart jack-hammered in her chest, but not in fear. In desire. This fierce, intense side of him, almost brutal in the animalistic stance, had her damp. Needy.

He flinched as if shocked by his actions. He swiped a hand down his face and expelled a breath. Shoving off the counter, he backed away.

She grabbed the ties of his pajama bottoms and hauled him back. "That was hot. You going all alpha and angry? Really hot, Noah."

His gaze was disbelieving.

Reaching between them, she palmed his shaft, satisfaction rising when he thickened in her hand.

His hands dropped to her hips, fingers flexing. "Raven, baby…"

"Have I also mentioned how much I like you calling me baby? Surprising, that. But I like it." Normally, she hated pet names. Her mother used them constantly. But coming from Noah, in that voice of his speaking through a haze of lust and skirting the edge of control, her knees weakened.

Sucking in a breath, he fisted the hem of her shirt, shoving it up to her waist. His gaze dropped. A groan rumbled from his chest. "You're not wearing anything under my shirt." His voice was breathless. Awed.

As if he needed confirmation, she shook her head.

Suddenly, they spun and her back was against the wall, him on his knees in front of her. Showing her his hands, he pressed one and then the other on the wall on either side of her hips, silently telling her he wouldn't move them. "Open your legs, baby."

The breath caught in her lungs, but she did as he asked, bracing her feet farther apart and using the wall for support.

He grunted his approval. His blue gaze held hers for a moment before dipping to her sex. Leaning in, he licked a path up her inner thigh and she shuddered.

Never, not once, had a man gone down on her. She'd never concede that kind of control and the vulnerability gave her pause. But this position, with him on his knees and her above him, didn't strike fear into her chest. Instead, she ached.

"Noah…please."

"Please, what?" He mumbled, licking his way up her other thigh, teasing her inches from where she wanted him.

Damn. *Damn, damn.* "Kiss me *there*."

Without hesitation, he brought his tongue between her folds and tongued her opening. Hot, wet strokes that had her eyes rolling back in her skull. The tip of his tongue flicked her clit and her head hit the wall.

"Oh God. Noah…"

"Right here, baby. You taste better than I'd imagined."

She whimpered, her hips bucking toward him. His tongue swirled, licked, penetrated, and she went mad. Her hands fisted in his hair, tugging, guiding, but he knew exactly what he was doing. In and out his tongue darted, easing back so he could nip her clit and then repeating the insanely delicious process again.

"Come, Raven."

She breathed his name, looking down at him. Something shifted inside of her, at seeing him between her thighs, her core aching. He was watching her, blue eyes severe, darkened by his own need. His hands flexed against the wall, as if the restraint were too much. The muscles in his forearms and biceps bunched.

A tingle shot through her, the only warning for the impeding explosion. She locked her knees, arched away from the wall and quaked through the onslaught.

He never let up, sucking and biting until the last of her tremors ceased and she couldn't breathe. When her legs gave out, he caught her.

Chapter Six

Noah stood and wrapped his arms around Raven's waist before she could fall. Half carrying, half dragging her, he stumbled backward into the living room until his calves hit a chair and he collapsed with her straddling him. She buried her face in his neck, and he remembered, almost too late, to keep his hands on the chair.

She licked his neck, sucking her way to his jaw. Her hands fumbled with the elastic of his PJs, tugging them down. He raised his hips in assistance until the bottoms pooled at his ankles. And then she had him in her hands, stroking with the perfect amount of pressure to make the world stop.

"Ah yes, baby."

He pushed a few strands of hair away from her face that broke loose from her ponytail and set his hands on her thighs. When she didn't object, he slid them up her belly to cup her breasts. Either she was lost in what she was doing or the touch didn't bother her. Wishing he could get a better handle on her triggers, he caressed her body, warily watching her to make sure he didn't push too far.

He ran the rough pads of his thumbs over her nipples and she sucked in a breath, stilling, eyes closed tight. He froze, waiting on a cue from her.

Her eyes flew open, hands leaving his cock to cup his jaw. She stared down at him, gaze searching, but damn if he could read her. She rose up, keeping his gaze transfixed to hers, and aligned their bodies for him to enter. He held his breath as she paused, suspending them between pain and bliss. And then she lowered her hips, taking him to the root.

If he were the kind of man who wept, he may have done it right then. She was his first lover not using a condom, and the words to describe the full sensation of her tight walls along his shaft hadn't been invented. There were none.

Her hands dropped to his shoulders and held tight. She released a measured sigh, as if remembering she was supposed to breathe. Then her eyes drifted shut and her head fell back, exposing her throat while the ends of her hair brushed his thighs. A thrust of her hips and he was snapped from his haze.

One hand splayed on her back to support her, he worked the other between them to where their bodies joined and circled her clit.

She cried out, clamping around him and thrusting with more force. He rose up to meet her, burying himself deeper every time and still never deep enough. Her fingers fisted in his hair, nails raking his scalp.

Fucking love that.

Bringing his mouth over her breast, he sucked, swirling his tongue around the nipple and biting gently. His arms banded behind her back, holding her to him so he could give the other breast equal attention. She mewled and arched into his mouth.

Their movements grew frenzied, bodies slapping and breaths soughed and untamed sounds that just drove him even closer to the brink. Just as he was about to beg her to come so he could plunge, her walls fisted around him, milking. She quaked in his arms. He drove twice more and stilled, face buried in her shoulder and mouth wide mid-bite. The roar as he came was muffled by her skin, but he felt it all the way to his toes.

She collapsed onto his chest, crushing her breasts against him. Unable to do more than lean back, he ran his hand up the delicate curve of her spine.

"We'll need some protein if we're going to keep this up."

He laughed, surprised he had the energy.

After a few moments, her breathing grew deep and she nuzzled into him. Something inside his chest pinched, not entirely painful, but unfamiliar. Spent himself, he reached for a throw quilt folded over the arm of the nearby couch and covered them. His last conscious thought was how damn nice it felt to have her slight weight on him.

■■■

Raven swallowed the bite of pizza she'd been chewing and looked at Noah from across the table in the kitchen alcove. Neither had wanted to cook, and she didn't have any clean clothes, which left going out not a viable option. He'd been quiet since their...nap in the chair.

"Are you sure you want me to stay the whole month?" She was still embarrassed as hell to have fallen asleep on him, curled up like a contented cat.

He looked up sharply and narrowed his eyes. "Yes." She opened her mouth, but he raised his hand to stop her argument. "I said yes. I meant it."

"Okay," she said through a sigh. "Tomorrow morning I'm going to head to my apartment and pack some things. I'll spend the night and come back here after work on Monday."

He seemed about to say something, but his cell buzzed on the table between them. The name "McCannon" appeared on the screen, unfamiliar to her, but Noah's face drained of color and his jaw tensed. Grabbing the phone, he rose. "Excuse me. I need to take this." He was across the living room and out the balcony door before she could respond.

Leaning back in her chair, she eyed the few pieces of remaining pizza. She forgot how much he could pack away. Then again, they had worked up an appetite. Grinning, she rose to wrap up the leftovers and then took her bottle of water into the living room.

Noah was still on the balcony, facing away from her and back tense. He'd thrown on a tee and sweat pants after their nap, but his feet were bare and it was freezing. Snow was in the forecast for later tonight. He seemed oblivious to the cold.

After disconnecting, he stared at the screen as if debating whether to shuck the thing twenty floors below. Bracing his hands on the railing, he leaned into them and ducked his head. His shoulders and forearms knotted with his grip.

Worry rose in her throat. Without hesitation, she crossed the room and opened the door wearing nothing but his T-shirt. Folding her arms against the biting wind, she stepped next to him, bouncing from foot to foot. "What's wrong?"

He closed his eyes and shook his head. Straightening, he swallowed and tucked a strand of hair behind her ear. "Nothing." He drew in a breath. "Come on. You're going to freeze out here."

Too cold to confront him, she led the way. Inside the condo, he stopped near the fireplace, gaze distant. Lost was not a good look on him, and hell if she could remember seeing it more than once. The night his parents died, the same expression had haunted his face. He had no other family and besides the guys who worked for him, not many close friends. It had always been just the two of them really, in a little bubble. What could possibly have him down-shifting that quick?

"You're scaring me. What's going on?"

He snapped to attention and shook his head. "Nothing. Just business." His gaze seemed to take her in for the first time since before their nap. "I...I know you want the details of my past, want to understand why I insist on security. But not now, baby. Just know that..." He briefly closed his eyes and ground his jaw. "They've killed people, Raven."

The hair on her arms stood. "What?"

He nodded, gaze distant, and then he sucked in a breath as if washing away what he'd said. "How about I introduce you to my shower so we can warm up?"

Her head jerked in whiplash. She opened her mouth and quickly closed it again. Okay, he was done talking. If he wanted her to know more, he'd tell her. Later. Her belly twisted in warning but, slowly, she nodded.

They stripped and stepped under the multiple showerheads, spraying from every direction. The man had a fabulous bathroom. She turned to tilt her head under the spray when she found him staring at the tile, jaw working a grind. Gone was the distance. Though he was lost in thought, anger was humming just under the surface.

"Maybe I should go home tonight. You obviously have something to work out."

His hands fisted at his sides, a hard, dangerous edge in his eyes. And she realized it wasn't anger she sensed, but rage. Seething. Building. He did not like her plan, nor would he look her in the eye. His steely glare was pinned to the wall over her shoulder.

Having never seen him like this, she paused. Noah could be intense at times, but she'd come to realize over the past couple days that when he was like that, it was the artist in him snapping pictures in his mind. Assessing the lighting. Lining up a shot. It was his passion, and now she understood what had always been niggling doubt before.

But this wasn't one of those times. The severity of him was shocking. He didn't want to talk, so there was no sense in pressuring him. There had to be other means to vent.

"What do you normally do to work off your frustration?"

Not one tense muscle moved, not even to look at her. Except his semi-hard erection. That part of him thickened, stood at attention. "I punch something in the gym. Or find another continent to take photographs. Or…"

He seemed beyond the gym right now, and she didn't think hopping a plane would be quick enough an escape. Her heart started to pound. She knew better than to fear him. He'd never strike out in anger, but damn if her skin wasn't flushing hot. Bottled rage and tension and alpha sexiness. With no outlet other than… "Or what?"

His gaze slowly slid to hers, and hell if he didn't look point-five seconds from snapping. "Or I fuck mindlessly."

Her girly parts clenched. Hard. "I vote for option three."

He flinched, barely perceptible. She'd shocked him. When he spoke, his voice was menacingly low and tight. "I'm not in a safe frame of mind to do that."

"You said mindlessly."

Sucking in a harsh, ragged breath, he closed his eyes. "Not doing this with you. I can't. You couldn't handle—"

"Try me." She wanted to give him what he needed. As one of the only people in his comfort zone, she didn't know what had set him off, but she wanted to fix it. Had a sinking suspicion she might be the only one who could.

His blazing eyes opened and pinned her in place. He made a motion toward her and came up short, hands fisting. Holding back. He studied her, long and steady. After too many moments, he must've seen the determination and honesty in her, because he let out the breath he'd been holding.

"Safeword," he ground out.

"What?"

"I need to know if I'm pushing you too far. Give me a safeword."

Shaking her head, she looked heavenward, wracking her brain. The tiles in his bathroom were a mossy-green color. "Sage."

She didn't even have time to blink before he was on her, pinning her between the shower wall and his hard body, water raining down over them. His mouth crushed hers, seeking entry. She opened and his tongue stroked hers, rough and demanding. Power radiated off him in waves, and it was damn hot.

He cupped her breasts with callused hands, slick with water. There was no finesse or coaxing from him, just need. He broke away to press open-mouthed kisses to her shoulder. She tilted her head for better access, shivering at the sensation. Electricity shot down her body and up again. Her own desire amped, needing him inside her.

She wrapped one leg around his hip, putting his hard length between her slick folds. He growled and thrust, hitting her clit, rubbing against her aching heat. Grabbing her ass, he spread her cheeks and ran a finger down her crease to where she throbbed, shoving a finger deep and curling it inside her.

"Fuck, you're so wet."

His hands left her and she whimpered at the loss. Spinning her around, he pressed her face first against the tile and molded his front to her back. Her breasts crushed against the wall, his erection between her cheeks. She arched back, urging more.

"What's your safeword, Raven?"

"Sage," she panted, unable to stand the insanity anymore. Her palms flattened on the wet tile, fingers curling.

His voice rasped her ear. "Use the word if you need it, baby."

And then he pushed inside with one firm thrust, filling her like she'd never been before. Relief released the knot in her chest. She cried his name, begged for more.

He grabbed a fistful of her hair and yanked her head back, closing his mouth on her throat. One arm banded around her, fingers pinching her nipple, the other was between her legs, stroking with the pad of his thumb. Strong thighs smashed into hers from behind as his hips pistoned faster. The tip of him nailed her deep, again and again, rioting her sensitive flesh with maddening, sweet strokes.

Incoherent words tore from his mouth, mumbled against her skin. "Too hard…never…been like…can't go…back." His arms tightened as if he feared she'd leave. Or maybe reason was beyond them now.

He stole her breath and she loved it. Her core clenched, nerves tingling and muscles stiffening on the cusp of orgasm. The explosion took her by surprise and her hands slipped.

But he had her. Never let her fall and never eased the punishing thrusts through her quaking. She may have screamed his name a time or twenty, because he was all there was in the moment and everything she ever dared to wish for.

Worry ticked in the back of her mind, but she shoved it aside. Somehow he'd unraveled her fears and pushed her past where she ever thought she could go. It had never been like this before. Intense, connected. Freeing.

He went rigid, clutching her hair in his fist and mouth wide on her neck. "Fuck, Raven." Spilling hot seed inside her, he jerked. Shuddered. Stilled.

Panting, he pulled out, stumbled backward and collapsed onto the stone bench with her in his lap. Grabbing her legs, he swung them around so she was curled up sideways on his thighs. His large hand rested on the back of her head, urging her cheek to his chest and held it there. The other arm circled her back. His chest rose and fell in rapid tangents as they both struggled for air.

"Not what I expected," he whispered, as if to himself.

His head hit the shower wall, but she didn't look up for fear of what she'd see on his face. This time was different. Something cracked inside him, inside her. A release of demons or an acknowledgement of them. She didn't know, but the change was an entity.

He stroked her wet hair. "Wasn't expecting this, Raven."

She closed her eyes, certain she knew the feeling.

Chapter Seven

Raven looked up when Nicole climbed the steps to her office. Not that she was getting much work done anyhow, but the intrusion grated on her raw nerves. She needed alone time, needed to think. It had been almost a week since she'd moved in with Noah, having agreed to continue on, and even though things were going swimmingly, she sometimes had trouble breathing.

The intimacy of sharing space with him was both jarring and comforting. They went from understanding each other as friends to knowing the tiny details only lovers could obtain.

He liked to sleep in the nude on his stomach but, by morning, he was curled along her back with a possessive arm around her. He hated the sound of teeth brushing and eggs cracking, but loved the click of her heels on the hardwood floor of his living room and the rustle of clothing when she undressed. He listened to soulful jazz when trying to unwind, country when he was happy, and cranked angry rock when attempting to drown out his day.

After he arrived home from work, the first thing he did was seek her out, a smile tugging at his lips. She made dinner, he cleaned up, and they showered together afterward. It was routine, just like she preferred, except for their love-making. There he always found new ways to pleasure her, only seeking his own after she was spent. He touched, and she let him. She didn't know if it was because it was him or if she'd been wrong in her needs all along.

Nicole sighed and slumped onto the chair in front of Raven's desk. "Two things. First, this Max guy is driving me batshit."

Max was Noah's bodyguard and, as of a few days ago, had been pushed onto Raven, regardless of her objection. Glued to her being, he drove her to and from work and wherever else she went, such as the coffee shop for lunch. She had no idea why. Noah wouldn't tell her, just said it was necessary. The dread pitting her stomach eased when she realized he was probably just taking precautions because of his mysterious past. Another thing he refused to talk about.

They've killed people, Raven.

She shuddered at the reminder, still not knowing what he'd meant.

"I can't do anything about Max." He was her shadow until Noah said otherwise. She hated to admit it, but having Max around brought a sense of security. She still hadn't shaken the crazy feeling she was being watched. Which was probably Noah's paranoia rubbing off.

"He just stands in the corner, watching. It's creepy."

Raven grinned. "At least he's good looking." She glanced at him through the glass wall and down on the show floor. Built like a wrestler, his brown hair was cut short in a buzz and he had a wide jaw. Long dark lashes complimented his brown eyes. He always wore a suit, not a wrinkle to be found. By her best guess, he was in his early forties.

"Word. Except I have no idea if he's plotting a world takeover or stripping me naked. His expression never changes."

Raven laughed. "Perhaps both. What's the other thing? You said you had two reasons for coming in."

Nicole wrinkled her nose. "Vincent Soreno is here to see you."

She barely resisted a shiver. She'd been hoping the would-be photographer had gone back to the lower forty-eight and not taken her suggestion to come back. "Send him in." When Nicole got up to leave, she added, "And sit in on this meeting, would you?"

By the end of the day, she was looking forward to getting home. The fact that she thought of Noah's condo as home she'd worry about later. Running through her day, she glanced out the window as Max drove them down the dark, snowy streets in a non-descript SUV.

Mr. Soreno might prove to be a problem. There was some justification in that he gave Nicole the creeps, too, but it offered Raven no comfort. A big, intimidating man, he'd been upset when she told him the shots just weren't strong enough to offer a showing at this time. Of course, he said he'd be back.

Other than that one blip, her afternoon was productive. She'd put the final touches on their opening for Saturday and got a head start lining up dates for Noah's. Or Hoan's. Whatever. She'd have to talk to him about it tonight. Glancing at Max in the front seat, she wondered if he'd be attending as their security. As far back as she could remember, Max was always around, hovering in the shadows.

"How long have you been Noah's bodyguard, Max?"

He glanced at her in the rearview. "Thirteen years, ma'am."

Wow. Since before Noah moved to Alaska freshman year. "You knew his parents?"

"Yes, ma'am. Good people. Shame about the accident."

"It was." It had hit Noah hard and made her face her own mortality. That one icy road could wipe it all away. "Who guards Noah when you're with me?"

"We have a full security team. You've only seen me, ma'am, because that's how Mr. Caldwell wants it."

She sighed. What wasn't he telling her? If it was serious enough to create an alter ego and lie to her, it had to be noteworthy.

They've killed people, Raven.

She shivered. "Do you know why he's insisting on my protection detail?"

He was silent a beat and changed lanes before answering. "Yes, ma'am. And no, I won't tell you. That's something to take up with Mr. Caldwell."

Except Noah wouldn't tell her anything. Then again, she hadn't pushed very hard either. For all she knew, it was his parents' old ghosts, someone who once threatened the former senator and now Noah was playing it safe. What would be the harm in telling her? He had to know she'd never do anything to risk or out him.

"He cares about you a great deal, ma'am."

She met his gaze in the rearview before facing the window. Why that statement worried her more than a security team was not something she cared to explore. There had been love between her and Noah almost from the first day. Kindred souls. Not romantic love, but just as enduring. This shift in their friendship didn't change that. She suspected friendship wasn't what Max meant.

"I care about him, too." She pressed her forehead to the cool glass. "And Max?"

"Yes, ma'am."

"Please stop calling me ma'am."

She swore she heard him grin. "Yes, Miss Crowne."

■■

"You told me the conviction was in the bag." Noah tossed his keys on the table and moved deeper into his condo. Two charter fishing trips after three guys called in sick with the flu was not on the agenda today. Neither was the impromptu phone conversation with his FBI contact, who was pissing him the fuck off. "Three weeks ago, you assured me it was finally done."

Noah rubbed the back of his neck. He never would've taken steps with Raven if he hadn't been handed the confirmation that the threat was all but gone. Then, out of nowhere, the tables turned and he'd been on edge ever since. His ulcers had ulcers. Those bastards could take her away from him in one pull of a trigger.

James McCannon sighed wearily into the phone. The flick of a lighter sounded, followed by the drag from a cigarette. He answered on an exhale. "Look, Noah. We weren't expecting Rizzoli to learn about where the evidence came from, nor the hit he put on you."

"No shit. But why does that matter? You said there were other witnesses and you had recordings of him talking about election funds." It should've been a slam-fucking-dunk.

McCannon's chair squeaked. "The timing of the contract is worrisome. His funds are tied up until trial."

Noah ground his molars to dust. "He got it from somewhere."

"And until we know who he hired, you need to stay on the down low."

McCannon had called with a "watch your back" warning just twenty-four hours after Noah had Raven in his arms. Finally. And there was Aubrey to take into account. He'd have to beef up security at her estate, even though Rizzoli didn't know the girl existed.

Raven was Noah's biggest concern at the moment. As his friend, she'd been off radar and of no consequence. In fact, so had Noah. Until he'd finally gathered enough credible evidence that the feds could lock the fucker up for life. Raven was under his roof now, and Rizzoli would have to be an idiot not to suspect. If there was a hit out on him, then Raven was already in the crosshairs. This was a clusterfuck, and he'd possibly put Raven right in their sights.

"I want to know if anything changes. And so help me, McCannon, if I find Rizzoli's contracted killer on Alaskan soil, the hell I'll deliver will make what Rizzoli's done look like a Sesame Street special. Got me?"

McCannon sighed. "Calm the hell down. Threatening a federal officer is a crime," he said lightly. When Noah didn't laugh, McCannon cleared his throat. "I know this has been a long time coming and it's been hard on you. Just hang in there. It's almost over. She's finally going to get justice."

"She'd better."

Noah disconnected and tossed his phone next to his keys. His late teens and entire twenties were buried neck deep in this mess, a mess that wasn't even his, and damn if he didn't want to start living his life without looking over his shoulder or putting those he loved in danger. He looked down to find his hands shaking. He fisted them and took a deep breath.

A glance at his watch told him Raven would be home soon. How long could he evade her curiosity? Part of him wanted to tell her everything, but the less she knew the safer she might be. He trusted her with his life, with Aubrey's if it came down to it, but he still had a gut feeling she didn't trust him. Not one-hundred percent. Regardless of the change in their relationship, she was holding something back. It pissed him off he couldn't figure out what.

Keys slid into the lock and the door opened. Raven stepped into the foyer and halted, Max on her heels. "You beat me home."

A funny thing happened in his chest when she said "home." He smiled, walking to her and taking her coat. She was moving slow and her expression was distracted. "You look tired."

"Yeah, long day. Not bad, just long."

Before he put too much thought into the act, he cupped her cheeks and kissed her forehead. Not a gesture he could ever remember doing. It spoke of tenderness he'd never known. "Why don't you take a hot bath? I'll order Chinese. We can eat with chopsticks by the fire."

She rolled her shoulders. "Sounds good." Glancing briefly at Max, she smiled and headed to the bedroom. "Goodnight, Max."

"'Night, ma'am."

Already in the bedroom, she cleared her throat loudly.

An out of character grin split Max's face. "Sorry, Miss Crowne."

"Better." The bedroom door closed.

Noah raised his brows.

Max's grin fell to half watt. "She doesn't like being called ma'am." He shrugged, the giant of a man's face reddening in embarrassment.

Right. "Anything unusual today?"

Max sobered. "No. She had a client come in but, other than that, she stayed in her office. I thought we might've had a tail on the drive back, but I was wrong. The car passed us before the turnoff."

He sighed and forced the tension from his neck. "Thanks. See you tomorrow."

Max looked like he wanted to say more, but he nodded and turned to go.

"Is there anything else?"

"She's asking questions," he said over his shoulder. He turned with his hand on the doorknob. "I don't think it would hurt you or Miss Aubrey if Miss Crowne had the answers to those questions."

Noah crossed his arms and regarded Max. He'd been with Noah a long time and, in that time, he'd never offered advice or spoken up unless directly asked or if there was a potential threat. Seemed as if Raven was getting under Max's skin, too. "Noted."

After his bodyguard left, Noah ordered takeout and switched on the fireplace while waiting for delivery. Pouring two glasses of wine, he moved to set them on the coffee table and signed for the food when it arrived.

Just as he was about to check on Raven, she emerged from the bedroom in a pink silk robe that barely covered her good parts. Long tendrils of midnight hair broke free from the clip on her head, framing her face. To contrast this sexy as fuck look, she wore large fluffy bunny slippers he'd given her for Christmas one year.

"Don't move." He went to the black room down the hall and retrieved a camera. When he returned, her brows drew together in frustration.

"Put the camera down."

"No. And wipe that exasperated expression off your face." He wanted the look she had when she first emerged. Sleepy and curious. And, damn her, she wasn't complying. Dropping his voice a baritone, he lifted the camera to his face. "Baby, look at me. After dinner, I'm going to untie that robe of yours and spread it wide. Do you know what I'll do next? I'm…"

Click, click, click, click, click. Fuck yes. That was it. Perfect.

She rolled her eyes and crossed the room to sit on the floor by the fire. With her in profile, the firelight cast shadows and light across her form. Before she could reach for the takeout, he snapped several more. When she looked over her shoulder at him, he stole the money shot—her lips parted, slight lift to her brows, warmth in her eyes and the light behind her. Impish and sexy.

As he lowered the camera, something pinched in his chest. His jaw clenched as he attempted to control the myriad reactions jostling inside. Something was off. He wasn't expecting this punch to his gut when he looked at her or the incessant need to have her. Not just under him, but beside him in all things. Hell, she'd been at his side for years. Lust was expected. He'd lived with it for a decade, like an extra appendage. Why did things feel different?

Shaking it off, he strode over and sat on the floor next to her. He opened a container, realized it was her chicken chow mein, and passed it to her before reaching for his cashew beef. Dipping his chopsticks, he pulled out a bite and chewed, watching her.

Her feminine characteristics were unique, which was why he'd wanted her on film. A mix of siren and innocence. Everything about her was contradictory. Dark hair, light skin. Brazen sexual abandon with innate fear lurking in shadow. A control freak, yet soft at heart. Where did she get such artistic perfection? She didn't resemble her mother at all but, then again, Raven wasn't Willow's biological child.

"How old were you when your mom adopted you?" They'd talked about it a time or two, but he couldn't remember.

Her chewing slowed, then she swallowed just as slowly. "Seven. Why?"

He shrugged. "Just curious. Do you remember anything about your life before?"

She faced the fire, chopsticks stabbing her food. "A little here and there. It's mostly small flashes. I don't know how accurate they are."

Talking about this bothered her, judging by the stiffness in her spine and avoidance of her eyes. She didn't put up walls against him, not often. "What do you remember?"

"I told you, it comes in spurts—"

"I heard you. Why are you getting defensive?"

She glanced up and let out a harsh exhale. "I'm not. I just don't like talking about it."

His spine turned to ice. Her personality, mannerisms, and inability to make love normally all blinked through his conscious. He liked her just as she was, but was pushing for more. Because she deserved that. Sexual creatures like her should never be contained, especially behind fear. Did any of her walls have to do with those formidable years?

"Why don't you like talking about it?"

She set the carton aside and hugged her knees to her chest.

The ice along his spine spread to other areas. "Raven."

She closed her eyes. Shook her head. Sighed. "Do you remember hearing in the news about that naturist group in California, Lambs of Christ? We were young when they disbanded."

Wondering what the hell this had to do with anything, his gaze got lost in the flames as he thought back. He'd certainly heard of them. They were one of those cult groups in southern Cali. "A little. Weren't the leaders arrested on weapons charges?"

"Among other things. I think most of the members, like my birth parents, went into it thinking they'd live in a small, Christian community to raise their daughter. By the time I was starting to babble, it was too late to get out." Her voice went reflective. "According to my mom, some tried to leave the group and were never seen again."

If he tried to move, he'd snap. That's how tight, how cold, her words left him. "You were raised in a cult?"

Her gaze whipped to his as if she sensed his tension. "All I know is what my mom told me. I have almost no memory of it."

She pried the carton away from his fingers before he could crush it to a pulp. Grabbing her wine, she leaned against the couch. "From what I understand, the kids slept in a separate bunker from their parents and were treated well. After their school studies, they helped farm the fields." She cleared her throat. "My parents died during the ATF raid. My mother was living in the area at the time, heard about a lot of the newly orphaned kids, and adopted me. A shrink told her it might be best to move me from familiar settings, so she packed us up and we've been in Alaska ever since."

The air slowly seeped from his lungs. He forced himself to draw more in. Two weeks ago, she'd told him she'd never been abused or assaulted. He'd believed her. Of course he had, but doubt niggled in the back of his mind there was more going on than her need for control. She may not remember it, but something had happened to her back then that made her like this today.

He doubted she even realized it. When they'd first started going at each other, she wouldn't let him touch her. Now, he did so freely, but he had to go slowly in the beginning. She didn't like enclosed spaces and hated surprises of any kind.

He looked over to find her watching him. Grabbing his own wine, he downed half the glass. They had sex often, in a multitude of positions. All but one. He never thought he'd crave the missionary position so damn much. The only time she panicked anymore was when he was on top of her.

"You won't let me make love to you on top. Have you noticed that?" Against the wall, her riding him, him from behind…didn't matter. She was fine. As long as they were vertical.

She frowned, confusion marring her face. "Yeah, I guess you're right."

Satisfied he'd put the notion in her head, he set his wine down and crawled on all fours over to her. She'd analyze what he said and dissect it until she figured out a solution. He just needed to set her on the path.

But now? He needed to sink inside her and forget the things she'd told him. If he let the vision of a younger version of Raven cement in his head, he'd need eight solid hours in the gym with a punching bag.

She grinned when he took her glass away. "What are you doing?"

Kneeling between her legs, he ran his hands up her calves. "Wondering what you have on under that robe."

The fire reflected in her eyes, lit with humor. "Why don't you find out?"

Clamping his mouth on her throat, he growled. "With pleasure."

Chapter Eight

A week later, with an Elements exhibit starting in twenty minutes, Raven turned away from the door in her office and sat on the edge of her desk, listening to her mother blubber about a recent breakup. She cradled the phone in one hand and plucked dead blooms from her potted plant with the other.

When there was a pause, Raven said, "I thought you were seeing someone named Daniel."

Her mom sniffed. "Oh no. Daniel was weeks ago. I thought things with Richard were going so well."

They always did, until a few weeks passed and Willow Crowne fell head over heels. Surprise, surprise, it ended shortly after that. Raven had had this conversation so many times, but it still pained her that her mom was hurting. "I'm sorry."

"Me, too." She blew her nose. Loudly. "Enough about me. How are you? Are you seeing anyone? Why are you calling me on a Friday night?"

Her mother liked Noah, but the two of them were a temporary thing, so no sense in telling her because it would only get her hopes up. They agreed to a month, and only one more week was left of their time. Her stomach churned. She ignored it. "Just checking in. I have a showing starting in a few minutes. But, since we're on the phone, I need to ask you something."

Weariness weighed on her shoulders. Between Noah exhausting her after work and a sudden rash of new nightmares, sleep was not a commodity. Ever since he'd brought up her childhood, she started remembering little tidbits. Google searches only brought up things she knew.

"Anything, honey."

Raven rubbed her forehead. "Where was I found after the Lambs of Christ raid? I keep having strange flashes and can't piece it together."

Her mother was silent, which should've warned her something ugly was coming. Her mother made talk show hosts look like mutes. "Honey, I..." She sighed. "When the shooting started, you and some of the other kids were locked inside one of the bunkers. Some of the leaders were there hiding out, along with your parents, planning an escape. The ATF kicked down the door and shots were fired from Lambs leaders. The authorities responded. You..."

Her fingernails dug into her palms. "What, Mom?"

She sniffed. "Your father pushed you to the ground and told you to crawl under the bed. He died right next to you. The agents didn't know you were there until a little while later. You hadn't moved. They thought you were dead, but it was just shock."

Just shock. As in her limbs freezing and inability to breathe. Her first panic attack had come before she'd moved to Alaska.

Making excuses, she hung up and stared out the window, trembling from hairline to toenails. All these years she'd thought she was a freak. Turned out, she was traumatized. The claustrophobia, the panic during sex while horizontal, made sense. Noah was right. She could handle any position but missionary. And she couldn't even remember the incident, yet it had forged a dark path for her all these years.

Feet shuffled behind her. Noah. She'd grown accustomed to his sounds, his scent, and his touch in their few weeks together. She could make him out from a thousand others while blindfolded. She wanted to go home, where he could bury himself deep inside her willing body and push this new knowledge from her mind. With him, she forgot to be afraid.

His gaze scanned the gallery below before he cupped her cheek. "What is it? You're pale, baby."

She couldn't do this now. She had a showing. Forcing a smile, she met his worried gaze. "Nothing. My mother. We just hung up."

"You sure? Your mother doesn't typically make you shake, not in fear anyway." One corner of his mouth curved.

She nodded. "I'll tell you the rest later. I'm fine."

His jaw tensed and he looked over her shoulder at the gallery as if to make sure no one was watching. His hand dropped from her face. "I want to fuck you on this desk one day. Thought about it every time I visited you at work. It'll have to wait, though. Your guests are arriving."

Heat replaced the cold. Her cheeks flamed. She suspected he said as much to scrap the edges of panic he must've seen, but now she'd have to go through the entire night with her sex aching. Turnabout was fair play.

"Noah, ask me what I'm wearing under this dress."

His gaze shot to hers and narrowed. His thigh brushed hers, sending sparks of need to her core. "What are you wearing under that dress, baby?" he asked in a rough, tight tone that skittered along her nerve endings.

"Not a thing. I'm commando."

"You're..." He ran his fingers through his wavy, blond hair. "Fuck, Raven."

Because he kept darting his gaze between her dress and her eyes, sucking in a breath when she'd told him what she wasn't wearing, she screwed with him a little. "Those were my sentiments. Figured going commando would make access easier. This is one of your favorite dresses on me, too, right? Does it drive you nuts that I'm commando?"

"Stop saying commando. I'm about to make us the gallery's focus by turning you into an exhibitionist."

She threw her head back and laughed. God. Zero to happy in ten seconds. Only Noah could do that for her.

Sliding off the desk, she wove around him. "I promise not to say the word *commando* anymore tonight, or remind you that I'm *commando* under my dress."

He closed his eyes and shoved his hands in the pockets of his expensive charcoal-colored suit. Tailor made for him, he looked attractive and like the wealthy man he was while wearing it. She wanted to peel it from him slowly, licking his exposed flesh along the way.

She stopped in the doorway. "Are you coming?"

"Not at the moment, but I'll rectify that later."

Unable to help it, she grinned. "Death by innuendo. Hell of a way to go."

He unclenched his jaw. "Go. I'll be down soon, when other parts get the memo and I'm presentable."

No way could she pass that one up. "You'll be *down* soon and I'm *commando*. Falling into my plan perfectly."

He growled her name and she left. Damn. She couldn't wait for tonight.

Hours, too many hours later, the showing was a success. Raven leaned against the wall and sipped her champagne as the last of the stragglers lingered. She knew exhibiting Wesley Freemont's work would pay off when he strode into her office six months ago. A good-looking black man, he was oddly charming with people for an artist. His underwater stills were incomparable. The public thought so as well. They'd sold out of every print.

Nicole ventured over and leaned on the wall next to her. She clinked her champagne flute to Raven's. "Here's to a successful exhibit. Where do you want to go for drinks afterward?"

It had become tradition for her and Nicole to have a celebratory cocktail after a showing. She'd forgotten. Glancing at Noah, she bit her lip. He was talking to Wesley, the artist of the night, so of no help to her. Much as she loved Nicole, she had been waiting all night to get Noah alone. And naked.

"I knew it." Nicole straightened. "I knew it. You're sleeping with Noah."

Raven glanced around, but thankfully no one was looking at them. "Do I have it tattooed on my forehead?"

Nicole flipped her long, blonde hair over her shoulder. "No, but he's been watching you all night like you're a forbidden dessert, and you haven't moved about the room without checking his position. When did this happen?"

Raven hadn't realized they'd been that obvious. "A few weeks ago. Friends with benefits, so not permanent."

"Why? I mean, you've been besties since college. After all this time, it seems kind of…romantic. I've wondered why you two didn't hook up sooner."

Raven took a sip of champagne to cool her dry throat. Romance was not their style or their intention. He'd wanted her, now he had her. It was two people colliding for sexual release. Those were the terms. Except the deadline in one week loomed closer every minute, and the thought of walking away left a hole in her chest. He'd opened her to a whole new part of herself she didn't know existed, but could she let down her guard with other lovers? Did she even want to?

"It's just sex," she rasped, staring into her glass. Why in the hell did that feel like a lie?

"Bet it's damn hot." Nicole sighed and slumped on the wall, her tone playfully sad. "I always hoped he'd look my way someday and take me. Now that he's been with you, I stand no chance."

Nicole had a crush on Noah, but Raven knew it was attraction more than actual feelings. Not for the first time, she thought about Nicole and Noah together. She was his typical flirt, both in personality and appearance. "What makes you say that?"

Nicole took a sip and swallowed, scanning the room. "I'm the girl next door. You're the wet fantasy." She shrugged. "Just the way it is. Some guys go for my type and most go for yours."

Pondering, Raven stared at her shoes. She wasn't a take-home-to-meet-the-parents woman. The idea of forever had never gelled in her mind or her heart. To be with one man every night, to leave herself exposed and blindly offer the kind of trust it entailed was never a road she wanted to start down. Without conscious effort, her gaze found Noah's from across the room. Her pulse throbbed, her blood rushing through her veins with breakneck speed. The heat and tenderness in his eyes left her dizzy.

Breaking the connection, she discovered everyone had left and Nicole was locking up. How long had she been standing there? She pressed a palm to her forehead and, God help her, her gaze was drawn to him again. He hadn't moved from the center of the room, hands shoved deep in his pockets and gaze steadily on her. The air pulsed between them.

Nicole walked over and took the champagne flute from her fingers, downing the contents. "I'll take a rain check on the drink. Looks like you have other plans." She swatted Raven's ass and headed for the door. "I expect details on Monday."

∙∙∙

Noah held the door for Raven and slid into the back of the limo after her. Once they were underway, he closed the partition so Max couldn't hear their conversation. He had two goals and two goals only tonight: to find out what her mother had said to upset her and to make her forget in as many creative ways conceivable.

But first… "Here." He pulled a box out of his coat pocket and handed it to her.

"What's this?"

"Open it."

She lifted the lid and gasped at the watch. Silver and gold, the face was small and the band adjustable. It also had a tracking device inside, just in case.

"I love it. Thank you."

He removed the watch from the box and clasped it around her wrist. "Do me a favor and wear it whenever you're away from the condo."

Her finger traced the face. "Why?"

Staring at her profile, he decided not to lie. "Because if something happens to you, I can find you if you're wearing it. The trace inside links to an app on my phone."

Her gaze slid to his. "You scare me when you talk like that."

Kissing her temple, he drew in her scent of rain. "Just a precaution, baby."

She didn't seem to believe him, but she leaned her head against the seat and closed her eyes, the streetlights playing with shadows on her pale face. "Nicole knows about us. She figured it out. I don't think she'll say anything, but give the word and I'll talk to her. I told her it was temporary and just sex."

He rubbed his jaw. It was sex, but it wasn't *just sex*. Somewhere in the past few weeks, he'd come to the realization. The "temporary" comment was what caused a sharp pang in his gut. And if that wasn't the most fucking twisted thing, he didn't know what was.

"What was the conversation with you and your mother about?"

She lifted her head and looked at him with haunted, dark eyes. "I asked her about the day of the Lambs of Christ raid. I've been having dreams, but nothing that made much sense."

She'd woken a few nights this week with her heart pounding against his chest and a scream trapped in her throat. He'd tugged her closer, unsure of what else to do, and skimmed his hands down her soft hair until she'd resettled. He nodded for her to continue.

She swallowed. "My father died trying to protect me from the shootout. Apparently, I was…frozen under the bed until the authorities found me."

Mother of God. A vise closed his throat. A primal, ferocious need to protect filled his chest. "Hell, baby." He tugged her onto his lap.

Pressing her cheek to his chest, she shivered. "I don't remember it. Which is a good thing."

He kissed the top of her head and breathed in the rain scent of her hair. "No wonder you can't stand any weight on you. Although you may not remember, part of that day stuck with you." He wanted to erase that fucking fear so bad he'd give everything he owned to make it so. And never, *never* again would he attempt to try the missionary position. Not until she gave him the signal it was okay.

"This is going to sound crazy, but I'm glad she told me. At first, it shook me, but it's like a weight's been lifted." She raised her head to look at him. "I guess I just needed an explanation or something. Makes me feel like less of a freak."

He ground his molars and held her jaw. He wished she'd stop calling herself a freak. It made him want to punch something. Repeatedly. To ease the anger, or perhaps settle his pounding heart, he crushed his mouth to hers, seeking entry. She opened immediately, always did, and with every stroke of his tongue the friendship lines blurred even more.

Inside the condo, he stripped her coat off and pulled her to him, her back to his front, face buried in her hair. For some reason, he couldn't make himself move, so he tightened his hold and stood with her in the foyer.

Her hands settled on his arms, which trapped her, cool from the elements outside. Tilting her head, she laid it on his shoulder and pressed her face under his jaw. "Come with me into the bedroom."

Yes. Anything she wanted.

Taking his hand, she led him through the dark living room and into their bedroom. *Theirs*, not his. He stopped in the doorway as her slender form wove through the room to click on the fireplace. Warm tones flickered over her skin, shining in her eyes. He made a move toward her, but she held up her hand.

With too much space between them, she bit her lip and reached behind her back to unzip her dress. The teeth unlatching was almost as loud as the blood roaring through his veins. Cupping the material to her breasts, she slid her arms out and let the red dress pool on the floor.

He forgot how to breathe. She was, in fact, wearing nothing underneath. He greedily took in her pale, milky skin, small, perky breasts and triangle of dark hair at the juncture of her thighs. The firelight bathed her skin, and he had to swallow a groan. His cock strained against his pants.

She tugged the duvet and sheets down and crawled into bed to lay down.

On her back.

A powerful, unknown in origin sensation shoved its way into his throat as she stretched, holding her hand out in invitation. Fuck film. He'd never need a camera to remember this, and damn if he ever wanted anyone but him to see her like she was at this moment.

The information her mother gave her about how—and where—her biological father had died must've given her the answers she'd needed to connect the dots on why she feared the missionary position. She couldn't remember that part of her past, but something subconscious did, and now that Raven understood, she would try everything to get past it. That was just who she was. Strong. A fighter.

Shrugging out of his suit coat, he stripped off his tie, keeping his gaze locked to hers as he unbuttoned his shirt. When it was tossed aside, he made quick work of his pants and walked slowly over to the bed.

He had to clear his throat twice to speak. "Are you sure, baby?"

She nodded.

Sitting on the edge of the mattress, he ran his fingers from her collarbone to her navel, earning a shiver. "What's your safeword, Raven?"

"Sage." She blinked up at him. "But I don't need it."

"You might," he said, his voice rougher than his breathing. "All you ever have to do is use the safeword, and I'll stop. Always. No matter what. I'll know you've hit your limit." He ran his fingers back up her taut belly to lightly trace her nipples. "We all have limits, baby."

And hell. She was his.

With great care, he slid under the sheet and rose over her, bracing himself on his elbows to not crush her. He waited, but her expression never changed. Still, to give her time to adjust, he brushed his nose with hers and kissed her lightly.

It was she who eventually cranked the heat, deepening the kiss and arching up to meet him. Her thighs spread, welcoming his hips between them. He kept his weight off, his palms on the mattress, and made love to her mouth. Her hands skimmed his shoulders, his back, as if relearning his body before eventually settling on his hips.

His cock throbbed, but he held himself in check. Lifting his head, he watched her as he slid his shaft between her folds, testing her readiness. Slick, wet heat met him.

"Raven," he murmured, easing back so the head of his cock poised at her opening.

Her dark eyes met his, not a trace of fear in them. "I want you—"

He pushed inside with one fluid stroke. Again, he paused, arms shaking with restraint. She wrapped her arms around his back and her legs around his hips, nursing him deeper into her soft, giving body.

He buried his face in her neck, his hold slipping. "Fuck, baby…"

"Noah."

That was all it took. His name on her lips, spoken in passion and not fear. A plea to give her what she needed. Damn if he could do anything else but give.

One arm worked between her ass and the mattress, angling her hips to take more of him. The other cupped the back of her head and held her against his rough kiss. He withdrew and pushed back inside, the glide slick and tight and hot. He tore his mouth away to suck in a ragged breath, dropping his forehead to hers.

He took her with slow strokes, and she met him with a moan, urging him on. She said his name, over and over. A plea. A demand. There was nothing better than hearing her say his name. Nothing. Sweat soaked their skin. Testing her, he drove into her a little harder, faster.

"Ah, Noah. *Yes, yes, yes.*" Her nails raked his scalp. Her legs banded tighter, heels digging into his ass and urging him for more. She threw her head back, and the scent of rain mixed with musk surrounded them.

He grabbed the headboard with one hand to keep them from drifting as he ground into her. Again and again. With each punishing thrust, she grew more demanding, until her walls clenched around his shaft and she cried out, holding his head to her collarbone as she came.

He followed, driving twice more, and strained. Violent shudders wracked his body until he was completely drained. Spent, he tried to roll them to the side, but she held him firm.

"No. Stay like this. Don't...move."

He rested the side of his face between her breasts and slid his arms around her, unsure of what, if anything, could be said after that storm. Her fingers combed his hair lazily, and he fell asleep just like that, with her holding him for a change.

Chapter Nine

How fitting her and Noah's last day together be Valentine's—a holiday they both despised and was the epitome of everything they rejected about romantic love. In the past, no matter who they'd been dating, she and Noah spent Valentine's Day together, usually watching an action movie in her apartment. Except this year, he demanded they do something different.

She glanced down at the dress laid out on her bed. This morning, she'd packed up her things and told Noah she'd return to her apartment after work. Their time was up. Other than a clench of his jaw and a tight nod, he had no response. She'd come home from the gallery to find the dress and a note. She'd tried to sever the physical aspect of their relationship cleanly, just as he'd wanted…as she'd wanted, even though a tiny part of her hoped…

Wear this tonight. I'm taking you out.

How did he even know the right size? And shoes, too. A thin slip of a dress, it was ankle-length and dark red, with the neckline coming to a V between her breasts and a slit going up one thigh. It felt like silk between her fingers. The shoes were black heels and three thousand dollars. Both Nicole and Raven had sighed over the pair on their last shopping trip.

Since when did he buy her expensive gifts?

Sitting on the edge of her bed, she reached into her nightstand for the key to her jewelry box and wrapped her hands around a small leather-bound book instead. Drawing it out, she set it in her lap. Years ago, a psychiatrist had given it to her and told her to write her thoughts inside. Like a diary or journal, it was supposed to help her come to terms with her memories. She'd never written in it, the pages blank.

She glanced at the dress and then the book. What better time to start than now, when her feelings were a kaleidoscope of crazy? Snatching a pen from the drawer, she cleared her mind and just wrote the first thing that popped in her head. She'd written two pages, hardly noticing what she'd penned, when the doorbell rang.

She whipped her glance to the alarm clock. It was almost seven.

"Shit." Running to the door, she carelessly tossed the book on the coffee table before turning the knob. "Max?"

He smiled. "Don't be too disappointed. I've been instructed to deliver you to dinner with Mr. Caldwell."

"Oh. I'm running behind. Give me a few minutes to change. Come in."

"I'll wait here for you."

"You will not. It's freezing." She grabbed the lapels of his coat and pulled him inside, though she suspected he let her. She'd never budge a man his size.

She shut the door and went down the hall. "Be right back."

He cleared his throat. "No rush, ma'am."

"Max," she said in a warning tone, shrugging out of her work suit.

"Sorry, Miss Crowne." His voice was deep and loud as it traveled to her.

Setting the clothes on her bed, she unzipped the dress. "I can hear you smiling." She stepped into the dress and twisted to zip the back.

"I can't help it, Miss Crowne. You're a very likable person."

Aw. Hell. "Thank you."

"You're welcome."

She rushed into the bathroom, brushed her hair, decided she didn't have time to putz with it, and spritzed her neck with perfume. Her makeup had survived the workday, but she touched up her lipstick and made her way to the living room.

Max gave an appreciative nod, holding out her long, black peacoat. "Very lovely, Miss Crowne."

"Thanks, Max. You're full of sweetness today." She placed her arms in the coat he held and turned to button it. His face was scarlet, but she didn't call him out. Chances were, he didn't get to converse with many people. If he stayed on her detail, she'd like to at least be able to talk to him. "Are you still my bodyguard?"

"Yes, ma'am…Miss Crowne."

"You should call me Raven, then."

Flustered, he opened the door. "After you."

They wove through the dark, icy streets of Tartok Crest in the opposite direction of Anchorage with the Northern Lights as a backdrop against a starry night. The moon was full and clear, illuminating the snow and storefronts. There wasn't much down this way except The Sound, and no restaurants were this far south.

"Where are we going?"

"I've been instructed not to say." He glanced at her in the rearview and then back to the road.

"Do you always do as instructed?"

"Most of the time."

Ha. Humor. "I instruct you to tell me where we're going."

He didn't laugh as she'd hoped, or even crack a smile. His jaw hardened and his gaze kept shifting from the rearview to the road. His entire demeanor changed from jovially reserved to alert and tense. Very calmly, he said, "Miss Crowne, please lie down in the seat and make sure your seatbelt is buckled."

Her heart stopped. "What's wrong?"

"Nothing I can't handle. Please do as I said."

Suddenly shaking, she lay down crossways on the seat and tightened her belt, cold sweat lacing her skin.

He pushed a button on the console to activate Bluetooth and, a second later, someone by the name of Hintz answered. Max shoved an earpiece into his ear. "We have a tail." He gave a handful of one word answers and disconnected.

The car changed lanes and Raven tried to swallow through her fear. What the heck was going on? And why was someone following them? For the entire three weeks Max had been her shadow, nothing even close to worrisome had occurred. The car swerved back again and picked up speed. She bit back a cry and dug her fingernails into her palms. Closing her eyes, she focused on her breathing to avoid a panic attack.

In, out. In, out.

"You can sit up now, Miss Crowne."

Blowing out a breath, she straightened in the seat and smoothed her hair. She shifted to look out the back window, but there were no headlights. "Max—"

He tapped his earpiece and said, "It's gone. Yes, I'm sure. No, sir. We're heading to you now. We had to circle around off route." There was a lengthy pause in which Max regarded her in the rearview before answering. "She's quite calm, sir."

She fisted her shaking hands in her lap. Calm, her ass. Fighting back tears, she glared out the window toward Prince William Sound. Ships, docked at the harbor, bobbed and swayed in the frigid wind. Some crab boats dotted the horizon. The Northern Lights reflected off the choppy water. Truly beautiful, a sight she'd never grow tired of...if her heart wasn't stuck in her throat and her limbs blocks of ice.

There was no deluding herself anymore. Though nothing had come of being followed tonight, Max's reaction was a slap of reality. He wouldn't have made her lie down if he hadn't thought bullets were a possibility. He wouldn't have called backup for a simple tail. Noah's security wasn't a precaution or because of his parents' old ghosts. He was living with a very real threat and had been since before they'd met.

The car stopped and she glanced up. They'd parked at a private pier on the edge of The Sound where a large yacht bobbed on the water. Lights illuminated the interior. Max came around and swept his hard gaze across the area before opening her door. On unsteady legs, she rose and hunched against the wind. He took her elbow and walked her to the edge of the pier.

A door snapped and Noah emerged by the railing of the boat. With one smooth, fluid motion, he leapt from the bough to the pier and stalked toward her, his blond hair catching the wind. She halted to watch him eat the distance, her relief so heavy tears blurred her eyes. He strode right to her, palmed her cool cheeks in his warm hands, and kissed her soundly.

"Are you all right?" His gaze swept over her before he crushed her against him. Tension radiated off of him. He shook from it. Cupping the back of her head, he held her to him and spoke in her ear. "I was fucking worried sick."

"She handled it well."

Noah spoke to Max over her head, his hold on her unrelenting. "Details."

"Dark blue or black Ford pickup. Newer model. It tailed us halfway enroute." There was a pause. "It was the same vehicle from two weeks ago. This time he wanted me to know he was there. After a mile, it turned off before Hintz could arrive for backup."

This had happened before? And she hadn't known?

"Fuck. We need to go back to the condo. We're too wide open here."

"Agreed. Hintz is meeting us here. I'll redirect him." Max's shoes crunched as he walked away.

Noah pulled her away from him, his hard, glacial blue eyes scanning her face.

Tears filled her eyes again, falling and freezing on her face. "I'm sorry. I don't know why I'm so upset. Nothing happened—" Her legs threatened to buckle.

"Ah, baby." He crushed her to him again, as if unable to let her go. "It would scare anyone. Hell, I still can't...Swear to God, I think I died when Max called." Bending, he swept an arm under her legs and carried her to the SUV with long, determined strides.

Her legs were frozen under her dress by the time they were driving again. Or maybe it was the shock because her whole body was ice. Keeping her sideways in his lap, Noah absently ran his hands up and down the length of them, cheek resting on the top of her head. He ordered Max to turn up the heat.

"I want you back at the condo. It has more security and we can protect you better." He paused when she didn't respond. "If you'd like, you can stay in the guestroom. If you don't want...to sleep next to me." His voice was strained and low, on the cusp of snapping like he'd done that day in the shower.

As her gaze transfixed out the window, her chest swelled. He wanted her to stay. Except it was just to keep her safe, not because he wanted to retract the agreement. At least, that was the impression she got from him. But then why bring up sleeping together? Did he...want to continue?

When had she started hoping for more? Between dinner a month before, when he'd blown their friendship out of the water, and right this moment, she'd found a semblance of normal with another person. Not just someone, but Noah. Her best friend, her anchor.

Stupid. People like them weren't capable of picket fences and ever-afters. Both believed fairy tales were full of crap. Marriage, kids, monogamy were fine for those that sought the lifestyle, believed in it. She and Noah weren't those people. At least, they hadn't been. Was she reading too much into his request?

"Raven?" He said her name like a prayer.

"Okay," she said, her voice dull even to her own ears. "I'll...stay. I need to stop by my apartment and get some things." And once they were alone again, he was going to tell her what the hell was going on. No more keeping her in the dark.

He cradled her closer in answer.

■■■

Noah followed Raven into her apartment and shut the door with Max on the other side to stand vigil. Wordlessly, she went down the hall toward her bedroom, so he plopped on the couch with his head in his hands. His *shaking* hands.

Ten years and he'd taken every precaution to avoid this exact moment. Looked like his FBI contact was right. There was a hit out on him. But why taunt Raven by following her instead of just taking a shot? Not that he wasn't grateful.

And he hadn't been with her. Max Gerard was the best, Noah wouldn't have hired him if he wasn't, but shit...*he* hadn't been with her. That little incident could've been something much more than a tail. Tonight was just a warning. Something could've happened to her, *and he wasn't fucking there.*

He'd stood in his condo this morning like a dumb fuck and had said nothing as she packed, despite how everything inside his head screamed not to let her walk. He thought he was being irrational, clouding the friendship line with sex, so he'd said nothing. But damn...

He swiped a hand down his face, gaze landing on a small book on her coffee table. Picking it up for a distraction, he skimmed the first page, recognizing her handwriting.

And though all this seems well and good—a rise from poor upbringings—I remain someone of little consequence. I linger in the shadows, letting the artists shine. That is their place, not mine. I merely give them the means. I much prefer it this way, for reasons I dare not pull from memory or I'll sink back into the dark.

The more he read, the bigger the hole in his chest grew.

So when my assistant strolled into my office on the second floor of Elements and set her palms flat on my desk one idle Tuesday morning, I had no way of knowing that this would be the moment everything changed. A series of dominoes tipping with a clack, all leading to an unexpected and crazy end. One I fear I won't ever recover from.

It was dated today. Nothing before it, nothing after.

Raven walked into the room and set down a suitcase.

Slowly, he rose and turned to her. "I'm something you'll never recover from?"

She looked at the book and then him, genuinely confused by his question. She waved her fingers for him to pass it over. He did, and she scanned the page and reared back. "I wrote this earlier today. Honestly, I've never written a journal before. I let my mind go blank and just wrote." She looked up. "Max arrived before I could read it."

For the first time tonight, his gaze took in the dress he'd picked out for her. She was as breathtaking as he'd imagined. Thin straps over her slender shoulders, the material clung to her breasts and flowed like water. Raven wearing red was instant dick CPR. Every time.

But it was more than that, more than the physical punch of lust she invoked. Raven was smart, strong, and compassionate. Elegant and hard-working. The only person who could drag a laugh out of him most days. She made him desire to be something better. Someone who could maybe be the lasting sort. To fall asleep beside and wake up with each morning. Who'd protect her at every turn and put her above all else.

In a way, he'd been doing it for years. Only now, he was aware.

In the journal, she'd said she was of little consequence. That couldn't be further from the truth. It didn't even leave him rattled to discover she was the most important person in this world to him, equaled and comparable only to Aubrey. It pained him to think she felt that way. He hoped to all that was holy he didn't put that view in her head. Didn't she get it? After everything the past month, the past ten years, did she not see his sun rose and set with her?

She made him...feel. After a lifetime of forcing emotion down and welcoming the numbness that separated him from attachment, she'd opened a door. And he was something she wanted to recover from.

He stepped forward. "Answer me. Please."

Tossing the book down, she leveled him with a look that nearly brought him to his knees. Desperation, longing, desire, optimism. It melded together in the span of seconds. Finally, she swallowed, her voice husky and raw when she spoke. "I don't know if it's possible to recover from you."

Just like that, the room tipped. The floor fell out from beneath his feet. The air evaporated. Yet neither of them moved. The clock on her wall kept ticking.

"Sage." It was the only thing he could think of to say, the only thing that seemed to make any damn sense. All things considered, he was surprised he could force the word out.

Confusion wrinkled her brows before they lifted in surprise. Her lips parted in a gasp. "Noah?"

Yeah. He was invoking the safeword. "It appears that you leaving is my hard limit." When she didn't say anything, he took another step closer. "I don't know what in the hell happened, but giving up on us because the time clock punched out doesn't feel right. What could it hurt to try?" He swallowed hard. "Stay, Raven. Stay and see where this goes."

She let out a breath, hand fisted over her chest. "I told you sex would change everything," she whispered, tears clinging to her long, dark lashes.

"You're still my best friend. I'd still do anything for you, anything in my power to protect you. Sex didn't change that. It enhanced it." He closed the distance until they stood toe to toe and she had to crane her neck to look up at him. He skimmed the back of his hand down her arm, linking their fingers. "Sage, baby."

She shook her head, the motion conflicting with the hope in her eyes. "God, Noah. You really want to do this? What do we know about relationships? Hell, people don't get more broken than us."

In his opinion, scars weren't a thing to hide behind. Having them meant a person went through hell and was still around to tell the tale. He dropped his forehead to hers. "If you can honestly say to me you haven't thought about it, that you aren't tempted to try, then I'll walk away. Can you say that, Raven?"

Her eyes fluttered closed, the pulse in her neck beating erratically. "I can't say that because you're right. I have thought about it, about…us."

He cupped her cheek, forcing her to look at him. Leaning in, he brought his mouth to hers, kissing her long and thorough and deep. He edged back enough to look in her eyes. "I think it's time you met my family."

Chapter Ten

To Have

Raven grabbed the armrests of her seat and pinched her eyes closed. She'd been in Noah's float plane before, but this was different. The helicopter didn't offer the same smooth ride or peace of mind. Sure, she was being silly, but with her stomach in her throat it was hard to think rationally.

After his rather cryptic announcement back at her apartment, Noah had told her to change into comfortable clothes and then ushered her out the door. God. He had a helicopter. His own helicopter. At his disposal. They'd taken off in Anchorage and were heading to destinations unknown somewhere north. He refused to tell her where.

She wondered what he meant by *meeting his family*. Having been introduced to his parents a few times in college before their fatal car crash, she'd known he had no other living relatives besides some distant cousins on his mother's side. What could he possibly have meant by that statement?

From the seat beside her, Noah patted her hand. "You okay, baby?" His voice came through her headset as he yelled over the noise.

Up front, Max turned to offer her a reassuring smile. "Almost there, Miss Crowne."

She nodded and faced the window. Several mountain ranges, lakes, and villages passed as the copter ventured overhead. They were low enough to make out some vegetation and lights from the houses at their elevation.

"I didn't know you could fly, Max."

He turned and grinned again. "Yes, ma'am. I have a license and everything."

"Ha," she barked. "Funny guy."

His shoulders shook with a chuckle, but he said nothing more.

Noah rubbed the back of her hand with his thumb, the coarseness of his skin causing her to shiver. The touch succeeded in calming her a bit. "Max flies me up to the estate once a month. He was an Air Force pilot before finishing his last tour and coming to work for me. You're in good hands."

Max threw a thumbs-up over his shoulder.

The next twenty minutes passed with nothing but the wide expanse of the rough Alaskan terrain. He was truly taking her to the middle of nowhere. She couldn't even make out any roads. Questions filled her mind, too many to voice. Noah wouldn't answer them until he was damn good and ready, so she bit them back and focused on the view.

The helicopter dipped left and Max's voice filled her headset. "We're here."

She didn't see anything but mountains. "Where are we?"

"The northern Kuskokwim Mountains, on the western facing ridge." Noah leaned forward. "Circle in from the other side so she can see."

"Yes, sir."

They were way west of Fairbanks, then. Though she'd never ventured out this far, she knew the land was too rugged for roads and no major communities were within range. Was this why he chose the location? To make it near impossible for others to get to him? Or…his family? The family she knew nothing about.

The helicopter dipped right, and Noah tapped her hand, pointing to her window. "Welcome to Aubrey Castle."

The breath caught in her throat. Though the structure didn't look anything like a castle, it was just as massive. With the rear snug against the base of the mountain, it seemed to be an extension of the land. Resembling a log cabin in design, the color of the exterior indicated redwood. Nearly the entire front was glass. Three stories tall, she could make out a launch pad on one side of the roof, balconies on the south end, and a wraparound porch at the base. Thick forest with spruce and birch were directly north, and a small lake with a spring to the southwest. It was…breathtaking.

They said nothing as Max brought them down onto the roof, shifted some gears, and stepped out to get Noah's door. A crisp, biting wind shoved into the passenger hold, causing chaos with Noah's blond hair. The whirl of the propellers overhead slowed and stopped.

Instead of getting out, Noah turned to her. "No one but my security team knows about this place. You need to understand that. Once we're inside and settled, I'll tell you everything. Just…be patient."

His clear blue eyes held hers, more exposed than she could ever remember seeing them. He'd never brought anyone here before, never trusted them enough. Emotion clogged her throat. She'd passed some test in his mind if he was taking this leap.

He cupped her cheek and kissed her mouth. "Come on, baby. There's someone I'd like you to meet."

She nodded, fighting tears, and stepped out after him.

Taking her hand, they crossed a windy tarmac and entered a door. Warmth immediately enveloped them. Pine and wood polish filled her nose as she glanced around. Telescopes lined the wall with windows, all directed up to the glass dome ceiling. A desk and a drafting table rested in the opposite corner. Globes and models of the solar system filled the shelves and tables.

Before she could get her bearings, the interior door opened and a girl rushed through. Raven caught a glimpse of wavy strawberry blonde hair before the girl ran right past her and launched into Noah's arms.

Noah released Raven's hand to wrap his arms around the bundle clinging to his neck with skinny arms and his waist with her legs. "Easy, my love."

Raven stilled, hand at her throat. "My Love" was ten, maybe eleven years old, and had her face buried in Noah's shoulder. She was wearing a long nightgown as if she'd been preparing for bed before they'd intruded.

Raven's heart started to pound, dread swirling in her gut. What in the hell was going on?

"I missed you," the girl slurred.

Noah closed his eyes and kissed her head. "I missed you, too. So much." He ran his hand up and down her back. "I brought you a visitor."

She lifted her head, still not having seen Raven, and waved at Max. "Did you bring me something?"

Max shoved his hand in his pocket and held out his palm. On his outstretched hand was a penny. "1956. Don't think you have that year, Miss Aubrey."

Aubrey. As in Aubrey Castle? Just who was this girl and why had Noah named an entire mansion after her? Not only that, but so far away from civilization it required them to fly to its destination.

As if sensing her confusion, Noah glanced her way and carefully set the girl on her feet. With her back to Raven, Aubrey took the penny from Max and held it up, examining it.

With his gaze still on Raven, Noah cleared his throat. "What do you say, Aubrey?"

"Thanks, Maxie. It's awesome."

Maxie looked like he was biting the inside of his cheek. "Very welcome, Miss Aubrey."

At that moment, Aubrey turned toward Raven. The girl froze in place. Her face was pale with freckles sprinkled over her nose and cheeks. Her eyes were a bright aqua blue, shades lighter than Noah's, and she was very thin for her height. When she turned to Noah, Raven's gaze lowered to her neck, where red, twisted scars ran from her ear down until disappearing under the nightgown. Her hand had the same scarring, indicating it covered the whole arm.

Burn scars.

Noah smiled and wrapped his arm around the girl's shoulders, dragging her to his side. "Aubrey, I'd like you to meet Raven. Raven, this is my niece, Aubrey."

Niece. But Noah had no siblings.

They stared at each other for a beat before Raven realized she might be scaring her. "Hi, there! It's so nice to finally meet you."

Aubrey looked up at Noah. "But you never bring strangers." The words were once again slurred, and her mannerisms indicated someone much younger than she looked.

Noah's expression was pained, but he kissed her hair. "She's not a stranger, my love. She's very special, just like you, and I'd like you to be friends."

Aubrey regarded her before she stepped out from under Noah's arm and crushed Raven in a hug. "I like friends."

"Me, too." She wrapped her arms around the girl, careful not to squeeze too hard for fear she'd break her. She smelled like baby powder, innocence. Typically, Raven wasn't fond of touch, but something about the girl called to her.

Raven met Noah's gaze over Aubrey's shoulder. Tenderness and apprehension filled his eyes. This moment obviously meant a lot to him.

He rubbed his neck and nodded at Max. The bodyguard stepped back outside and brought in their luggage, Aubrey holding Raven in her death grip hug the whole while. Max moved past them and into the hall, their bags in his hands.

Noah sighed. "Come on, my love. It's getting late. How about we get Frances to whip you up a snack and then it's off to bed."

She let go of Raven and turned to him. "But you just got here."

He ran a hand down her soft waves. "We'll be here all weekend. Lots of fun to be had."

"Really?"

"Cross my heart." He swallowed, glancing at Raven and quickly away. "Scoot. We'll be down in a few minutes." When they were alone in the room, he kept his gaze down. "She's excited. Let's get her calmed down and we can talk."

After the five dollar tour, Raven could do little more than gawk. The house had a library, solarium, indoor pool, gym, and media room, all in addition to the observation deck from which they'd arrived. The live-in caretakers, Frances and Jeff Brisbin, were in their mid-sixties and regarded her with friendly reserve. There was more security throughout the house, who never engaged her outside of a nod.

The living room, den, and kitchen were all front-facing, with floor to ceiling spectacular views of the lake, spring, and forest. Massive wood beams in the slanted ceilings, hardwood floors with decorative rugs, stone fireplaces with raw-cut mantles…it was a decorator's dream. Even the candles and throw pillows were tasteful, the kitchen a mix of slate and stainless steel. The second and third floors weren't just bedrooms, but suites, each one complete with its own bath, kitchenette, and living room. The house was bigger than a freaking hotel!

Frances gave Aubrey a snack and dished out some soup for her and Noah, since they never did get dinner. Though Raven didn't have the stomach for food, she ate to be polite. While she did, she watched Noah and Aubrey together from across the long dining table big enough for a White House press conference. Aubrey was a delightful, if not somewhat lonely child, who obviously loved her uncle a great deal. In turn, Noah was crafty and funny around her, illustrating none of his usual intensity.

More questions than answers pushed around in her skull, shoving for space and attention. He had a girl—a niece supposedly—hidden away in the middle of nowhere, who had burn scars on her arm. Though the girl seemed educated, she was socially awkward. Bodyguards were everywhere, milling about. The house had a security system that could trump NASA. There was a panic room, for goodness sake!

After an hour, Noah sensed her growing unease and bid everyone a goodnight, claiming they'd tuck Aubrey in for the evening. Raven didn't know whether to be relieved or worried she'd finally get her answers.

Just who the hell was Noah Caldwell?

With Raven leaning against the doorframe, Noah pulled a blanket up to Aubrey's chin and leaned over the bed to kiss her forehead, reassuring her he'd be there come morning. Her blonde hair spread out over the pillow, her blue eyes sleepy, he had to resist not rubbing the ache in his chest. His whole adult life had been about protecting this precious little girl, when he'd barely been of adult age himself.

And she needed her sleep. "I love you." He rose and headed for the door.

"Love you more. Does she like coloring?" Aubrey asked through a yawn.

Noah lifted his brows, pleased Aubrey was sending out feelers for Raven. In no time, they'd be past the awkward phase and Aubrey would love her to no end. That's how she rolled. Her trust was never-ending. "Raven's a master colorer."

Aubrey laughed. "That's not a real word."

Raven smiled, exhaustion in her features. "I don't know about master, but I can hold my own. How about we get right on that after breakfast tomorrow?"

Leaving Aubrey to her slumber, he and Raven worked their way through the second floor suites where Aubrey's caretakers slept, as well as the security team. They climbed the stairs to the third floor and to his suite on the far end of the house.

Just as she'd done since arriving, Raven took in her surroundings quietly. He'd designed and built this house from the ground up, carefully selecting everything from the region to the light fixtures. He wondered if she liked it. Somehow, that was important to him. He wasn't expecting how it would make him feel having her here. So right, so…perfect.

She crossed the polished bare hardwood floors of the living room, decorated in plush brown leather furniture and rustic tables, to stand by the glass wall facing the lake. Moonlight bathed her face in ethereal wonder. In the distance, the Northern Lights flashed and danced across the sky. His fingers itched for his camera, but he didn't think she'd appreciate that at the moment.

He dug in his pocket and extracted a small box. Walking over to stand behind her, he held it out to her. "Your Valentine's present."

She craned her neck to look at him, pretty brown eyes wide. "You didn't have to do that. I…we…"

"We were supposed to be finished. I know, but I can't seem to quit you." He brushed his knuckles down her cheek. She closed her eyes and leaned into the touch. The need to strip her down and bury himself inside her was fierce, but he had a lot of explaining to do and he wasn't sure she wouldn't still leave him afterward. "Open it. To warn you, I've never bought a Valentine's gift before."

She smiled. "Never got one before, so my expectations are low." She flipped the lid of the velvet box and drew in a sharp gasp. "Oh, it's lovely."

Reaching around her, he pulled the small ruby heart from the box and slid the chain through his fingers. Raven was simple sophistication and not flash, so he had to refrain from buying the largest rock he could find. "There's just something about you and the color red that makes my blood roar." Unclasping the chain, he brought it to her throat and fastened it behind her neck. It rested perfectly above the swell of her breasts.

She fingered the charm. "I love it. Thank you."

He wrapped one arm around her from behind, tugging her flush against him. Dipping his head, he used his other hand to sweep her hair off her shoulder and kissed her neck. "You're welcome. Feel free to wear that, and only that, to bed later."

Laughing, she turned in his arms. "Done." She stroked his chest over his white shirt, her smile faltering. "Noah…"

He exhaled and dropped his forehead to hers. "Come sit down. I'll answer all your questions."

She nodded and took a spot on the couch, leaving his arms unbearably empty. She was expecting him to sit next to her by the expectant expression, but he couldn't sit down to do this. Frankly, it wasn't a story he'd told in years, for so long it would seem as if it were someone else's life if not for Aubrey.

Rubbing his neck, he figured starting at the beginning was best. He could only wish he wasn't throwing ten years of friendship and one month of sweet bliss out the window.

Chapter Eleven

Noah swallowed and turned away from Raven, facing the window and the view, but not truly seeing it. He shoved his hands in his pockets and tried to prepare himself for what rehashing his past was going to do to him, to her.

"My mother had a daughter through a previous marriage when she met my dad. Fresh on the political circuit, they got married quickly and had me. Melissa was eight years older than me and spent a lot of time with her dad, so we weren't exactly close. Neither of us harbored any resentment, there was just such a big age gap."

Pressing his palm to the frame, he leaned into his hand and hung his head. "She married Mario Francesco when I was ten, and none of us had any idea he was a legal aid for Rizzoli. My father was part of the Democratic Party and went up against Rizzoli in a few elections. Mario found out about misused campaign funds, but that was the tip of the iceberg. When the feds dug deeper, they found money laundering and drug pushing out of New Jersey. We didn't see a lot of Melissa during those years, either because the family wouldn't let her or it was some misguided way to keep us safe. They'd had a son, Jonathon, but he barely recognized us."

Forcing himself to look at her, he turned and checked her reaction.

Pale but calm, she nodded slowly. "Go on."

Nervous energy skimmed under his skin, so he paced. "The summer before my senior year of high school, she got pregnant with Aubrey. Jonathon was five. The feds were coming close to gathering enough evidence for an arrest on Rizzoli. Mario was turning over particulars to avoid prosecution which, of course, Rizzoli didn't know."

Bone tired, he crossed the room and sat on the table in front of her. The ingrained part of him needing her near was pacified by the move. "My father was concerned enough to have me looking into colleges as far from the east coast as possible. That's how I settled in Alaska." He swallowed hard, his gut churning.

As if sensing the story was about to take an ugly turn, she closed her warm fingers over his hands. "Do you need a minute?"

He shook his head. He'd had nothing but minutes, endless agonizing minutes that accumulated into years. Better just to spit it out fast. "The summer after graduation, Rizzoli found out what Mario was up to and had Mario and Melissa's house burned down to the ground. With them inside."

She gasped, fingers tightening over his. Her eyes welled. "Noah."

Waving away her sympathy, he got up to stand by the window again. The pressure in his chest expanded, the vise around his throat cinching. The fucking worst part was coming. "Two days after the funeral, I got a call from the FBI asking to meet. Turned out, a neighbor of Melissa's saw the house burning and called the fire department before running into the blaze. He wasn't able to save the others, but he got Aubrey out."

He paused, but there was no way to garner composure for the rest. He let himself break for the first time in a decade. "She had second degree burns on the left side of her body. She was only eight months old and couldn't escape the crib." His voice cracked. Tears blurred his eyes, falling hot and heavy on his frozen cheeks. His chest cracked open.

Raven came up beside him, her eyes wet. Smoothing her hand down his arm, she linked their fingers. She moved in front of him, not wiping away the tears or offering pithy condolences. None of those things helped one fucking bit. But he was grateful, so damn grateful, she was here.

He wiped his face with the back of his hand and looked over her shoulder, still hearing Aubrey's cries of pain in his head. "A month later, when she was stable enough, they transferred her in secret to a hospital in Anchorage. While she was recovering, I used my inheritance and the money from her life insurance to build this house, with everything a little girl could ever need. My parents never knew she survived, and it killed me not to tell them, watching them grieve with no hope. But I had to keep her safe."

His gaze slid to Raven's. Held. "I hired the Brisbins to be her caretakers, who were down on their luck and could never have children. She has a tutor who lives on site four days a week, a team of security that never leaves." He shook his head. "And I started college like nothing had happened, visiting once a month on the pretense of mountain climbing or fishing." He swallowed. "For ten years."

She cupped his jaw with both hands, soothing away some of the ache with just her touch. "What about your parents? They died, what, two years later?"

He nodded. "The FBI couldn't link their accident to Rizzoli, but we suspected." Grabbing her wrists, he held them tightly. "You have to understand, I'd never put you at risk. From the moment we met, I've had a guard following you at a distance, just in case. I've had a private investigator gathering evidence, but Rizzoli was slippery. It took this long to get a good amount so he couldn't wiggle out of charges. The FBI has enough to lock the bastard away for good." He shook her. "That's why I made a move with you. It was supposed to be over."

"Okay," she said immediately, wrapping her arms around him, her scent of rain calming his erratic heartbeat. "I believe you." She rubbed his back in slow methodical circles. "But what about the truck who followed us tonight?"

It seemed so long ago, but it had been tonight. He hated this fucking holiday, not that it had anything to do with his past. "A week after you and I…" He waved his hand, unable to put words to what was between them. Sex wasn't the label to slap on it anymore. "McCannon, my FBI contact, called to tell me there was a hit out on me. Rizzoli's funds are inaccessible, but he got around that somehow, had money hidden somewhere."

Her gaze grew distant. "That's what that call was about at your condo. The day you got upset and we wound up in the shower."

His teeth gnashed. "Yes." She'd shocked him that day, taking his punishing thrusts and endless supply of rage. There was something utterly healing about being with her, sinking into her soft, supple flesh and letting the world fall away. Though he didn't think sex would fix his riotous emotions tonight, his erection thickened, needing her. Always needing her.

He sighed. "Rizzoli never had any interest in me. Moving to Alaska was more precaution than anything, but then Aubrey happened…" He shook his head. "I wanted justice, so I pushed. Got evidence. Rizzoli found out about my involvement the same night I told you the truth." He grabbed her shoulders. "I won't let him hurt you. The trial will be over soon. The contract out on me is a last ditch attempt at revenge. I'm all that's left of my family. He doesn't know Aubrey exists."

She blew out a breath. Her gaze swept over him, the moonlight at her back and heart in her eyes. No one else ever got to see this side of her. The yielding, vulnerable person she hid under all that control.

Threading her fingers in his hair, she tugged his head down to hers. "None of this is your fault. None of it."

He suspected she knew a thing or two about irrational guilt. No, he wasn't responsible for this clusterfuck any more than she was for her own parents' deaths. Still, the thought of that bastard taking her from him gave fear a whole new name, made wrath bounce around inside his skull until thinking was a pipe dream.

Hell, he was teetering between pushing her away to keep her safe and drawing her closer for the same reasons. Tonight, they'd found her. And it scared him so damn bad he hadn't drawn in air since. There were two people in this world he'd die for, and tonight, both were under the same roof.

Sensing the shift in him, or maybe she just knew what he needed, she brought her mouth to his and kissed logic out of his head. Her tongue danced with his, her arms banding around him like she was just as fucking lost.

Clothing flew across the room. But always, his mouth came back to her kiss. To heaven. Naked, shaking, he laced their fingers and pinned her hands above her head to the cool glass wall. She brought one leg up, then the other to wrap around his hips, arching her back and forcing her pebbled nipples to rub against his chest.

Reality eked in and he tore his mouth away. "Is this okay? Your hands..." Restraint and her weren't friends, but they were vertical and he was throbbing to the point of pain. Tonight, he needed to dominate. To feel like he had some measure of control again. But not at the risk of her mental well-being.

"Yes," she breathed, rolling her hips to rub him between her folds. "Now, Noah."

God help him. She was so wet. Ready. With a slight shift, he aligned their bodies and, with her hands still gripped in his, he locked his gaze to hers and thrust deep. Soft, wet flesh enveloped him, accepted and welcomed him into her body. There was nothing else like it, nothing like being inside her.

Absolutely nothing.

Her pupils blew as she let out a needy whimper, and he was reminded how much he fucking loved that noise. Her eyes drifted shut. She ground against him when he stilled, seeking more. But he had to watch her, just for a moment. He couldn't take his eyes off her. Her black hair, damp with sweat, her soft porcelain skin, midnight lashes fanning her cheeks, flushed face, lips parted in desire, and breasts rising and falling with rapid breaths.

Perfection. *His.*

"Noah..."

"Right here, baby." He took a step forward, so there wasn't a breath between them, wedging her between the glass and his body. He was close to snapping, and he shook with the need to let go. She'd handled it once before, but he was in a much darker place this time. As if he needed the reminder.

The bastard had found her. Anything could've happened. If they got their hands on her... Fuck. Image after gory image filtered through his mind, closing his throat. His eyes burned.

He growled. Thrust. *Yes.* She was here. He was inside her.

She begged for more.

He gave it to her. Rearing back, he drove right back in. A string of unintelligible curses followed, because... She. Felt. So. Damn. Good.

His fingers squeezed hers, while her walls clenched him. Her cries blended with his grunts. His muscles strained to keep them upright, to keep up with the brutal pace. Burying his face in her neck, he opened his mouth wide to have a muffle for the frenzied, animalistic sounds escaping. Their skin was slick with sweat. He pistoned faster, feeling the pull all the way to the muscles in his back, his ass.

He punished himself. He punished her.

Just as his balls tightened and he knew he couldn't hold out much longer, she shook with an orgasm, clamping inner muscles around his shaft and wrenching a scream from him. He came so damn hard, falling to his knees, still buried inside her with her back pressed to the glass.

He forced his thrusts to shallow, gliding slowly to ride out the last of their quaking.

Scared to open his eyes, to move, he fought for air and released her hands. She immediately wrapped her arms around him, breath hot in his ear. His chest ached, his throat beyond ravaged.

What in the hell was happening to him? To take her like that was…reprehensible.

Fumbling, he sat back on his haunches and pulled her to him as if she wasn't already molded like second skin. It wasn't enough. Twisting, he fell on his ass to lean against the glass with her in his lap. Not enough. He drew his knees up, cinching her higher. His arms banded around her back, up to her shoulders. Frustration ripped through him.

Not…fucking…close…enough.

"I'm sorry, baby. I'm so sorry."

∙∙∙

Not knowing what else to do, Raven encouraged, and then forced, Noah into the bathroom. He preferred to shower at night and, after such a long, stressful day, a bath was a decent way to unwind before crashing.

The room was just as generous as the one in his condo, but the color tones were dark blues and grays instead of mossy green. The shower wasn't as luxurious, but the tub was big. The room smelled like him, like spice and comfort, even though they'd just arrived, and she realized, after a moment, that it was from oils he'd dripped into the water.

He climbed in and she followed, sitting behind him and urging him to lean against her. Since making love, he'd been silent, and she suspected the guilt was eating away at him. The desperation, the sheer frustration rolling off him afterward, was heart-wrenching.

Tears threatened when she thought about everything he'd been through, been forced to endure by no fault of his own. Lesser men would have let his parents take the girl or had the FBI put her into witness protection.

The love he had for Aubrey was undeniable. At eighteen, he'd given up his freedom to raise her, without any support system other than a bank account. Had it been her, Raven didn't know what she would've done. He'd always been kind, thoughtful. But who he was? Deep down? She hadn't even scratched the surface until tonight.

Trying to fight back tears, she took a washcloth from a ledge and dipped it in the water before running it over his shoulders. His head fell back against her, the fight leaving him as his muscles relaxed. With an arm over his chest, she squeezed water over his pecs, his stomach.

He sighed, as if enjoying her taking care of him for a change. Running his hands down her calves, he grabbed her ankles and crossed her legs, caging him in her hold. She followed his lead and wrapped her arms around his neck. He placed both hands on her arms, as if worried she'd let go.

She kissed his shoulder and rested her cheek there. "I'm going to smell like you after this bath."

He made a noise of agreement in his throat. "I like it when you smell like me." He caressed her arm, staring at the water. "You smell like rain. Your shampoo or soap. I can't tell. As much as the scent turns me on, there's nothing sexier than you smelling like me. I notice it most after making love."

She smiled. "You smell like Christmas cookies. Cinnamon."

Breathing out a laugh, he dropped his hand to her leg and stroked. After a moment, he stilled. "I didn't hurt you, did I? Please tell me you don't have bruises from—"

"Hey." She kissed his temple, letting her lips linger. "I'm fine. There's nothing wrong with a little rough sex. In case you didn't notice, I enjoyed it." She paused, trying to conjure a way to lighten his mood. "Although, I was a little worried we'd fall through the window."

"Bullet-proof glass. No chance." His voice was flat, making her worry ebb higher.

"In that case, we should do it again."

"I'm serious, Raven. I couldn't take it if I hurt you. When I'm like that, I—"

"Shh," she cooed in his ear. "You'd never hurt me. And I have a safeword, remember? I didn't invoke it." She didn't know what to do with him like this. It was as if he'd given up. Slipped into some form of depression where guilt had the reins.

He pressed his palms to his eyes and shook his head. "I made a mistake." Her stomach cramped when he sat up and slipped out of her arms. "I never should've gotten you involved in my mess. I should've stayed away from you. It was selfish."

Hugging her arms to her chest, she studied his shoulders and back. Sinew and bone and muscle in perfect symmetry. A chill crept up her spine. Not twelve hours ago, he'd tossed out the safeword when they were supposed to be ending it. It was *him* who'd asked her to stay. It would've been hard, but they would've gone back to their friendship, stronger for having experienced what they had together. But no. He got her hopes up, stood in her living room, and pleaded for more.

She wiped angrily at her tears, hating them. Not one to cry, as it only stripped composure, she straightened and swallowed past the worst of it. "You regret it." Stupid, weak voice. How could that be hers?

He turned his head and regarded her over his shoulder. How dare he look tormented. "Of course I don't regret it."

"I'm not daft, Noah. *A mistake* is a pretty obvious remark." She'd been a lot of things in her life. Invisible, controlling, cowardly. But never a mistake. The sharp stab in her gut twisted.

She rose from the tub and reached for a towel. He made no attempt to follow, just hung his head and viewed the water. Not waiting around to dry off, she wrapped the towel around her middle and headed for the door.

"I'd never regret a single second with you."

She turned, heart pounding, vision graying.

He still didn't look her in the eye, but his gaze landed on the ruby heart necklace she wore. "I made the mistake of not waiting until things were completely neutralized before engaging you. After a decade, I guess I was just sick of not having something for myself. You have no idea what it's been like—" Abruptly cutting himself off, he shook his head and rubbed his neck. "It was selfish. And now you're in danger."

Taking a step forward, she opened her mouth to speak, but he interrupted anything she might've said.

"Go to bed, Raven. I'll be in soon."

Angry, hurt, and—damn it, moved—she backed into the bedroom. Rooting through her suitcase, she found her pajamas and stepped into them. She lifted her head and her gaze landed on a picture on the wall she hadn't noticed before. Between him telling her about Aubrey and everything after, she hadn't paid much attention to the suite.

Stepping closer, she realized it was a black and white photo of her on the couch in her apartment, knees drawn to her chest, a glass of wine in her hand and head thrown back laughing. It must've been from her surprise party a few years ago, because that was the last time she remembered him with a camera. There was another next to it of her from college, wearing a red coat and beret, standing near a snow bank on campus. Another of her sitting on a kitchen stool in his condo, looking over her shoulder at him with a wry grin. That had to have been his housewarming.

Pressing her fingertips to her lips, she started to shake. There were no other pictures in his bedroom. Just...her. His condo in Anchorage had photos he'd taken of Gallivanting Adventures, but here...here was *personal*.

She strode into the living room. More pictures. Of Aubrey, his parents, a couple she assumed to be his sister and her husband. *Her*. The only one of him and Raven together was a selfie she'd taken last year with his new phone. He grinned over her shoulder at the camera, arm wrapped under hers and hand over her collarbone.

Her heart tripped in her chest. Doubt edged, even though the obvious was staring her in the face. Attraction was one thing. Friendship another. This seemed like...more.

The floor creaked behind her. She turned to find Noah leaning against the doorframe to the bedroom wearing a pair of flannel pants and nothing else, arms crossed over his chest.

It was criminal to be that attractive.

He studied her as if gauging her reaction. After a moment, he swallowed and glanced at the pictures. "I couldn't have any personal photos in Anchorage, in case he came looking for me." He shrugged and pushed off the doorframe, closing the distance. "But that's not what has your pulse tripping." He skimmed his fingers over her throat, gaze watching the path. His voice dipped lower when he spoke again. "What are you thinking? I'm having a hard time figuring it out."

She released the breath she hadn't realized she'd been holding. "There are a lot of me." She pointed to the wall.

She immediately regretted the slip the minute the words left her. She didn't want to know the reason. Really, she didn't. Facing that, while everything else was happening, was another complication she couldn't handle. Denial, her old friend.

One corner of his mouth lifted, his eyes softening. His thumb slid over her lower lip, releasing it from her teeth. "You're an important part of my life. Why wouldn't I have pictures of you?"

Well, when he put it that way. "And what about the pictures in your bedroom?"

His grin was a weapon of mass destruction. She'd swear it. "You're an important part of my fantasies, too." His gaze raked over her face, sliding into photographer mode. "Pose for me." When she tried to say no and back away, he hauled her right back. "Pose for me, not Hoan."

"You're the same person."

A slight shake of his head told her just how wrong she was. "No one will see them, if that's what you prefer. I've wanted you in front of my camera from day one, Raven. Don't deny me. Please."

God. How could she argue with that? "No one will see them?"

"Just you and me." He stepped closer so that their bodies brushed and shared heat. "You're too fucking beautiful to share with the world anyway."

A gale force wind expelled from her lungs. "Hell, you're smooth. No wonder women go all gooey around you."

Leaning in, he slid his mouth over hers and spoke against her lips. "I'm honest. And there's only one woman in this room. Pose for me."

Did her knees just go weak? Yes, yes they did, damn it. "Okay."

Chapter Twelve

They woke late in the morning and, though Noah wanted to burrow under the covers and make love to Raven, Aubrey was no doubt anxious for them to come down. He didn't get to see her near as often as he wanted and Skype just wasn't the same.

Aubrey drilled Raven with questions while they ate breakfast. Raven took them in stride, patiently answering each one. He'd never seen her around kids, but she was a natural with Aubrey. Afterward, they went to Aubrey's art room to color, and he got a great shot of their heads huddled together working on the same drawing. That one was going up on the wall before they left.

He'd been anxious to get Raven alone for the shots he wanted, but late light would be better for what he had in mind. He sat back in the chair in Aubrey's room, listening to his two best girls chat about stuff and smiling at how full his heart was. Odd, that.

Finished with the picture, Aubrey held it out for Raven. "To take home."

"For me? Really?" She grinned and swiped a strand of strawberry blonde hair off Aubrey's cheek, the gesture maternal. "I know just the place for it."

After they talked a few more minutes, Noah stood. "How about a walk outside? The temperature is supposed to be in the double digits today."

Aubrey bounced, tugging on Raven's sleeve. "I can show you my tree house!"

"Lead the way."

They bundled into their gear and walked across the front yard toward the woods. Jeff decided to join them and fell into step next to Noah, with Aubrey and Raven several paces ahead.

"They're getting along well."

He glanced at Aubrey's caretaker, noting the lines on his face were deepening, a testament to how time marched on. Ten years ago, Jeff didn't limp from arthritis. His dark hair had thinned on top during the past decade, too, and was now more gray than brown.

Returning his gaze to the girls, he smiled. "Like old friends. It's a good sight."

"Aye." They walked silently a few paces, the wind brisk off the mountain. "Does she know everything? Raven? You've mentioned her often enough, but we were a little surprised she came."

He nodded. "I told her last night. She knew some of it beforehand." He stopped and turned to Jeff. "I trust her with my life, with Aubrey's, or else she wouldn't be here."

Jeff raised a gloved hand. "Say no more. I understand." He glanced at the girls, then around the land. "What's your plan for when the trial is over?"

Blowing out a breath, he shook his head. "Hell if I know. I keep waiting for McCannon to call and say they let Rizzoli go on a misdemeanor. It hardly seems real."

He started walking again, uneasy that the girls were getting so far ahead. The location was distant from civilization and roads, but wildlife was still a factor. Bears, lynx. Just as he thought it, an eagle flew overhead.

"Aubrey will need an adjustment period," Jeff said, head down against the wind.

"Yeah. We'll acclimate her slowly." She had a private tutor and Skyped into a classroom via the public school system for a few hours a day, but it wasn't the same as physically being there. Aubrey hadn't even been shopping before. The risk of her being seen was too great. "Will you and Frances stay on? We'll bounce back and forth, I'm sure, but you're like family."

"You know we will. Whatever you need. We love that kid an awful lot, Noah."

Thank God for the Brisbins. He wasn't a praying man, but he didn't know what he would've done all these years without the two of them to help raise Aubrey. "I tried my best, Jeff," he said quietly. His poor niece had never known friends, never known normal. "Doesn't seem like enough."

Jeff slapped him on the back. "Don't beat yourself up too hard. You were just a kid yourself. She's healthy, she's happy."

She's alive.

They edged the tree line and he grinned. Raven stood at the base of the tree house, gawking up at the structure.

"I'll have you know, this is no tree house. This is a Pinterest board."

He laughed. It was pretty fantastic. Around the base of a thick spruce was a thin, winding staircase that led to a small platform twenty feet up. The tree house was designed to resemble a much smaller version of the main house and was held up by four thick beams. All four walls had windows and insulation.

"Come on!" Aubrey shouted from the top. "Or are you afraid?"

Raven grinned. "Funny. I'm not fond of heights, but I can manage this."

As she took the first step, Noah ducked off to the side, camera ready. Waiting until she rounded the first curve and he could get both her and Aubrey, he held firm. He'd waited hours sometimes for the perfect shot, often in the shittiest of elements. This one was important.

And there it was. Raven looking up, her small hand covered in a blue glove holding the railing, the sapphire of her coat stark against the snow, and Aubrey looking down at her in a pale pink coat, a grin the size of the Pacific. Raven's dark to Aubrey's light. Color popping. Fucking perfect.

Jeff held out his hand. "Go stand over there. Let me get one of you guys together."

Reluctant, he passed the camera and climbed the steps. Standing between them on the small porch, he put his arm around both of them and smiled. Didn't matter if the picture was blurred to hell. That one was going above the mantle in the den.

"Raven, Noah. Come down here. I'll bet you don't have many pictures of you together. Noah's usually behind the camera."

Noah thought about the one in his living room, a selfie from his cell phone, and cringed. "He's right. Come take a picture with me."

Grabbing her hand, they walked down the steps, where he glanced around for a unique spot. A few feet away was a fallen birch. Straddling the trunk, he patted the spot in front of him. She mimicked his pose and sat between his legs.

"Stand on the trunk, Jeff, would you? Angle the camera down."

"You're so bossy," she whispered, craning her head to smile at him.

He dropped his forehead to hers, unable to hide his own grin. "You usually don't mind."

Staring down at her, he forgot Aubrey, Jeff, the camera, and his own name. The honey in her eyes was more prevalent in this dusky light, her impossibly long lashes framing them. Her cheeks were pink from the wind, her hair cascading over her shoulders and back. She stole his breath sometimes. His chest swelled, both painful and pleasant, as the sensation twisted.

"Got it," Jeff called.

Noah took the camera from him, no idea what kind of pictures were taken while he'd been lost. He'd upload them in his suite later.

Raven called Aubrey down from the tree house. "I don't know about you, but I'm freezing. You wouldn't happen to have hot chocolate up at your big, fancy house, would you?"

"Of course we do." Aubrey rolled her eyes, smiling as they walked ahead.

Raven bumped Aubrey's shoulder with hers. Aubrey bumped back.

Without even thinking, he brought the camera to his face and clicked the button several times. Lowering it, he paused to watch them. A lump formed in his throat, one he couldn't swallow past.

Jeff nodded and took off after them.

When Noah got back to the house, he went straight for his suite, leaving the others to their hot chocolate. Once in his office, he pulled the memory card and waited for the pictures to upload. Just as he suspected, the shot of Raven and Aubrey was spectacular. He printed two eight-by-tens, as well as the one of them coloring. Scrolling through, the three of them Jeff took wasn't half bad, so he set that one up to print as poster size to mat and frame for the mantle.

He paused, rubbing a hand over his jaw. Staring at him and Raven, that sensation from before crept back into his chest. Jeff had taken three pictures. One with Noah's chin on her shoulder from behind, her head down. Another with her face turned to look at him. And the last with their faces close. They both were grinning in all three, but something was different about his expression in the last shot—right when he experienced the pressure behind his ribs the first time.

He shook his head. Not the first time. He'd had the feeling before, or something similar. Except each time he felt the odd ache, it grew with each episode. He set the pictures to print and leaned back.

As a friend, he'd loved her for years. As a man, he'd desired her. Now that both worlds had collided, it was messing with his head. He'd always been able to separate friendship and desire before. There was a difference between loving someone and being in love. So why did the love he felt for her go deeper, shove stronger than two months prior? He wasn't capable of settling down or striving at forever. Neither was she.

Rising, he went to his drafting desk. Losing himself in measuring and cutting, he worked until he had mats for the new pictures. From there, he sifted through his endless collection of frames until he found the right ones. He decided on black for the shot of Raven and Aubrey, a red pine for the three of them, and a clear floating frame for the three pictures of him and Raven. That one was particularly tricky and it took time to space them evenly, to center on the glass, before applying the backing.

He strode into the living room and scanned the wall, deciding where to put it. He had plenty of space, but adding these would clutter the current layout. He took down all the pictures of Raven and hung them in his bedroom instead, then went back and rearranged the living room wall so that he hung the new frame in the center and the family ones around it. Satisfied, he carried the others downstairs and aligned the picture Jeff had taken to center the den mantle.

Finally, he let out a sigh and…The house was dark. He quickly cast a glance at the clock and was shocked to find it almost eight o'clock. Hell, he'd lost the whole day. Aubrey usually went to bed at this time.

Climbing the stairs to the second floor suites, picture in hand, he caught Raven's soft voice coming from Aubrey's bedroom. He stopped in the hallway, hand poised over the knob. Through the partially opened door, he could just make out Aubrey in bed, with Raven sitting at her hip.

Aubrey laughed at whatever Raven said. "He's always like that. Takes tons of pictures and then goes upstairs to frame them right away. He's so impatient."

Raven breathed a laugh that drifted like smoke. "Men can be very impatient. But I'm glad he was busy so we could hang out."

"Me, too." Aubrey fell silent for a moment. "He says I can maybe go visit him in Anchorage soon."

"That'll be fun. We can go shopping or grab some lunch."

"Yeah, but…"

The sheets rustled on the bed. "But what?"

Aubrey took her time answering. "My scars. What if people don't like me?"

Noah pinched his eyes closed and tilted his head back. She'd never mentioned anything like that to him before, and it killed him she worried about it. Most of the scarring could be hidden by clothing, but it was another factor to take into account when…

"Listen to me, Aubrey. If people don't like you because you have scars, then that's their problem. You don't want to know them anyway."

He could fucking kiss her right now for that alone.

"Do you think they're ugly?"

Noah crept closer to see what Raven would do, and was stunned stupid when she lifted Aubrey's arm.

"Let me have a look at them," she said gently.

Pushing up the sleeve of Aubrey's nightgown, Raven tenderly skimmed her fingers over the red, marred flesh of Aubrey's forearm to just below the shoulder where the worst of the damage had been. She didn't offer a quick platitude or pretend the scars weren't there. She addressed them head on.

Raven tugged the sleeve down. "I think you're very brave. And I don't think there's anything ugly about you."

Everything inside him froze. He swayed, throat closing, fingers clenching the frame of the picture somehow still in his hand. Tears burned behind his lids.

Fucking…hell. Slowly, he staggered from the door to gather himself, pacing the hallway—once, twice—until he was certain he had his emotions under control and his chest was no longer bleeding out.

He closed his eyes and drew a deep breath before knocking. They were talking about hair products when he walked in, plastered a grin on his face, and held up the picture he'd framed for Aubrey's room. "Got a surprise for you, my love."

Leaving Noah to have a few minutes of private time with Aubrey, Raven climbed the steps to the third floor and stopped in the living room. Aubrey wasn't kidding. He'd printed and framed the photos already. The arrangement was different, too. Three shots of her and Noah were together in a floating frame, with family portraits around it.

Studying them closely, she could scarcely believe the couple was them. They resembled a jewelry ad or greeting card. So happy, carefree. Loving. God, they looked…real. Not friends with benefits, but the genuine article.

Panic threatened, her chest growing tight with too little air. She fought it. Seeing them together shouldn't frighten her. This was Noah. Protective, loyal Noah. He was the same person and so was she. The only difference was the physical relationship.

She glanced again at the pictures and knew she was lying to herself. A man didn't look at a woman like that if he wanted only sex, if he had any intention of returning to a safe friendship. He was slipping into love, and they swore they wouldn't. She'd spent the majority of her life afraid, keeping others at a distance because the thought of falling in love, of trusting someone that deeply, was an incapability. It wasn't even until recently she understood why.

No more responsible for her past than Noah was for his, she swallowed hard and pushed the last of the panic away. Noah had her trust. She'd done things with him she'd never allowed with other lovers. If she were to even try a committed relationship on for size, it should be with someone like him. No one was shoving them down the aisle or saying anything about forever.

That had been her issue all along, because what man wanted a woman who would only accept him into her body on her terms? You couldn't build a marriage, a life, on those relationships. Somewhere along the way, she gave up on the hope for normal and accepted her lonely fate. It hadn't even crossed her mind enough to upset her, to think twice.

Until now. Noah wasn't them, and she had the suspicion he was silently begging her for everything she had, even if he wasn't yet aware. His touch, the kind words, the endearing way he looked at her, all bespoke of what he wanted. And he wanted her.

At this point, what could it hurt to try? Lines had been crossed. Feelings were involved. Except she didn't know how to voice her emotions. She straightened. But, because of Noah, she did know how to express them. When they made love, she could tell he was pushing for a little more every time. She'd give him that more.

And she knew exactly how to get started.

Determined, she walked into his office and grabbed his camera off the desk and made her way into the bedroom to set it on the bed. Stripping, she made a trail of breadcrumbs in the form of clothing from the door to the bedroom. She turned off all the lights and set the fireplace kindling. Then, taking the comforter from the bed, she wrapped it loosely around her body, exposing her back and bunching it in her fingers at her chest. She stood by the wall of windows, facing the extraordinary view, and waited, knowing he'd be up soon.

He didn't disappoint. The suite door opened and closed, followed by a pause in his footsteps. A groan emitted from down the hall and she grinned.

"Raven?"

She didn't answer, but his footsteps drew closer, stopping periodically as if picking up her clothes along the way.

"Baby, I hope to hell you're still awake."

He stepped in the room and drew up short, surveying first her and then the camera she'd left waiting for him. Recognition dawned in his eyes. "Fuck, Raven. Do you mean it?"

Since he seemed hesitant to move, she looked at him coyly over her shoulder. "Go ahead, Noah. Take some pictures and then take me."

He drew in a harsh breath, hand drifting to the bulge behind his zipper. "Don't move."

Facing the window again, she grinned.

Several clicks filled the room before his rough voice cut the quiet. "Turn your head. Yes, that's it." He moved around the room. "I'm so goddamn hard, baby."

"I'm so damn wet." And she was. Her sex ached and her folds were drenched with this new foreplay. "You're wearing too many clothes."

He groaned painfully. "No. I take them off and the camera's a distant memory. I want you on film, knowing no one else will see you like this. Mine. Just for me."

Her lids drifted shut as a tremor coursed through her. "I want to see your reaction, Noah. Strip and I'll drop the blanket."

Cursing, he shed his clothes while she turned to watch. His thick erection sprung up to his naval, swelling under her gaze, and she realized how badly she wanted to take him in her mouth. She'd only tried oral with a couple of other partners, and always while they were tied down. What would it feel like having his hands thread her hair while she pleasured him?

As if reading her thoughts, the smooth, corded muscles of his body tensed and shifted as he moved. He gripped his cock and stroked, camera ready in the other hand.

"I'm taking you in my mouth when you're done."

His hand stopped. So did his breathing.

She walked to the bed and sat at the edge, still clutching the comforter to her chest.

His eyes tracked her movement. He opened his mouth to speak, but closed it again, clearing his throat. "In all these years, you're the only woman who's made me desire to pick up my camera and throw it aside in the same blink."

Because she knew he was telling the truth, and it equally scared her and turned her on, she distracted him by letting go of the comforter. It pooled by her waist, exposing her breasts.

He brought the camera to his face, taking several shots. "Put your hair over your shoulder, baby. Yes." The camera clicked. "Lay back." *Click, click.* "One arm over your head. Good. The other, dip it below the duvet."

She set her hand on her belly, gaze locked on him. Sliding her hand lower, she bit her lip and closed her eyes.

Click, click, click.

"Touch yourself, baby. Fuck, yes. Are you wet?"

"Very wet. Wanting you." She parted her folds and spread the slickness over her swollen clit, arching her back. Her head flung to the side, lost in the sensation.

"Imagine it's my fingers there. That's it, baby. Does it feel good?"

Click, click, click.

"So good." Tension built in her body, already on edge. Her fingers stroked faster, harder. "Going to come, Noah."

He groaned low and deep and long. "Come for me, baby." His feet shuffled closer, moved to her left. *Click, click, click.* "Need to see your face when you climax. It's a gorgeous sight."

His low, rough voice caused a delicious shiver. Her nerve endings fired. Her breath caught. She bowed off the mattress. Screamed his name.

Click, click, click.

Then, *crash.*

Chapter Thirteen

Noah dropped the camera and was between her thighs before her tremors ceased. Crashing his mouth to hers, he pushed for entry and stroked his tongue inside, doing with his mouth what he wanted to do with his cock. He had no idea if she was serious about giving head, didn't know if that was a trigger for her, so he kissed her like his life depended on it, because his sanity did.

She wrapped one leg around his waist and rolled him to his back. He cupped her neck, holding her to him. When she raked her nails down his chest and her mouth followed the path, he thought he'd blow. *Lower, lower.*

He grabbed her hips. "Only if you want to, baby. If it—"

"I want to," she moaned against his nipple, taking it between her teeth and sinking in.

His head hit the mattress. "Holy fuck."

She grinned against his flesh, licking her way down past his naval to...

"Holy, holy fuck."

Her tongue swirled around his head, darting into the slit and spreading the moisture beading. His cock was so full with seed the veins protruded. His balls tightened. She licked her way down the underside of his shaft and it was all he could to hold it together when he wanted to shove his fingers in her hair and his cock farther in her mouth.

She urged his thighs apart. He complied, allowing her more room to work. Fisting his base, she worked her lips around his size and brought her hot, wet mouth down, taking half of him in one try. Breathing ragged, his clutched the sheets so he didn't grab her. Forcing his hips not to move proved difficult. Sweat broke out on his forehead, dripping down his temple with the restraint.

Hollowing her cheeks, the pressure increased as she pumped her fist while sucking him off. He groaned. Begged. She went back to teasing the hell out of him, licking his head and down his shaft. Her hand closed around his balls and massaged. He pressed his palms to his eyes, the torture, the pleasure, almost too much. She was driving him fucking mad, and he goddamn loved it.

When her other hand worked between his cheeks, he stilled. She slid her finger along his crack, applied pressure to his hole. She massaged the tight muscle, but didn't penetrate. His heart pounded as he tried to decide if he liked it or not.

She lifted her head, gaze meeting his, ceasing all activity. "No?"

He looked at her, poised over his cock, lips wet, her hands on his body and where. "Honestly? I don't know."

She slid her hand out and the loss almost gave him his answer. "Have you ever before? It can be very pleasurable."

He was beginning to think anything she did would be its own form of rapture. "I've done it to my partners." Not often, though. "Never had it done to me."

Nodding slowly, her hair fell around her face, the ends caressing his stomach. "Same here." She sat back on her haunches, hands on her thighs. "Trust me?"

"Of course." There was never a doubt. He searched her gaze, missing her hands on his body. "Go ahead, baby. Touch me."

She paused, and then dipped her fingers between her own legs, coating her middle finger in her wetness. Slowly, she slid it between his crease again. Before he knew what hit him, her other hand was fisted around his base and her mouth was swallowing half of his cock. Her slick finger massaged his ass, working the tight muscle in a rhythm mimicking her tongue.

Sensation overload. He was at the brink of coming that fast.

Tongue swirling. Mouth suction. Hand pumping. Finger penetrating.

He barely had time to register the slight pressure in his hole, the mild, yet pleasurable burning, before his back tightened with an oncoming orgasm. She twisted her finger, and the nerves in so sensitive an area lit a fuse of need, building the pleasure. Her other hand fisted him harder. Her head bobbed faster. He hit the back of her throat and went blind.

"Coming," he growled. "Coming, baby." This time he yelled.

She waited until he started spilling before she slipped her finger out, lifted her head and straddled him, fist pumping as his seed shot out in hot spurts over his chest. Still coming, quaking, he thrust into her deft hands, the glide unimaginable. Finally able to touch her, he fisted his hands in her hair and dragged her face to his. Mouth wide open in pleasure as the last of him spilled out, he screamed through the strongest fucking release he ever had.

When his muscles unlocked, his lids opened to find her right there, breathing the same air and satisfaction in her eyes. Though it wasn't nearly enough to thank her, he kissed her with everything he had, wrapping his arms around her slender back.

Later, after he'd carried her to the shower and washed, she curled under the sheets and drifted off. Unable to look away, he fetched his camera from the floor, pleased he hadn't broken the thing when he dropped it before, and took several pictures of her sleeping. Stalker? Maybe. Smitten was more like it.

Yes, that's exactly what he was with Raven Crowne. She surpassed every fantasy he had where she was concerned. Enamored, lost, and smitten. He couldn't complain. He even saw it coming.

■ ■

Raven lifted her brows at Nicole and bit back a smile. Nicole, just as amused, widened her eyes, pleading with Raven to stop.

Michael Hawthorn, Hoan's agent, was more than a little surprised by her assistant being in the meeting to set up the exhibit. And by Nicole's low-cut peach dress, which molded to her curves. His gaze kept drifting, even while he fiddled on his phone to check his event calendar.

He smoothed a hand down his tie. "I think the end of March would work best. What do you have open?"

Nicole checked her ledger. "The twenty-eighth? That's the last Friday."

He nodded and adjusted his tall frame in the chair. "That works. When do you need the pieces by and how many?" As it had been since he'd arrived, his tone was clipped and curt. Gone was the smooth, amused man who'd strolled into her office a little more than a month ago to initiate Noah's reveal.

They both looked to Raven. "Nicole will oversee this show, so you can deal with her directly. I'll step in if need be."

On average, Nicole typically handled the details once Raven signed an artist. Where Raven focused on the catering, online and media aspects, Nicole worked the rest, like sending the photos out for framing, handling sales, and setting up displays. Just because Hoan was a big name didn't mean she was pulling her assistant off the exhibit.

Nicole crossed her legs, completely unaware Mr. Hawthorn followed the movement with his eyes. "We should meet with Mr. Dwell to establish—"

"No. You deal with me and me only."

"But…" She looked at Raven, tucking her long, strawberry blonde hair behind her ear.

Raven nodded. "I'm aware of Mr. Dwell's aversion to the public eye. I agreed to his terms. Mr. Hawthorn will act on his behalf."

"Okay," Nicole said slowly. "In that case, I think thirty pieces would do it, but we can adjust that number for what he has ready."

They worked out some minor details and agreed to another meeting early next week before Mr. Hawthorn left and Nicole went back to work.

Raven finished the catering menu for a showing next Friday and called it an early day. Noah had a fundraiser tonight his company was sponsoring and she needed to get home to prepare. She shuddered. Black tie affairs were not her thing. Too many people, too many eyes. But Noah had asked her to attend as his date, and she found she could deny him very little.

She looked at Max, hovering just outside her door. "We need to stop by my apartment on the way home. Is that all right?"

Rising, she grabbed her coat, but Max was at her side and took it from her, holding it while she shrugged into the sleeves. His manners were so traditional she wondered why he was single. He was a good-looking man, too.

"We can go wherever you like, Miss Crowne, so long as I have you back in time for the fundraiser."

He pulled out his cell and thumbed a text, probably notifying the team that they were leaving and changing routes. Ever since the night they were followed, Noah had been freakish about security. Now she understood the serious reasoning behind it, and was grateful to have Max around.

On the way to her apartment, Raven glanced at Max in the front seat, studiously checking the mirrors. His brown hair was cut short, curled slightly at the ends. He had a wide jaw, which was always clean-shaven, and kind, observant eyes. Easily six feet tall, he could take up space in a room just by his size, yet he went unnoticed, more gentle in nature than commanding. The strong silent type.

"Why are you still single, *Maxie*." She grinned at Aubrey's nickname and the blush that rose up his neck.

He cleared his throat. "I prefer Max, Miss Crowne. Or Mr. Gerard. I only let Miss Aubrey call me…Maxie."

"Nice dodge of the question. Bravo. I'll let you slide." She crossed her arms and leaned back. "You're very good with Aubrey. What's the deal with the pennies?" She'd wondered about it at the time, when he'd given one to Aubrey, but with everything else, it had escaped her mind since.

"She was studying the Depression and currency with her tutor last year." He shrugged. "I thought it would be neat for her to collect a penny from every year in circulation. She has a book in her room."

Aw. "I like you, Max. A lot."

He chuckled. "Mutual, Miss Crowne." Swallowing, his face fell stoic again. "I'm glad he told you about his past."

Pressing her fingers to her lips, she stared out the window. "Me, too." The details of Noah's story passed through her head. "If Rizzoli is in prison, why the need for such high security?"

Max checked the mirrors. "A contract has been taken out on Mr. Caldwell's life." More mirror glances. "Andre Rizzoli's assets have been seized, but somehow he got the funds to order the hit."

It was the most she ever got out of Max, and it hurt to hear as much as it scared the ever-living shit out of her. She shook her head, angry and sick this happened to him. "Why Noah, though? He had nothing to do with any of this." Neither did poor Aubrey.

"The FBI only had enough to bring Rizzoli to trial because of the evidence Mr. Caldwell's investigator dug up. Rizzoli found out." His grip tightened on the wheel, the first sign of aggression she'd seen out of him. "It's revenge."

Her pulse beat thready. "Is he going to get off?"

"Not this time. He got careless. Made too many mistakes. He also has no clout to tamper with witnesses or buy off a judge." He glanced at her in the mirror. "Once we find this goon he hired, you'll be much safer. No one will hurt you."

She nodded as they pulled up to her building, not entirely sure she believed him. If someone really wanted to hurt her or Noah, a few men standing guard wouldn't stop them for long.

They walked down the hall to her apartment and found two men standing outside. One of them, who looked about thirty and dressed in a similar black suit as Max's, held up a hand. "We swept the apartment first and found a problem. We're waiting on the cops."

She shook in her heels and crossed her arms over her chest. "What kind of problem?"

His jaw hardened when he looked at her, his eyes filled with regret. "Someone tossed the place."

"What?" She tried to shove him aside, but he wouldn't budge. "Move, now."

"Let her through," Max said, sidling up behind her. "Don't touch anything, Miss Crowne."

The security member turned the knob and stepped aside, allowing her past. She got three feet before she halted and lifted a shaking hand to her mouth.

Her furniture was overturned, pictures smashed, drawers emptied. The floor wasn't even visible through all the clutter. They'd even broken her dishes in the kitchen. She trembled in anger, in fear, at the violation that left a thick, dirty coat over her skin.

Max set a reassuring hand on her shoulder from behind. "We should go. Let the cops handle it."

"Yes," she agreed, turning. She couldn't stand another minute in here, a place that had once been her refuge, where her and Noah had spent endless time together as friends. Tainted, all of it tainted.

Her gaze fell on the inside of the door. She froze, not believing her eyes.

Pinned to the door with one of her kitchen knives was a note, written with lewd scratches in black marker.

He's not who he seems.

Her gut turned to ice. This wasn't a random break in, nor someone just looking for drugs or quick cash. God. They'd been in her apartment.

The door crashed open. Max pushed her behind him with one arm, drawing a gun with his other. She fisted her hand in his jacket to keep from falling but, before her heart could start beating again, he relaxed and put his gun away.

"I almost shot you."

Noah, jaw tense, ignored Max and stepped around him. "Are you okay, baby?"

She nodded, sagging in relief, and went willingly into his arms. Would she ever stop shaking? "We got here after it happened."

He tightened his grasp, running his hands up and down her back as if to warm her. "What were you doing here in the first place?"

She opened her mouth to speak, but two young male officers strode in and eyed the mess.

"Before you do anything, you need to see this." Max kicked the door shut, revealing the note.

Noah tensed against her. He and Max shared a knowing look. "Out," he growled. "Get her out and somewhere safe."

"Hold up." The black officer raised his hand. "Start at the beginning." He took out a pad of paper. "Which one of you lives here?"

"She does," Noah said. "And that's about to change."

Raven didn't even have the strength to argue. Besides, she could never live here again. Not after…this.

The next hour dragged endlessly, scratching her nerves raw and trying her patience. She'd been through the same story eight times on when she'd last been to the apartment, who she thought the note referred to, was anything missing…

Sending in the crime scene techs, the officers weren't hopeful on getting any prints or evidence. She didn't care. They knew exactly who was involved and had no choice but to keep silent. The FBI would deal with it, and catch Rizzoli's man. They had to.

All she could think the whole time was, what if she hadn't agreed to extend the time with Noah? When he'd stood right here in her living room and used the safeword, she'd been so nervous she'd almost said no. She could've been home when the guy who'd done this had come. It could be way more than just her apartment he'd trashed.

She shuddered. "Let's go home."

Chapter Fourteen

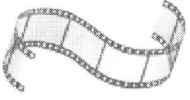

Noah checked his watch and pulled Raven closer to his side in the backseat. "We only have an hour until we need to be at the charity event."

He wanted to say fuck it and cart her back to Aubrey Castle until all this blew over, but too many people were depending on him. His company hosted this event every year. Proceeds went to a battered women and children's shelter. A twisted way for him to try to save Melissa and Aubrey, a decade too late.

"Do we have to go?"

"You don't, but I do." He kissed her temple and closed his eyes, imagining all the damn things that could've happened to her. "I'd really like you to come, though. It might take your mind off everything." He'd get a few glasses of champagne in her and take her home, where he'd fuck the memories from her head.

It was a good plan.

"I'll go, since it'll make you feel better."

She didn't like crowds and, after her day, the fact she'd do this for him stirred emotions to the surface. "Thank you," he whispered against her hair.

She didn't say much on the rest of the drive or in the elevator. As she stepped into their bedroom, he leaned against the doorway while she took in the items he'd laid out on the bed. The dress he had his assistant buy, but the other purchases were all him.

"Do you like them?"

Confusion wrinkled her forehead, but she stroked the pale yellow dress. "It's beautiful. You really need to stop buying me things, though."

He walked into the room and sat on the edge of the bed, pulling her between his legs. "I have more money than I know what to do with. I like spending it on you."

She eyed the dress again. Sleeveless and knee-length, it would show a lot of her soft skin and leave him hard all night. The black heels he would ask her to leave on afterward.

He reached for one of the two small boxes and opened it, showing her the amber necklace and matching earrings. The silver etchings holding the yellow stones were simple, but unique.

She gasped and touched her throat. "Noah. God. They're lovely."

"They match the little bit of honey in your eyes." He removed the ruby heart necklace, pleased she still wore it. "Take off your clothes, baby. Let me dress you."

Seemingly too stunned to argue, she slipped out of her work suit and laid it on a chair. When she came back between his legs, he dipped his fingers in the band of her panties and slid them down her thighs.

"What are you doing?"

"Dressing you." He reached around and unclasped her bra, watching it drift down her arms and to the floor.

"I think you mean undressing me."

He smiled. "I'll do that later."

Removing the jewelry from the box, he clasped the necklace at her nape, then put the earrings in before brushing her hair over her shoulders, letting his fingers linger in the strands. Because of her skin tone and sharp contrast of black hair, the photographer in him could study her for hours. A muse to shadow all others. Certain hues just drove his artistic eye insanely happy. This color was nearly as perfect on her as ruby or sapphire.

He lifted the shoes and waved for her foot. Once both were on, he grabbed her hips and kissed her naval. "When we get back home tonight, I'd like you to wear this, and only this." Just the bling and the shoes. His cock swelled as his gaze traveled the length of her. "So beautiful."

Her fingers threaded in his hair. "Or we could stay here," she breathed, head falling back as he traced a finger up her inner thigh.

"Anticipation, baby." Grabbing the last box, he removed the lid for his favorite present and held up the black thong with one finger. "Do you know what these are?"

"I'm pretty sure I can recognize panties."

Hmm. She had no idea. Holding them out for her, he waited until she stepped into them and they were in place, then he held up the small remote that came with the thong.

"Do you feel that hard little button over your clit?" He brushed his knuckle over the dime-sized mechanism sewn into the thong. She drew in a breath. "Put your hands on my shoulders. Good. Now, hold on."

He pushed the switch on the remote, sending shallow pulses through the thong and right to her core. Her eyes went wide, fingers digging into his shoulders. She moaned and then whimpered, slowly grinding her hips. Heat scored her cheeks.

He cut the switch. "You like, baby?"

Air rasped between her lips. "Oh, my God."

"I'll have the remote in my pocket. Anytime I see that you're thinking too hard, or if I just want you to remember what comes later, I'll flip the switch."

"That's entirely unfair." Her breathy response and heavy lids were answer enough. This step didn't upset her. She was willing to try new avenues.

"I'd like to push more from you. Nothing that makes you uncomfortable or that will hurt." He cupped her mound, pressing his heel against her clit. "You like this." Not a question.

"Yes." She swallowed and met his gaze. "I'm going to embarrass us terribly. Something tells me it'll be rather awkward to orgasm between dinner and dessert at a table full of strangers."

Dropping his forehead to her stomach, he laughed, the sound almost rusty. The tension and worry over earlier disappeared. Hands on her hips, he reluctantly eased her back. Helping her step into the dress, he zipped the back and shooed her to freshen her makeup while he got dressed.

They didn't have much time before the event started, but when she walked out of the bathroom, he wanted to make them late. Very, very late. The dress fit her slender body perfectly, the heels adding a sexy punch. She'd put her hair up in a twist at her nape, exposing the long column of her neck. Even now, he couldn't wait to unleash the knot and wrap her strands around his fist.

She stopped and raked her gaze over him. "I don't need vibrating panties. You in a tux is orgasmic enough." The carnal look in her eyes as she stepped closer had his pants too damn tight.

"Stop, baby. We're going to be late."

Pressing her body to his, she grinned and grabbed his ass. Hard. "The sooner we leave, the sooner we can get back." She nuzzled his neck and licked a path to his ear.

His hands fisted, wanting to touch. "Have mercy, Raven."

■ ■

The charity function was in a ski lodge hotel on the northern tip of Anchorage. People were bustling about and socializing as she and Noah walked into the open lobby. A massive fireplace was lit in a corner, the inlaid stones traveling up to the thirty foot ceiling. Exposed beams and crystal chandeliers added to the rustic chic décor. Several round tables were scattered through the room, covered in white linen. The centerpieces were pinecones in a lead glass bowl, dusted with silver glitter. A bar was set up on the far wall with an amazing ice sculpture of a whale's fin.

"Geez, Noah. You really go all out." She liked that it wasn't pretentious. Classy, not pompous. Her shoulders relaxed. She took a glass of champagne from a passing waiter. "So, what goes down at this shindig?" Having not attended his event before, she didn't know what to expect. In the past, she'd donated money on behalf of the gallery and waited for him to tell her about it the next day.

"There's a table in the back with silent auction donations. After dinner, people dance, I say a few words, and hope to get home before the smile freezes on my face." He slipped an arm around her waist and pulled her to him, his other hand dipping into his pocket. "You give me even more incentive to get home."

A slight pulsing shot between her thighs, vibrating her core. She drew in a sharp breath and leaned on him as her panties grew wet. The sensation stopped as soon as it started, leaving her knees weak and her humming with need. This was so unfair. Fun, but unfair.

"Payback's a bitch, Noah," she murmured. "I can torture you for hours." Leaning in, she whispered in his ear. "I'll kiss my way down your chest and take you in my mouth so deep you hit my throat. Then I'll stop to lick circles around your tip. Can you feel me humming around your cock?" He tensed and sucked a harsh breath through his nose. "And my hands? Oh, the places they can roam—"

Someone slapped his back, making him jump. "Noah! How are you?"

Noah swiftly drew her in front of him, hand on her shoulder and erection against her ass. "Jack, good to see you as well. How's the lumber business?"

"Can't complain." As an older gentleman in his sixties, he had a nice smile and a shock of white hair. "And who's this lovely creature?"

"I'm sorry," Noah rasped. "Where are my manners? This is Raven Crowne. She owns Elements Gallery down in Tartok Crest. I'm lucky to have her as my date for tonight."

She held out her hand. "Nice to meet you."

His handshake was firm. "You, too. The wife and I were in your gallery last year. Beautiful building."

"Thank you." She smiled and covertly stepped back against Noah's straining erection to tease him again. His hand gripped her shoulder hard. "You own a lumber yard?" When their guest started yapping, she bent slightly, pretending to adjust the strap of her shoe, thrusting her ass even more firmly to Noah's crotch. And wow, he grew thicker as he inhaled a sharp breath.

So, so much fun.

After Jack walked away, Noah leaned over her shoulder, breath hot against her ear. "If you move from in front of me before I get control of this hard-on, I'll set the switch for your thong to go off every five seconds." A fast vibration of her clit punctuated his point.

Squeezing her thighs together to ebb the throb, she almost regretted the tease. Almost. "In case you were wondering, I'm drenched right now. All for you. I can't wait to get you between my legs so you can feel just how wet."

He cursed under his breath, fingers tightening on her shoulders. "You drive me insane."

"Likewise." She smiled, deciding to have mercy on him, and took a tiny step forward to break their below-the-belt contact. Her gaze scanned the room and spotted a woman at the bar eying them curiously. "Who's that woman in the black dress?"

He followed her gaze. "Veronica, my assistant. You've met her before."

That was Veronica Fields? Legs that went up to the moon and a rack barely contained in her dress? Raven had met her before, years ago, long before she became Noah's right hand in business. She didn't remember her being this...sultry. Her blonde hair was in a loose, sexy knot on top of her head, fingernails red as she strummed them on the bar. Even her eye makeup was applied to enhance her mysterious, smoky lure.

"What's wrong?"

Raven turned away from the woman, not liking the surge of envy. "Nothing. She's beautiful."

Noah glanced over at Veronica as if considering her statement. "Yes, she is. Does that bother you?"

She was shocked to find it did. Day in and day out, he worked beside that woman who was everything Raven wasn't. Not better, just different. Veronica called him at all hours, too.

"Have you slept with her?" Swiftly shutting her eyes, she rubbed her forehead. Her cheeks heated in mortification. Dear God. She'd just become one of *those* women, too insecure to release her claws from her man. "Don't answer that. It was out of line."

Turning her to face him, he rubbed his thumbs under her jaw. "Have not slept with her and never plan to. I keep business and personal separate." He studied her face and slowly shook his head as if awed by what he found. "I never thought I'd say this, but your jealousy is hot. It bothers you that I may have been with her."

She drew in a slow breath and exhaled. "Jealousy is not hot. It's a cover up for lack of confidence." Which she'd never had before. How unbecoming. And all over a ten second glance from halfway across the room. "I don't know what's wrong with me." For all she knew, Veronica was happily married. Or a lesbian. Or asexual.

A smile softened his eyes. "Jealousy means you're invested. In us, in this. And though you have absolutely nothing to worry about, I like knowing you don't want me with anyone else. Reverse the roles and I might go a little caveman if another guy hit on you." He kissed her forehead. "Relax, baby. You're the only woman on my radar."

Well, hell. Someone mop up the puddle she just melted into.

They got separated later when he went to refresh his drink and she got pulled into a conversation with the wives of some crab fisherman. Just before dinner, while among of group of men who worked for Noah, he set the vibration off in her panties. Engrossed in the story one of the guys was telling, she was too shocked to hide her gasp.

"Are you okay?" The youngest one, an attractive young man in his early twenties who did fishing charters, touched her back.

Noah set off the panties again.

She closed her eyes and sucked in a breath. At the last minute, she grabbed her ankle. "I'm good. Just twisted my ankle. Darn heels." She laughed to play it off, and the conversation continued.

She narrowed her eyes at Noah in warning. He raised his glass and grinned.

Dinner involved discussions on the increase in seal population. The salmon was delicious, along with wild rice and steamed broccoli. Noah hated the vegetable and she could tell he was itching to move it to her plate like they'd do if at home. Afterward, while he was called up to say a few words, Veronica slid over to claim the spot next to Raven.

"We met a long time ago, but I'm Veronica."

She forced a smile. "Raven. I remember. You did a nice job planning the event." Noah wouldn't have been involved in the fine details of the evening, which meant this was Veronica's doing. Raven respected how much time and effort went into putting together these affairs.

"Thanks." She watched Noah, tilting her head toward Raven. "You're the first date he's brought in the five years we've been doing this." She paused to flick her a glance. "I know how close you guys are. I'm glad you came."

It kind of made it hard to dislike the pretty vixen if she was nice. Focusing on Noah, who asked the orchestra to begin, she fumbled with what to say. "How late do these things usually go?" Because as Noah strode closer, all she wanted was to strip him out of that tux. Tall, rippling with lean muscle and confidence, he ate the space toward her.

"He usually cuts out after the first dance. The charity means a lot to him, but he hates these functions."

It grated her nerves Veronica knew that, but it wasn't exactly a state secret and she did work closely with him. As a matter of fact, according to Noah, Veronica pretty much managed most things about Gallivanting Adventures so he could be free to do other things. It dawned on her just how successful Hoan Dwell was, and that meant traveling a great deal. In the past, she'd always assumed he was doing something for the company or on vacation when he'd been gone for those short spurts. Instead, he'd amassed a fortune taking brilliant photographs.

Noah nodded at Veronica and leaned over the back of Raven's chair to speak in her ear. "Dance with me?"

"Sure," she said, rising and taking his hand.

He led her onto the dance floor, where several other couples were swaying, and gently tugged her to his chest. "Did you like the reminder that you're mine while you were fawning over my men?"

Resting her hands on his shoulders, she smiled up at him. There was a seductive draw to how he said *mine* that caused a shiver through her body. "I wasn't fawning, I was conversing, and I see your point on the jealousy thing now."

Grinning, he spun her around and brought her back. "We can leave after this song." They moved a few slow turns while his gaze swept over her face, her hair. "We've never danced together."

Thinking back, she nodded her agreement, acutely aware of the gorgeous body against her and the spicy scent of him. "Not much opportunity. Our friendship wasn't really like that anyway, was it?" She much preferred how things had evolved.

His expression sobered, jaw hardening and eyes heated. "There's a reason I didn't touch you often, and it wasn't to torture myself. In the back of my mind, I knew it would be like this. That I wouldn't be able to stop."

Heart thundering, she glanced away and forced a swallow. "I'm not complaining and I'm not asking you to stop."

"Look at me." He waited, his eyes intensely blue when she met them. "I don't think I'm capable of stopping."

"Then don't." She stilled. Held his gaze. And decided for all in. These feelings were raw and scary, but she was with him, so nothing could be more right. It wasn't a declaration of love or forever, but it was a step closer. Proof he wasn't alone in this adventure.

Wary relief flashed in his eyes before he shook it away. "I want to take you home now."

"No complaints from me." An idea sparked. "I'll meet you by the door. I have to stop at the restroom."

He nodded once. "Don't be too long. You've had me in pain half the night with your antics."

Leaning up on her toes, she brushed a kiss over his mouth. "And you've had me on the brink of orgasm the whole night. Give me five minutes."

In the restroom, she took off her panties and shoved them in her purse. She stopped in one of the stalls and then washed her hands, getting a good look at herself in the mirror. Her features were the same, but her reflection was different. Softer, perhaps. More open.

Happy. That was it, exactly. After a lifetime of battling depression one way or another, or settling for safe and content, she hardly recognized joy when she saw it staring back at her.

All she had to do was hold onto it. A task she'd yet to manage.

Squaring her shoulders, she left, determined to try. And when she found Noah standing by the door, her coat on his arm and lazy smile on his face, she knew she was walking in the right direction.

Chapter Fifteen

Noah climbed in the back of the limo after Raven, waiting until Max shut the door and had them underway before speaking. "Did you have fun?" He closed the partition for privacy.

She grinned, her face in contrasting shadows and moonlight. "It had its merits."

He pulled the remote for her thong from his pocket. "Like this?" Suspicious of her grin, he pushed the button, but instead of her writhing in her seat, his other pocket vibrated. "You took them off? And put them in my pocket?" He grabbed her waist and slid her across the seat. "Nimble little minx. When did you do this?"

She nuzzled his neck, her nose cold from outside. "Just now as we were leaving." Her voice dropped an octave. "But don't worry. I'm still wet. Know what else?"

After spending the night fighting a raging hard-on, he wasn't sure he could take anymore. "What?" He closed his eyes and fought to keep his hands to himself until they got home. It was only a fifteen minute drive.

"I bought you something, too." She nipped his earlobe. His dick jumped. "You'll have to wait until we get upstairs. But I'll give you a hint. It's sweet." Her tongue darted out and licked his pulse. He was losing the battle not to touch. "Oh. And, Noah?"

His head fell back against the seat when her hand on his chest drifted lower. "What, baby?"

She stopped just short of the mark. "If my panties are in your pocket, that means I'm…commando."

He growled and hauled her sideways across his lap, her head in the crook of his arm. He'd never been so damn hard in his life. Her laughter died when he slid his hand under her dress, up her thigh, and parted her folds.

"Fuck, you are wet."

Her lips parted, eyes closing. "Told you…"

He sank his thumb inside her heat. Nowhere near filling her, but preparing her body for what he had in mind. He should've known she'd be ready for him. She always was, as mindless as he when it came to lovemaking. She arched, gasping. He dragged his lips over hers, swallowing her moans. Pulling out, he spread the slickness over her clit, pinching the swollen nub before driving his thumb back into her.

"God. Yes, Noah."

Raven did several things when aroused that took him from hard to painful. Saying his name in her breathy, throaty voice was one of them. He bit back the urge to rub his cock and stroked her instead. A quick glance out the window and he confirmed they were a block from home. He increased the tempo, making her writhe and buck over his lap, ratcheting his need higher. Just as she was nearing climax, he withdrew his finger and kissed her mouth.

She whimpered and clutched his coat.

"We're home and we're both coming with me inside you." When she straightened in the seat, dazed and looking ready to snap, he grinned. "The wait will be worth it."

Through the lobby, in the elevator, to the suite. That was his singular focus while dragging her behind him. Inside the condo, he took off his coat and hers, tossing them on the floor. He backed her up several paces to the kitchen while shucking the tuxedo jacket and loosening his tie.

Her hands fell on his shirt. And ripped. Buttons flew, pinging across the room.

Restraint? Gone.

In the kitchen alcove, he grabbed her hips, spun her around, and planted her face first on the closest flat surface—the table. Kicking her legs apart, he reached for his zipper. "Tell me now if you're not okay."

She turned her head, panting. "Don't you dare stop."

He released his cock and shoved his pants to his ankles. Bunching her dress in his hands, he hiked it to her waist, aligned himself, and drove deep. He stilled, relishing her heat.

Fucking heaven.

She cried out and pressed back, seeking more.

Unraveling her hair style with one hand, he wrapped her strands around his fingers and tugged her head back. "Okay?"

"Yes. Please…"

He reared, slamming into her with another thrust. He ground against her ass, circling his hips to give her more of him. She begged, called out his name. No way would he last. Not after the cock tease at the event and not with how far gone she had him. Her soft, giving flesh hugged him tight, and if they did this dance a thousand times, he'd never tire of it. Of her.

He put his arm between her pelvis and the table so she wouldn't bruise and curled his body over her back. His open mouth found her exposed throat and latched on. *Mine.* "Grab onto something, baby."

She reached back, closing her fingers around the edge of the table as he pumped. "Oh, God. Harder."

He gave her harder. Faster. The table banged the wall. The fruit bowl toppled. His grunts were muted by her skin. As he pistoned into her with breakneck speed, she cried out with each brutal, blinding thrust.

"Ah, yes." She screamed his name as her walls clamped around his shaft, pressing back urgently onto him through her tremors.

Throwing his head back, he roared, following instantly, spilling inside her and riding out the shocking intensity. Even when spent, he still rocked inside her slowly, seeking every bit of pleasure her body wrung.

She pressed her forehead to the table, her palms flat on either side as she fought for breath. His own hadn't restored yet. While he had her this way, he unzipped her dress and worked it over her head, then kicked his pants from around his ankles.

She rolled beneath him to her back, arms sprawled on the table. "I didn't give you my present."

Didn't she get that she was the best damn gift? The only one he'd ever need. Leaning over her, he kissed her slow and thorough. "Let's get to bed and you can show me after I recuperate."

Laying side by side in bed, he on his stomach and her on her back, they held hands and stared at each other in the dark. He'd never shared intimacy like this with anyone else, in or out of the sack.

Taking in her thick lashes, haunting eyes and full mouth, he knew it wasn't just her physical beauty that sucked him in. It was her. He was a fool to think they could ever go back, a fool to think he'd never succumb once she was beneath him. He always figured he was incapable of falling in love. His tremulous past and constant hiding made trying impossibly stupid.

But he'd fallen long ago. His brain had known before his heart caught up. He was just waiting for her, for the day he could have her.

Except he'd pushed too soon and he'd put her at risk. And he loved her so damn much that he should let her go, for her physical safety as much for the emotional. Money couldn't buy what she deserved. A normal life, a guy who wasn't so fucked up he'd rather view life through a lens.

Yet his fingers tightened around hers instead of releasing.

"What are you thinking?" She turned on her side to face him. "Your mind went somewhere dark. You get a wrinkle right here when something upsets you." Her finger smoothed the crease between his eyebrows. Her thumb brushed his lower lip. "Are you worried you were too rough?"

"No." She'd tell him if he had been. She was honest about her needs and demands. Another reason he was sunk deep. There was nothing sexier than a woman open to her body, her pleasure, and not afraid to test herself. It had taken some time, but she'd done that. Pushed herself past the fear, sought the answers, and grasped for him during the ride. As if he was the only one she craved in the interim, the long haul.

He rolled to face her, lifting his hand to tuck a strand of hair off her cheek. It would not be wise to tell her how he felt until all this crap was past them. He had no right loving her in the first place. She needed to draw her own conclusions about what she wanted before he said something that would no doubt make her feel trapped. She'd lived her life in a cage, in one form or another. He would not be an additional confine. He suspected she wasn't ready yet anyway.

"I think you need my present now. You're obviously thinking too much." She rose and padded out of the room naked, with the moonlight caressing her skin.

He turned to his back and slung an arm under his head, anticipating her return. Not for her gift, but to observe the elegant sinew of her body as she walked, the graceful poise of her posture, the way her dark hair cascaded over her shoulders. He could spend the next eternity just watching her.

She had her arm behind her back and a sly smile on her face when she strolled back in. Kneeling on the bed next to him, she whispered, "Close your eyes."

Fighting a grin, he did as she asked. She set a cold, hard cylinder in his hand. He opened his eyes to find a can of whipped cream. He threw his head back and laughed. Hell, she was perfect.

She bit her lip. "Not exactly diamonds, but I've always wanted to…experiment with food. I heard it can be very stimulating." She shrugged, pink tingeing her cheeks.

He'd not done much erotic food play himself. A strawberry here or there, some chocolate syrup once. "Don't be embarrassed." He snagged her around the waist until she sprawled over him. "I want you to talk to me when you want something." He eyed the can. "You want to use this on me or the other way around?"

"Both." She took the can from him, shook it, and popped the top. "Where would you like me to start?"

"Don't care, baby." This was her fantasy. He was only happy to oblige.

Bringing the nozzle to his mouth, she sprayed some cream over his lips and leaned in, licking the sweetness from him. He groaned when she'd finished and cupped the back of her head to kiss her deep. Her tongue, cool from the cream, blended with his heat as their tongues danced. He could get lost in her kiss, in the moans purring from her throat.

Breaking away, she straddled his thighs and added a dollop of cream to each of his nipples. When she closed her mouth over one, he held her hair off her face and pressed her to him. She swirled her tongue and nipped the hardened bud. He hissed a breath and bucked, wanting inside her. Moving to the other nipple, she tortured that one until his fingers were clenching her strands.

He tugged her head up so he could look in her eyes, heavy-lidded with lust. His shaft thickened. "Your mouth is a thing of beauty, baby."

"In that case…" She sprayed a generous amount on his cock.

He sucked in air at the cool sensation, his heart pounding in anticipation of her hot mouth. "Can I hold your head?" he rasped.

"Yes." And then her tongue was on him, licking with firm strokes from base to tip. She swirled around the crown and, before he could beg for more, she licked his slit and brought him into her wet mouth.

"Holy fuck." He bucked before he could catch himself and cupped her head. "I'm sorry," he ground out and released her, his cock throbbing for more.

With a pop, she freed him from her mouth, took his hands, and replaced them in her hair. Fisting his base, she looked at him from under her thick lashes. "Be as rough as you want, Noah. I like it."

And with that, she went back to work, causing his eyes to roll back in his head with pleasure. Hollowing her cheeks, her pressure increased, and he couldn't stop himself from thrusting into her. Her hand worked his base, her tongue did some insanely awesome swirl to the underside of his shaft, and his tip hit her throat.

After moments, he realized she wasn't letting him go deeper than she could handle with her hand holding his pelvis, so he tested things by being rougher. He thrust up and brought her head down, fucking her mouth like he'd been dreaming of doing. She moaned around his cock, vibrating him all the way to his balls.

"Hell, baby. You feel so goddamn good."

Bringing his knees up, he spread his legs wider, holding her head and curling his upper body to see better when he thrust. His back tightened, his balls drawing up. He issued two more thrusts before warning her he was close. She didn't let up, and his eyes watered holding back. Tension corded his arms, his shoulders, and neck.

"Raven, I'm coming…" He rasped air. "Baby, come up—"

Too late. He let loose with a roar, head thrown against the mattress and hands clenched in her hair. His back bowed with the velocity of his orgasm. His release streamed in jets, powerful and hot. She sucked him deep, swallowing, wrenching shudders from him until his vision grayed.

He was still soughing for breath when she released him and kissed his stomach. He closed his eyes tight, grabbed her under the arms, and hauled her up his body.

Holding her to him, he struggled for air. "Two minutes. Give me two minutes and, swear to God, I'll make you see stars."

She laughed and kissed his jaw.

"You swallowed." He was still in awe. Most didn't, and he didn't really care, but she had for him. It had to have brought out bits of her claustrophobia with him holding her the way he had when he'd come and her mouth full with his cock.

She made a sound of contentment. "Salty and sweet. I like watching you lose control, knowing I can do that to you."

Control. He had none with her. She didn't seem to either. The constant power play, the give and take between them, brought out pleasure on both sides. Neither minded taking the reins or letting them drop.

His mind whirled with possibilities. Not since they made love the first time in the missionary position had she tensed during sex. Nothing they'd done triggered her panic. He'd wanted to test her boundaries, and it was time.

Running his hands down her shoulders, he lightly gripped her wrists and held them with one hand behind her. She stilled, but didn't object. Carefully, he rolled them so she was on her back and her hands trapped between her and the mattress. He held her wrists in place. Propping himself up on his other elbow, he rose over her and looked in her eyes.

She swallowed hard, gaze roaming his face.

"Okay, baby?"

His heart beat out of his chest when she nodded.

■ ■

With her arms trapped behind her, Raven's breasts thrust forward, her back arched, and her hard nipples brushed against Noah's broad chest. Her pulse hummed, her heart pounding. There was a trace of apprehension under the surface but, mostly, she was aroused. Curious.

Still holding her wrists, Noah reached for the whipped cream and spread a generous amount on each breast. She held her breath when he dipped his head to lick it away, hot mouth against cool skin. Her nerves fired, creating sensual heat over her body and throbbing between her legs. When he finished lavishing one breast, he moved to the other, just like she'd done to him.

She was panting by the time he was finished and he grabbed the can again. He made a long vertical line between her breasts, to her naval, where he sprayed two additional lines to create an arrow pointing down.

Without looking up from his task, he rumbled, "In case there was any doubt what direction I was headed."

She smiled and quickly gasped when his mouth was on her again, using teeth and tongue and lips to eat away the cream. "Noah…"

"I love it when you say my name."

"Noah," she repeated, begging.

She writhed beneath him, body tense with need. A cold sensation hit her between her thighs and over her folds when he added cream, but it did nothing to douse the fire. She looked down at him, head between her legs and eyeing her sex like he was starving.

His gaze met hers. Slowly, he slid his free arm under her and grabbed each wrist with his hands, still keeping her immobile. Tugging down gently until her hands were nearly under her bottom, he encouraged her shoulders back farther, her spine bowing. Her breasts thrust out more, the sensitive peaks wet from his mouth and puckered.

The position was binding and erotic at the same time. She was completely at his mercy, open for him. The loss of control caused a ripple of desire instead of her usual panic.

"Put your legs on my shoulders, baby."

When she did, his mouth closed over her sex and she screamed. He licked the cream from her folds, along her wet opening, and over her clit. She thrashed in his embrace, using the leverage of her position to press into his mouth. His tongue penetrated her, sending shivers of bliss along her spine.

Being pinned down, helpless to move and seek pleasure only on his terms, was enticingly explosive. Give and take. Pleasure and pain. Sweet, sweet torment. Her muscles coiled as her body tensed to explode.

"I'm fucking hard again, baby. Look what you do to me. I can't get enough of you." He rose to his haunches, knees spread, lifting her hips from the bed, her ankles on his shoulders and his hands still firmly holding her wrists. His heated gaze intense, it swept over her body, his thick shaft poised at her opening. "Gorgeous. You're goddamn gorgeous."

And in that single held breath, she was. All her life, she'd stayed in the shadows, not wanting attention, uncomfortable with it. He was the first person to look, to actually see her as she was, and demand she do the same. No man had ever made her consider herself beautiful. It wasn't even anything she'd contemplated. But she knew, without doubt, that she was to him.

He thrust into her, slow and deep. So, so deep. He thickened inside her, filling her like no one ever had before. Body, soul. Heart.

Her throat tightened. Moisture formed behind her lids.

"Look at me," he pleaded.

"I'm okay. Give me a second."

"Look at me." A demand this time, rough and frantic in concern.

She lifted her lids, tears blurring her vision. He made the motion to let go of her arms, but she shook her head. "No. It's not that." Wet tracks coursed from her eyes, down her temples, and to the pillow.

"Then tell me." His face twisted in worry. He didn't even seem to be breathing.

She didn't know what was wrong, how to put to words these emotions she'd never experienced. So how was she to voice it to him? Helplessly, she shook her head, a sob catching in her throat. God. She was crying during sex. What next?

At once, his gaze softened and his body relaxed, as if he understood the assault within her. He released her wrists and wrapped his arms around her back, bringing her up to meet him chest to chest. Without breaking their connection, he stretched his legs out, rooting himself deeper inside her body. She held onto his shoulders as if the world would tilt again.

Pushing her hair back from her face, he looked in her eyes and thumbed the tears away. "Me, too, baby." He kissed her with tender brushes of his lips and gentle strokes of his tongue, saying so much without speaking a word.

Her hand slid down his chest, where the steady beat of his heart pounded against her palm. She wasn't alone with the emotions. He was right there with her, telling her through touch and actions it would be okay. They were still them, the same people, stronger now.

He eased back, blue gaze steady as they shared air. "It's not as frightening as I thought it would be," he whispered. Then he kissed her again, hugging her close while he brought his hips up to move inside her.

Heat stirred within her again, but different this time. Stronger. Softer. Scarier. She ground against him, unsure whether to panic or cry anew. It was all so overwhelming, dizzying.

He matched her movement, rocking into her with slick deep strokes, gliding against her flesh and creating friction. Need uncoiled inside her, shoving everything else aside to come together with him. He buried his face in her neck, clutching her to his chest as if letting her go would cause pain.

When they splintered, they did it together, and when they collapsed on the bed and fell asleep, it was together. She could only wonder for how long.

And, as her eyes opened the next morning, with her laying on her stomach, his head propped in his hand and fingers stroking her spine, the question was still in her mind. He was watching her closely, gauging her mood.

She sighed. "What are we doing, Noah?"

His hand stilled, his gaze searching and contemplative, mouth in a tight line. "Don't do this. Don't freak out."

"I'm not freaking out. I'm here, aren't I?"

He didn't respond, but a muscle ticked in his jaw and wary hope looked back at her.

She bit her lip. "We had a time limit and kept going. Nothing's been spelled out. I don't understand what we're hoping for by doing this. I don't even know what to say if someone asks about you."

Expression unreadable, he swallowed. Long moments stretched. His voice was a gravelly whisper when he finally spoke. "You tell them I'm the man who's in love with you."

Chapter Sixteen

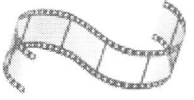

Raven hadn't moved one muscle. She lay on her stomach in his bed, eyes wide and lips parted in disbelief. He'd thought about holding back until she was ready to hear the words, but he'd lied to her for too long. Lied to himself.

No more.

And since they couldn't build a relationship if they kept halting any forward progress, he decided to say it all. If she ran, she ran. He'd chase her. To the ends of the earth and back. "I don't want a few months with you, I want a lifetime. You're all I want. That doesn't mean deciding right now and we don't need to rush whatever's happening to get to the end game. We can keep doing this for the next fifty years, if that's how you want it, Raven. As long as you're here with me."

Slowly, never taking her gaze from him, she sat up and hugged the sheet to her chest. He didn't move because something told him she needed the position above him to feel safe. So, he remained on his side, head in hand, calmly watching her as his heart jack-hammered out of his ribcage and his muscles grew rigid in fear she'd walk.

Thing about Raven? She didn't trust people. Whether that had to do with a childhood she hardly remembered or whether she didn't trust herself was moot. The point was, he'd broken through, when all others had failed, and that meant something.

When it was obvious she couldn't or wouldn't speak, he said the rest of the diatribe which had shoved around in his skull all night. "I've loved you a third of my life, and I think I've been in love with you for half that long. Don't say it back to me unless you mean it. You trust me with your body, and that's more than any man before me. But you don't trust me here yet." He pressed his hand to her chest and left it there. "Until you trust yourself, you'll never be able to love me." He swallowed. Hard. "I'll wait. I'm not going anywhere."

Pressing a palm to her forehead, she glanced away, gaze lost in thought. "We don't know if we can make this work, Noah. Neither of us has tried a relationship."

"We don't know it *won't* work. And we are trying, right now. We have been for weeks." The alternative was not having her at all, and he couldn't live through that. He'd lost everyone he ever cared about but her and Aubrey. He'd stop breathing if he lost either.

He could've wept when, instead of moving away or avoiding, she placed her hand over his on her chest. "How do you know I don't fully trust you? Or myself?"

Because she had to ask, that's why. "You know the moment I knew I was in love with you?" He stared into her eyes to ram home the difference. "When Max called to say you were being followed. My first thought as you walked toward me on the pier was I couldn't live without you." He'd rather that bastard kill him than harm one hair on her head. "If anything ever happens to me, you're the one I'd want raising Aubrey." That night he walked in on Raven and Aubrey's conversation about her burns made his chest ache to think about now.

Her eyes widened. "I don't know anything about parenting."

"You think I did at eighteen? No. You muddle through, for the best of the child. It's scary and hard and sometimes the only reward is an *I love you* at the end of the day." He sat up, her gaze tracking the move. "You don't trust that you can do the job. Be a parent, a mother. Whether it's Aubrey or your own someday." He slid his hands to her waist and pulled her closer. "I don't think you can. I *know* you can. That's trust. That's love."

Her pretty brown eyes filled again, tears clinging to her lashes and spilling down her cheeks. "You'd trust me with Aubrey?" She spoke so softly he barely heard her over his pounding heart.

"I already do."

She shook her head as if to deny his words, but then closed her eyes.

He pulled her sideways into his lap, hugging her hard. He got the sense she was trying to pull away from him, even though she didn't move, but he held tight. Raven didn't conform well to change and she hated being pushed, but he needed her to know how he felt. "I'm not asking for anything, baby. Just stay with me. The rest will come."

After long moments, when she didn't respond or flinch or cry, he had his answer. The knots of tension uncoiled in his gut and he flopped back on the bed with her sprawled over him. He'd never get tired of touching her. She was a damn balm to his soul. Running his hand up and down her back, he kissed her temple and started to doze off.

"Noah?"

"Hmm?"

She paused. "You're very comfortable."

A lazy grin split his face at her complicated statement wrapped in simple. She was staying.

▪▪▪

While Noah slept, Raven dressed in jeans and a black turtleneck sweater and padded into the kitchen. Coffee brewing, she leaned against the counter and bit her lip.

Her head was woozy with everything he'd said but, oddly, she didn't feel trapped or pressured. Being with Noah was easy. Maybe too easy. Sometimes, she kept waiting for the other shoe to drop and for him to say he'd hit his emotional limit. After all, for his entire adult life, he'd had no one close to him to latch onto. There were security people and caretakers. And her. But he was used to being alone, depending on only himself.

Logically, he should be as wary as her. Instead, it was the opposite. He knew what he wanted and went for it with courage she wished she had. She didn't even know why she was like this. Her mother was a sweet, compassionate person who'd given Raven everything a little girl required. They didn't have a lot of money, but she'd never gone without.

The missing element was inside of her, and she had no clue how to get it back. Maybe this all boiled down to survivor's guilt or abandonment issues, as her pediatric shrinks once diagnosed. If so, Noah was the best medicine available. With him, she was...free.

She poured herself a cup of coffee and sat in front of his laptop at the kitchen island. Now that she had some time, she could look up this Rizzoli person who'd made Noah's life hell. No doubt, Noah had told her everything, but she was curious to see faces and find out how the trial was going.

An hour and two cups of coffee later, Raven stretched, closing the browsers. The prosecution had just rested their case on Friday and the defense was set to begin Monday. The press was leaning toward a conviction and she didn't see how any jury could let the man off on all the evidence.

Just as she was about to close the laptop, a Skype invitation popped on the screen from Aubrey. Grinning, she opened it and waved.

"You're using Noah's computer?"

She laughed. "Just doing some internet surfing. How are you? I had a blast visiting. Maybe I can come up again in a couple weeks?"

Her grin was just as infectious as Noah's. "Awesome! There's tons we didn't get to do last time, like swimming and stuff."

"You're on. I'll talk to your uncle to see what we can arrange." She got up to refill her coffee, taking the laptop with her. "Check this out." Raven turned the screen around to show Aubrey the picture they'd colored on Noah's fridge. "Best spot in the house."

They chatted for thirty minutes about hair and clothes when Aubrey was called away by Frances for lunch. "Can we Skype again? When are you coming back to visit?"

The mix of excitement and loneliness in her voice broke Raven's heart. Her throat tight, she smiled. "We can't come this weekend, but let's shoot for the next. And you can call me anytime." She bit her lip, not knowing how much Aubrey knew about the trial. She and Noah never discussed Aubrey's knowledge of her past. "To play it safe, why don't we just plan to Skype on your uncle's laptop here?"

After saying goodbye, Raven dropped her elbows on the counter and grinned. She hadn't known Noah's niece very long, but she was a darn great kid who made it easy to like her. Just like her uncle. For a moment, she wondered what it would be like to have normal. The three of them sitting around the dinner table, talking about their day. Planning what to do for the weekend. Tucking Aubrey in for the night or checking out a grade on her math test.

The images didn't make her heart pound or her lungs collapse. A warm sensation filled her chest instead, possibilities blooming. Noah had said no pressure. He just wanted her to stay, to keep going as they were in the hope that she'd feel the same. Less than two months ago, she'd have laughed if someone told her what she'd be doing right now.

Before Noah, sex was a swift release and nothing more. Often, it was more hassle than it was worth. Heading to the club, watching the members from the shadows, picking the right man who had sub tendencies. Exhausting. Her day had been programmed to the minute, even Friday dinners with Noah. She went to work and she came home. There had been no excitement, no spark to break up the monotony.

How had she not known what else was out there, how good it could be?

Her gaze landed on a binder between the microwave and a seasoning rack. Rising, she slid it out and opened it. Index cards and scraps of paper were pressed neatly into page protectors, all with the same similar handwriting. Some of the pages were yellow and worn, some a bit newer, but all contained recipes. Casseroles, cookies, soups, bread.

She leaned on the counter and scrolled through the binder. They were definitely his mother's recipes he'd told her about their first night together. She'd offered to cook a few of her dishes for Noah, but was shocked she found herself thinking she wanted to make them all. Maybe not right away, but slowly, night after night, working her way through Noah's memories.

The last page's entry said "Noah's Favorite." Italian meatloaf. Straightening, she headed for the door to see if the guards were outside.

Max nodded in greeting. "Miss Crowne."

"Can you take me to the store?"

In answer, he pulled his cell out and thumbed a text. "Ready when you are, Miss Crowne."

When they returned, Noah's housekeeper, Mildred, was at the condo and dusting the living room. She met them in the kitchen, where Max set the grocery bags he'd insisted on carrying down on the counter.

"Mr. Caldwell is sleeping," Mildred said in her thick Russian accent. "Is it alright if I change the sheets and vacuum on Monday? Yes?"

Raven had met Mildred months back, but the housekeeper never directly asked her for orders. Unsure of protocol, she took in the elder woman's gray hair wrapped in a bandana and chubby form in the maid's uniform. Surely Noah wouldn't care if some things got put off for a couple days.

"That would be fine." She glanced in the direction of the bedroom. It was early afternoon. She'd never known him to sleep that long. Noah was an early riser. "We got back from the charity event late last night. He must be really tired from that." Or their fun afterward. She blushed and turned away to find Max exiting the condo. "Where are you going?"

Confusion on his face, he pointed to the door as if to say, *duh*.

"Keep me company. Please?" There was no need to have him stand sentry outside the door if Noah was sleeping. She pointed to the kitchen island when he didn't move.

He nodded, made his way over, and sat on one of the stools.

"I don't need to make dinner?" Mildred eyed the grocery bags.

Raven bit her lip, hoping she wasn't stepping on her toes. The housekeeper had been taking care of for Noah for eight something years. "Not tonight. I...like cooking."

Mildred nodded, seemingly pleased, and commenced with her duties.

Raven smiled at Max, wide-eyed in relief, as if just avoiding a thrown-down. She hadn't wanted to offend the housekeeper.

Biting back a grin, he thumbed a text.

She shifted around the kitchen, putting groceries away and getting the Italian meatloaf going. Once it was in the oven and Mildred had left, Raven started the side dishes and looked into the living room.

"I'm getting worried. He never sleeps like this."

As if on cue, Noah's bedroom door opened and he emerged wearing flannel pajama bottoms low on his hips and a white T-shirt that did nothing to hide his gloriously sculpted body. His blond hair stood up at odd angles and he unconsciously ran his hand through it.

Sidling up next to her, he kissed her cheek. "Morning, baby." He reached for the coffee pot and shook the carafe as if stumped it was empty.

"It's late afternoon. You slept the whole day."

He squinted at the clock, then their bodyguard, who was busy trying not to pay attention to them. "Hi, Max."

"Sir."

Noah rubbed his neck. "Anything wrong?" His voice was more coarse than usual and his blue eyes were hazy.

"No, sir."

"Max was keeping me company while I cooked dinner." She wrapped her arms around his waist. He was hot to the touch. She pressed her hand to his cheek. "You have a fever."

He grunted. "Not feeling great." Wrapping his arms around her, he rested his cheek on top of her head. "Need more sleep. When's dinner going to be ready?"

"An hour or so. Why don't you go back to bed?"

"Not if you went to the trouble of cooking." Releasing her, he leaned against the counter and rubbed his forehead. She already had a bottle out and was pouring two pills in her hand when he asked, "Where's the aspirin?"

He swallowed them and shuffled into the living room, where he piled two blankets over himself and flopped sideways.

"There goes our weekend."

Max grinned. "I'll be right outside if you need me."

Her cell chimed a text as she moved to turn the burner down on the noodles. She fumbled to unlock the screen while stirring the pot with the other hand. A photo popped up.

She froze, the hairs on her nape standing erect. Someone had texted a picture of the note from her apartment, the one stuck to the door with a knife. Shaking, she looked up to call for Max when another text came through.

You're not safe. I know where you are.

She yelped, shaking so fiercely she knocked the pan off the stove and to the floor with a loud clatter. Buttered noodles went flying everywhere.

Noah was on his feet and moving her way when Max ran around the corner and skidded to a halt. Both men eyed the mess and then her.

"What's wrong, Miss Crowne?"

She couldn't seem to move. To breathe. A vise squeezed her chest, cutting off air. Her fingers fisted the phone, trembling violently.

Noah took the cell from her grip and passed it to Max, pulling her to his chest. She tried to absorb his warmth, but she was so cold. Shaking so hard.

Max stiffened. "Sir." He handed Noah the cell and pulled his out. Within moments, he was pacing in the foyer, barking orders into the phone.

Noah thumbed through the message, jaw clenched, eyes glacial. "Son of a bitch." He tossed her cell on the counter and pulled her to him again. One hand came up to cup her head. "He won't get to you. He won't touch you. Swear to God, he won't, baby."

She nodded, because she figured that was the right thing to do. But Noah was wrong. They got her number. It would only be a matter of time before they got her. Right?

Max rounded the corner. "McCannon's coming to pick up the cell. Hintz is getting her a new one, with a new number. We've got a man at the gallery at all times and one downstairs. I notified the team on Miss Aubrey."

But instead of the news calming Noah, his arms banded tighter. "She doesn't leave your sight for two seconds." He sucked in a harsh breath and swayed on his feet.

"Understood."

"Not two seconds..."

"Shh," she cooed. Her stomach rolled with nausea and dread. "Let's get you back in bed. I'm safe right here."

For now.

Chapter Seventeen

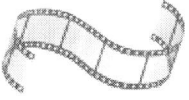

Noah groaned and rolled over in bed, assessing if anything new hurt before opening his eyes. Alas, his bones were no longer liquefying from fever and nothing seemed to be aching. Thank Christ. He hadn't been sick like that in ages.

Hell, what day was it?

Instinctively, he reached out for Raven and found the bed empty, the sheets cool.

Vague memories of her force-feeding him chicken soup and aspirin sprang to mind. He remembered waking periodically to find her watching movies or reading next to him.

And the text. She got that damn threat…when?

Shit. He sat up too quickly and grabbed his head as the room spun. Stumbling to his feet, he made his way into the living room. "Raven?"

His housekeeper, Mildred, came out of the guest bathroom. "She's at work, Mr. Caldwell. Are you feeling better?"

"Yes. Thank you."

He didn't like Raven being at the gallery. All those windows and… He closed his eyes and bit back a curse. He couldn't run her life. That gallery meant the world to her. If he had to live through the heart-pounding worry, he would. His team would keep her safe.

"May I clean your room, Mr. Caldwell?"

He blew out a breath. "That would be great."

"Would you like me to heat you something to eat first? Miss Crowne, she's a keeper. She made your mama's meatloaf."

Turning his head toward the kitchen, he stared as if he could see through the fridge door. "Did she?" he muttered, wondering if the dizziness was from emotion or lingering illness. The room seemed to vacuum of air, leaving a static hum of electricity in its wake. His mom used to make him meatloaf on his birthday because it was his favorite. That must've been what Raven had been cooking the other night.

"Mr. Caldwell?"

He flinched and cleared his throat. "No, thank you. I'm not very hungry at the moment."

Scratching his head, he headed to the kitchen to grab coffee and then he needed to shower off the remnants of fever. If he felt this gross, he could only imagine what he smelled or looked like. Raven left a letter on the kitchen counter. Picking it up, he poured a cup of coffee and read it over the rim of his cup.

My new cell number is programmed in your phone. There's leftovers in the fridge. I hope you're feeling better. xoxo

A silly, stupid grin split his face, and he didn't care who saw. A mundane, normal note, something a wife would leave for her husband. Happiness filled the empty spaces in his chest. He liked this. A lot. The dynamic between them was comfortable and familiar, yet he never tired of their love-making or conversation. They had, quite possibly, the perfect relationship. He just had to convince her of it. Or keep her sated long enough she didn't panic anymore.

Shoving off the counter, he retrieved his phone and shot off a text. *Miss you. Is everything okay? You have at least two guards?*

Sigh. Yes, master. I have Max as my shadow and some cutie named Jones in the main gallery. Nicole's eying him like candy. I may hook them up.

He barked out a laugh, first at her antics and then over the fact that she typed the word "sigh" in a text. *Cutie? He'll be fired at once.*

lol. Glad you're feeling better. McCannon says they got nothing on the text. It came from a throw-away. Police are done with my apartment. They got nothing. Can we just send in exterminators to fumigate?

He rubbed his jaw. The news wasn't surprising, but it was still disappointing. *I'll take care of the apartment.* He thought about ways to distract her from all this, remembering how she'd trembled in his arms after receiving the text. *Don't leave work without me. I'll pick you up.*

K. xoxo

Another thing he loved? The way she started putting X and O after everything. Damn, he was sunk.

He called for his guard.

The front door opened and Hintz stepped inside, filling the entire doorway with his size. "Yeah, boss?"

"We're leaving in twenty. Have two guys ready."

"You got it."

Noah showered and changed, grabbing a banana for the road. On the counter by the sink was Raven's watch he'd given her, as if she'd taken it off to cook and forgot about it. As an afterthought, he shoved it in his pocket and left.

Along the way, he called McCannon and got the same story Raven texted, but he was assured the FBI agent had put a man in a car outside Elements, just in case. Noah suspected Rizzoli's hitman already had an in with her, or had made contact before. He had no basis for this, but his gut was rarely wrong. All of her exhibits and meetings with artists just left her wide open for attack. He didn't like it.

And it seemed like the guy was screwing with them. Texts and notes and car tails. Almost like he was taunting them. Any professional would've had this wrapped up by now.

The pitting sensation in his gut dropped when he saw her apartment again. The bastard had left no drawer unturned. "Box up her books and knickknacks," he said to the guards. "Leave the furniture." He'd send a cleaning service in for the rest.

Making his way to her bedroom, his hands clenched at the violation. Her panties and clothes were strewn everywhere. Her jewelry box was broken in pieces on the dresser. Hell. Nicole had given her that.

"I need a box," he shouted and thanked Hintz when he brought one.

He threw most of her clothes into garbage bags for charity. She could be upset if she wanted, but it was all polluted. He'd buy her new clothes. Most of the ones she wore had been transferred to his place anyway. Kneeling in the closet to pack her shoes, he found pink paper on the floor.

He collected the letters he'd written and leaned against the doorframe. Seemed like a long time ago, after all that had happened. A desperate, lonely man had penned these, wishing for something he couldn't have. And now that he had her, they were threatening to take her away. He rubbed his thumb over the stationery, surprised she'd kept them, even more surprised at the well of emotion rising in his chest knowing she had.

A few other miscellaneous items littered the closet floor. He put them in the box and rose. Before leaving the room, he texted a list of things for his assistant to purchase and shot it off to Veronica, asking that she have them delivered to the condo.

Leaving the rest to a cleaning crew, he headed to the Super's office downstairs and gave him a check covering the remainder of Raven's lease.

As they pulled away from the building, regret tore at him. They'd had many Friday night dinners and good times as friends in that apartment. He sighed and rested his hand on the box beside him. They'd evolved since then into something not even he had hoped for. And no way in hell was he letting anything come between them.

• •

"What would you like to do for dinner?"

Raven glanced up at Noah, leaning on the doorframe to her office. He wore faded jeans and a black Henley under his thick down jacket. And she thought him in a tux was sexy. "Hi. You look better." She closed her program and reached for her coat.

He nodded to Max, who stepped out. "Don't put that on yet."

"My coat? Why?"

From her office viewpoint, she watched Max and Jones set the alarm code, cut the lights, and went out the front door.

"Alone at last." His grin was wicked. He shoved off the doorframe, turned off the lights, and strode toward her with only the dim hall light at his back.

"What are you up to?" Was it possible to swallow your own tongue? In his predatory gait, he drew closer, and her heart pumped. How did he do this every time?

He tossed his coat on a chair and rounded her desk, setting his hands on her hips until her ass met the edge. "I told you I had a fantasy about you and this desk."

She forced an exhale. "You can't mean—"

"I do mean." His head dipped closer and he kissed his way up her neck to her ear. He inhaled deep and groaned. His hands slowly worked up her skirt, until the material bunched at her waist.

Oh, God. That…was too good—his hands parting her thighs and callused thumbs rubbing over her flesh. "Someone will see." Her head fell back. She held him to her, contradicting her argument, and she shivered.

"The lights are off, the doors are locked, and my men are outside guarding the building. No one will see." He unbuttoned her blouse and spread it open, revealing her white bra. Cupping her breasts, he licked his way from her collarbone to suck at her nipple through the lace.

She couldn't think when he was touching her. He set her on fire. Embers that never cooled. By no means had things ever grown boring or routine between them. Each time they crashed together, it was more explosive than the last.

"Reach behind you and swipe the stuff off your desk."

Panting, she turned her head to look at her perfect order. Neat piles and everything in its rightful place. She couldn't. No...but, ah. He latched onto the other breast.

He eased her panties past her knees, grinning against her damp nipple through the bra, then yanked the cups down, thrusting her breasts out for his viewing. "Come on, baby. Swipe the desk. You know you want to."

She moaned when he cupped her heat, pressing his palm to her mound and continuing the assault on her senses by kissing her neck. His fingers flicked over her clit, spreading the wetness, and wrenching another moan from her chest.

Insanely needing his skin against hers, the drugging heat and more of his scent, she gripped the hem of his shirt and tugged it over his head. She paused to admire the ridges of muscle, skimming her fingertips over the dips and peaks, relishing the power when he sucked in a breath at her exploration.

"I love your body, Noah." She swirled her finger around his navel.

His mouth crushed hers, his tongue pushing past her lips to mate with hers. Desperate. Demanding. The edge of reason. Stepping between her legs, he grabbed her backside, spread her cheeks and ground his erection against her core, sending her into orbit.

"Do it, Raven. Swipe the desk. I'll lay you out and pound into you. You'll come so hard—"

She flung her arm back, sending everything atop her desk crashing to the floor.

He wasted no time. He unzipped his jeans, shoving them to his thighs to free his erection. She reached for him, stroking the soft skin over his hard shaft as he lifted her onto the desk. He grabbed her wrists, pinned them behind her back, and thrust deep.

Ah, God. *Yes.* So, so full. She could feel every inch of him gliding against her walls. Hot and hard.

She tried to ease back onto the desk and lay across the top, but he held her wrists firm. Her spine bowed, the top of her head nearly against the wood and body arched off the surface, rooting him deeper. He pulled out, until only his tip remained inside. The withdrawal was too much. She needed…she needed…

"Noah, *please.*"

"Is this what you want, baby?" Using her bound arms as leverage, he brought her down onto his shaft at the same time his hips jutted forward.

They collided. Hard. His pelvis ground into her clit. His thick cock shoved deep. Every nerve ending charged and fractured. She moaned. Begged. As if fueled by her response alone, he repeated the motion, faster, harder.

And she came in a blinding rush of wet heat, clenching around him to hold him inside, desperate to keep him there. Her muscles quaked. The air wheezed from her lungs.

"You're mine." His voice was raw and strangled, as if each word was torn out. "Never get enough of you. Never."

Cursing under his breath, he continued the motions, building her back up. Drawing out, driving deep. Manipulating her body to his will, until another orgasm ripped through her with no warning. Lungs seizing and muscles contracting, she screamed in bliss as he slammed into her.

He pumped hard twice more and threw his head back as he held her to him. With hot jets, he came, his body poised stiff over hers. Releasing her wrists, he collapsed onto her chest, palms pressed to the desk on either side of her head.

His hot breath panted against her neck. "You let me bind you." He lifted his head to look down at her. Awe and something she couldn't pin down shone in his blue eyes. "You let me bind you the whole time. Not once did you panic."

She hadn't thought about it. So ensconced in pleasure, she hadn't had time for fear. The only thing in her head was how he touched her and tasted her and took her like an animal. She'd loved it.

The truth hit her hard. He'd been right when he'd said she didn't completely trust herself. But an ingrained part of her trusted him to take her there.

He cupped her cheeks, face twisted as if he wanted to say more but was forcing it back. After a moment, he dropped his forehead to hers. "Come on, baby. Let's get you home."

Chapter Eighteen

"To another successful show." Nicole clinked her champagne flute to Raven's. "We sold out."

Raven grinned and scanned the thinning crowd. Another thirty minutes and they could call it a wrap. "She's very talented. I knew her work would sell."

Her gaze scanned the far wall where twenty exquisite pieces hung in symmetry. Their artist, Gloria, had an eye for unique architecture, but her show on native Inuits was spectacular. The only hitch tonight had been when a tourist mistakenly called them Eskimos—a derogatory insult in these parts. The poor man hadn't known better, and Nicole had diverted a scene by whisking the guy off to the food table and flirting until the artist had stopped seething.

"I assume, by the way Noah's stripping you naked with his eyes, that we're not going out for drinks?" Nicole tilted her head.

Guilt slammed into her. This was three shows now where she'd bailed on Nicole. "I'm sorry. Can you blame me?" She regrettably tore her gaze away from where Noah was talking to a small group.

Nicole sighed. "No, I can't blame you. He's so lickable." She took a healthy sip of champagne. "I need a man."

"You've had many lovers, as recently as two nights ago, if memory of our conversation serves." Nicole wasn't easy by any means, but she enjoyed the opposite sex.

"None of them look at me like that." Nicole pursed her lips, pointing to where Noah was still watching from across the room. "And the sex is boring. I mean, forget Fifty Shades. I'd take twenty-five shades. In any color. Doesn't have to be grey."

Raven laughed. "How about next Friday? Just me and you, wherever you want to go. We'll see if we can find you someone a little naughty. That's your problem. You pick nice guys."

"Sure. Why not?"

Raven made her way across the room, attempting not to draw attention, and plastered a smile on her face. Her steps faltered. Something wasn't right. Intuition stopped her dead. Not sure what was wrong, she glanced around trying to find the trigger for her unease.

Her eyes trained on a thin red laser beam of light shining in from the window, stopping on her chest. Like one of those toys for cats to chase.

Noah screamed her name.

Heart pounding, she turned toward him, confused.

Noah yelled for Max, his body poised to run. He lifted his arm, as if in a plea to stop, as two of his guards moved in on him. Fighting them, he tried to shove them aside, arms flailing. "*Nooo*." His voice bounced off the walls.

Shielding him, his guards dragged him to the floor.

Wait. Shielding him? From what?

Oh God. What was happening? The breath caught in her throat. Terror froze her in place, her limbs useless blocks of ice.

Glass broke. Chaos ensued.

Guests screamed and ran. The front door flew open. Two men with guns raised entered the foyer. A crack echoed, booming through the room, rupturing her eardrums.

The air punched from her lungs as someone launched into her side. They hit the floor hard, her facedown and a man covering her. A sharp pain seared her hip from impact. His muscles were tense, hard against her back. He had his hand on her forehead as a buffer between it and the bamboo floor. His weight was crushing.

Hot, shaky breath fanned her cheek. "Stay down, Miss Crowne," he grated. "I've got you."

"Oh God. Max?"

He groaned as if in pain. Drew in a harsh breath. "Yes, ma'am." His body shifted slightly, as if looking over his shoulder. "Just a minute more. The feds are chasing him on the street."

Chasing who?

"What's happening?" A sob rose in her chest.

Oh God. Was Noah okay? Where was Nicole?

"It's okay, Miss Crowne. I've got you."

A violent shudder ripped through her body. Max held her tighter, pinning her to the floor.

"We're clear!" Someone shouted from behind them, making her flinch.

Max eased up enough for her to roll over. His pained gaze swept over her before his arms gave out and he momentarily collapsed on top of her. With a groan, he raised himself again and muttered, "You're okay, you're okay," as if needing to assure himself. He rolled to his back next to her, panting heavily.

"Raven!"

Oh, *Noah*! Thank God.

She sat up, trembling from head to toe. Disoriented, she pressed her hand to her forehead as the room spun. Where was he?

The men who'd charged the front door were walking around, issuing patrons out of the gallery. The cops? Feds? Was the hell had happened?

Why couldn't she stop shaking?

"Raven!" Noah rushed across the room, dropping to his knees beside her. He looked like he didn't know whether to kiss her or kill someone. Anger and concern shone his eyes, in the twist of his mouth. Then, he stopped breathing.

"You're hit." He craned around. "Get me an ambulance!" When he turned back, his breaths were soughing and his hands frantically ran over her body. Tears welled in his wide, blue eyes. "Where, baby? Where are you hit?" His hands pressed, searched.

She looked down to find blood on the front of her mint green dress. Panic clawed at her throat. But...

No holes. No pain. The cold numbness of shock began to recede. "Not mine," she whispered. "Not mine."

She shoved Noah aside and crawled to Max, still laying on his back. Her trembling hands, red with blood, cupped his cheeks. "Max?"

"I'm fine...Miss Crowne," he grit through clenched teeth. "A through and through. Don't think the bullet hit anything vital."

She looked down where his large hand covered his side. Blood seeped out from under his fingers. "Oh God, *no*. You got shot."

"Raven." Noah touched her shoulder, but she shrugged him off. Max was hurt and it was her fault. He had protected her, shoving her to the ground and covering her body. Just like...

Just like her father had done all those years ago in that bunker.

Guilt slammed into her, churning her stomach. "Let me see, Max." She eased his hand away. Blood oozed from a small hole. So much blood. His white dress shirt clung to his skin, soaked. Anger and panic rose up to choke her. She pressed her palm to the wound. "You idiot! You got shot. For me?"

Max slid his gaze to hers, his hand covering hers on his wound. "Worth it. Just doing my job. Will be...good as new tomorrow."

The past few minutes caught up with her and she broke. Tears blurred her eyes.

Two of their guards knelt beside Max. One gently took her wrist and removed her hand from Max's side. He pressed a towel to the area with enough pressure for Max to grunt. "Medic's on the way."

"Raven, baby. Let me look at you. Are you hurt?"

She whirled and wrapped her arms around Noah's neck, burying her face in his shoulder. "No. I'm...not hurt." Terrified and sick with guilt and confused, but not hurt. Absorbing his warmth, his safe embrace, she breathed him in and clung.

He cradled her to his hard body, standing and backing them away from his team. Pulling her from him, he cupped her cheeks. His gaze dropped as if to verify she was okay.

"Are you sure?" Frenetic worry rounded his eyes, wrinkled his brows. He looked on the verge of homicidal and more than a little lost when his jaw clenched. His hands shook against her cheeks. Tension radiated off him in thready pulses.

She swiftly nodded, wanting to assure him and concerned about his mindset. He was the steady one, the rock. If he crumbled, there was no hope for them tonight. More tears spilled, trekking down her cheeks. She looked around, seeing Nicole with a group of people standing outside talking to an officer. Relief flooded her.

"Ah, fuck." Noah hauled her to him, arms banding her back. "I thought he got you," he whispered for her ears only. "I thought he got you."

She closed her eyes to the desperate tone in his voice and hugged him back, still reeling from the events. Breathing in his cinnamon scent, she tried to uncoil the muscles straining her neck and shoulders. Noah had her in his strong arms. She was okay. He was okay.

"I'm fine, Noah."

"You guys sure know how to throw a party." A man strode over to them, stepping around glass shards. His gait was lithe, like that of a martial arts practitioner. Tan suit wrinkled, tie askew, he shook his head. His dark blond hair was graying at the temples and his mouth had fine wrinkles at the corners. Dark brown eyes surveyed the room and fell back on them. "Everyone all right?"

Noah tensed and turned. "What the fuck, McCannon? I thought you had men outside? How did he get a shot?"

McCannon put an unlit cigarette between his lips and left it there as he spoke. "We did, and your men were out there, too. He was tucked into a back alley."

Raven regarded the man Noah referenced as his FBI contact. He was in his mid-forties and, though he had a screw-all demeanor, his eyes said he carried a piece of every case with him.

Two paramedics brought in a stretcher and got to work helping Max. Tears threatened again. He'd put himself between her and a bullet. The realization of "his job," as he'd put it, slammed into her. Max could've died. Protecting her. She pressed a palm to her forehead.

Noah slid his arm around her waist and looked down at her.

McCannon pulled out his phone, swiped the screen, and turned it toward her, holding it out. "Have you seen this guy hanging around?"

The wanna-be artist who gave her the creeps.

She nodded. "He's been in here a few times. He...wanted a showing." She looked between the two men. "He said his name was Vincent Soreno. Who is he?"

"Vincent Soreno is right. We're pretty confident he's the hired assassin." McCannon sighed. "Dumb shit didn't even bother to change his name."

Noah tensed. "That *dumb shit* just shot through a window with five bodyguards inside and three FBI agents outside. He nearly put holes in her. And me. He *did* shoot one of my men."

McCannon pocketed his phone. "We'll get him. He got away by the skin of his teeth."

"Pardon me if I don't hold my breath." Noah pulled them out of the way when the paramedics brought Max by on a stretcher. He set his hand on Max's shoulder and squeezed, quiet appreciation in his eyes.

Raven eased out from under Noah's arm and leaned over the stretcher. Having no idea what to say to Max, she smiled. He was pale, but didn't appear to be in much pain. "Thank you. I'm sorry I called you an idiot. You scared me."

He waved her comment aside. "See you tomorrow, Miss Crowne."

"You will not."

He smiled and winced. "Day after, then."

She stood and watched them wheel her bodyguard away, everything so surreal. Red and blue lights. Glass everywhere. Blood on the floor. On her hands.

"Come on, baby. Let's get you home."

▪▪

Noah sat on the bed and stripped off his tie. After the shooting, he couldn't stomach the thought of staying in Anchorage, so he had their driver take them right to the airport and, by helicopter, they flew to Aubrey's Castle. Thankfully, his niece slept through the noise and allowed him and Raven to enter the third floor suite without interruption. He was hoping he'd be in a better frame of mind in the morning.

Listening to the water from Raven's shower, he stripped out of his clothes and tried to block the images from earlier from his mind. But they kept coming. Raven with a scope target on her chest. Her underneath Max on the floor. Noah being too far away for too long, wondering if she'd been hurt. Agonizingly long moments where he hadn't known if she was alive or dead.

Running his hands through his hair, he flopped onto his back. If Max hadn't been so close to her, it could've been her who had been shot, with a much more fatal wound. He pressed his palms to his eyes, remembering the heart-stopping moment he thought she'd been hit. He hadn't drawn breath since. Was still suffocating.

He should've never touched her. Never brought her into this mess. He'd been selfish and, because of him, she could've died. All his security and the damn FBI, and the bastard almost got her. Most importantly, he'd never aimed for Noah, confirming his belief that Rizzoli was out to take her from him as punishment. Revenge.

The water shut off. He tried to get himself together for when she stepped out of the bathroom, but it was futile. Blood all over her. The gunshot still ringing in his ears. The desperate, frightened look on her face.

Fuck it. He should leave her here. She'd bitch and moan, but she'd be alive. There were no accessible roads. The only way in or out was to fly. A full security team, bullet-proof windows, alarm system, and panic room. She'd hate him for taking her away from the gallery, from her life, but she'd be alive.

The bathroom door opened with a quiet click, steam billowing out as Raven emerged with a towel around her middle. From his prone position on the bed, he held his breath when she stopped in her tracks. Her gaze raked over his naked form, not a sensual exploration, but a full study.

Worry ratcheted in his gut. She hadn't said much since they'd left the gallery. Her creamy skin tone was paler than her norm, her pretty eyes distant and unfocused with shadows under them. He had the distinct impression she thought this was all her fault. It made him sick.

"I don't have any clothes," she said at last. Her voice was flat, as if mustering any emotion took too much effort.

"We'll find you something to get by." He sat up and braced his elbows on his thighs, scrubbing his hands over his face. He'd thrown away the dress she'd worn tonight, but he hadn't thought to stop by the condo and get her some things. He'd just wanted her as far away from there as possible.

"Do we know how Max is doing? Can we call the hospital?"

"In the morning, baby." The shot passed through Max's side and exited into a wall. Judging by the location of the wound, Noah doubted the bullet had hit anything vital. Max was ex-military and tougher than steel. He'd be okay.

Yet his bodyguard had softened toward Raven since under her detail. Max looked at her with amusement and adoration. Not romantic by any sense, but he was growing to care for her a great deal. Just tonight, after the agents had the scene secured, Max had checked her out first before succumbing to his injury and standing down. Helpless,

Noah had watched from under the bodies of his own security men, needing to get to her.

Looking at her now, Noah could understand why Max liked her so much. Hell, it was impossible not to love Raven Crowne. Hadn't he tried for years to deny his feelings?

She stared at the bed, unmoving, not blinking, as if trapped in her memory. He had to do something to snap her out of this, but he wasn't right in the head either. Something told him if he didn't act fast, all their progress would regress. She'd be afraid of touch again, of submitting her body to pleasure. Worse, she'd panic and find a way to call off the relationship.

Unsure of what to do, he stared at the floor. Hell, if he could find a way for her to unsee everything, to just lose herself in his touch and...

He straightened, looking at his necktie he'd tossed aside. "Raven, come here."

Like a robot, she walked over to stand between his knees.

Gently, he released her hold on the towel and let it drop. "Trust me, baby."

Finally, she looked him in the eye, but there was nothing in hers. A blank page. He'd seen the look before, when her depression had a stronghold and she was too tired to struggle. Yet it had been years since it had metastasized, and the fact that it was here now had his own panic tripping. He could do everything in his power to keep her safe, take care of her by making her eat and sleeping next to her for comfort, but he couldn't fight this for her.

She blinked slowly, as if to question what he said. "I do trust you."

Of that, he had little doubt. But his beautiful woman still didn't trust herself. "Lay down on the bed for me."

She crawled to the center of the mattress and lay on her back, watching him. He walked to the closet and grabbed another tie, then picked up the other one he'd dropped before making his way back to the bed with both. She swallowed hard, trekking his movements, and he swore a flash of heat and curiosity lit her eyes before it was gone.

"Put your hands up over your head." He kept his voice calm, but authoritative.

She stared at him long moments, biting her bottom lip. "What are you going to do?" Judging by her expression, she knew exactly what he intended. And she wasn't saying no.

He straddled her hips, keeping his weight on his knees and off of her. Laying one tie over her breasts, he ran the other through his fingers. "I'm going to bind your hands to the headboard. You'll be able to get free at any time. And then I'm going to blindfold you."

He had no clue if this would work. She'd either give in to her body's needs and succumb to passion or she'd snap and slip further into her head. After everything they'd been through, it was time to take her here, like this. Time to give her the ultimate test.

Her throat worked a swallow. A shallow breath escaped her parted lips. She was not unaffected. Color rose in her cheeks as she eyed the tie, then brought her arms up over her head, crossing her wrists.

His shaft thickened in response. Leaning forward, he bound her wrists together and threaded the tie through the headboard rail. She tested the strength, but didn't remove her hands from the loose knot. Then he held up the other tie, carefully covering her eyes and knotting it behind her head.

Her lips parted in a sharp gasp. He brushed his thumb over her bottom lip and grew harder when she sucked it into her mouth.

He ran the heel of his hand over his swollen cock. "You know your safeword."

"Yes." She bit her lip again. "I...don't need it."

He ran his gaze down the length of her. Hands tied, blind to his movements, and still trusting him. Her breasts rose and fell in a fast rhythm, thrust out for his viewing pleasure from her position. The dark rose of her nipples puckered, begging to be sucked.

All night. He could do this all night. Fuck, he wanted his camera.

Placing his palms on the bed, he leaned in to speak against her lips. "You are so fucking beautiful, baby."

Chapter Nineteen

To Keep

Raven let out an uneven breath against Noah's lips, his words ringing in her ears. To him, she was beautiful. Not a head case or too much effort. Even though she knew her attributes, he was the first man to make her feel beautiful. And, it seemed, she was enough for him.

Whether pushing limits or just making love, there was always a fever, a need. He was patient and understanding. History told her their heat would cool over time. Except the desire wasn't waning or depleting, as she'd expected. He still wanted her just as much as their first night together.

Hope bloomed in her chest. She'd always trusted him, and the attraction was obviously there. Because of him, she'd experienced unimaginable pleasure. Normal was possible now. Every time he touched her, she fell deeper and deeper for him. Not just the idea of a relationship, but theirs. Them, together.

It was exciting and frightening. Beautiful and scarred.

She tested the binding around her wrists, cinched above her head, still loose enough for her to escape. But she didn't want to escape him. The blindfold took away the ability to see what he would do, but she wasn't afraid. Not of him. Her heart pumped hard and fast in anticipation, knowing he'd bring her to the brink and they'd plunge together.

The situation forced her other senses to kick in. His scent of cinnamon and arousal was strong. The heat from his body enveloped her. His breathing was slow, measured, as if forcing himself into control. He still straddled her hips, but no weight fell on her as he held himself above her body. She ached for him to touch, the apex of her thighs throbbing.

His lips brushed across hers, feather light and warm. "I love you, Raven."

She stilled, trying to process how she felt hearing the words. He'd told her before, but not using that actual phrasing. At the time, a surge of happiness and trepidation shoved around in her chest. He'd told her not to say it back unless she meant it, that he'd wait. The words were on the tip of her tongue. She did love him, was quickly falling in love with him, yet something held her just over that edge, not ready to plummet. Suspended in air.

I love you.

The warm whisper of his words caressed her. She shivered, liking the way his emphatic voice rang true. Noah didn't throw words around, didn't say things he didn't mean. Her heart beat faster.

She opened her mouth to speak, but he closed his lips over hers. He kissed her with determination and purpose, as if needing her to believe him. Stroking his tongue with hers, he commanded submission, not of her body, but her heart. She gave him all she could.

He broke away to speak against her mouth. "I love you so goddamn much I can't think, I can't breathe unless you're near me. You have me, all of me. Don't give up on us." Tension coiled his muscles when he eased his body down to hers.

All at once, like a blow to the chest, she realized just how scared he must've been back at the gallery tonight. He feared losing her to herself and to the man senselessly after them. She'd been numb with shock until he'd put the restraints on her wrists and the blindfold over her eyes. He'd had to take her sight away for her to see him.

Wanting to touch him, to soothe the worry, she made to slip out of the binding, but his hand pressed down over hers, stopping her attempt.

"Please, Raven." His tone was quiet, desperate. He rested his forehead to hers and sighed.

She forced a swallow. "I'm not giving up on us. I'm here."

He stilled for a moment, as if absorbing her words.

When he shifted, the light dusting of hair on his chest rasped her nipples. Heat flared over her skin. She drew in a breath, biting her lip. With his hands at her sides, he kissed her cheeks, her mouth, then her neck. His tongue traced a path from her shoulder to her collarbone. She shivered. Moaned.

"You like that, baby?" When she nodded, unable to speak, he said, "Where to next?" His fingers inched down to race circles on her breasts, the coarseness of his skin deliciously contrasting hers.

She'd never been so grateful for an outdoorsman who worked with his hands. The artistic side of him seemed to know where to draw the most response.

"My baby likes that." His fingers circled closer to her nipples, but never quite reached where she needed him most. "Would you like me to touch them?"

"Yes," she moaned.

The pads of his thumbs brushed over her erect peaks. His breathing grew as ragged as hers. Without being able to move, to see, every touch was heightened, setting her on fire. She arched, the air trapping in her chest.

He shifted, sliding down her body to kneel between her thighs. So frustratingly good. His fingers moved lower, over her naval and grabbed her hips. Then he paused, and she imagined he was staring at her with that intense expression of hunger. She grew more wet, the slight chill in the room drifting over her drenched folds.

Without warning, he ran his finger over her clit. She cried out, but he was moving down, over her sex, not staying where she ached for him. Lower yet his finger moved, to the tight ring of her puckered hole. He rotated his finger, massaging, but not penetrating. A nervousness she was unaccustomed to feeling charged, sending trembles of need straight to her core. She gasped, pressing down on him. Heat flared.

"Soon, I'll take you right here. Do you want that?" His voice was hoarse, tight. She loved him like this, when he was all consumed with her, with need.

She thought about his question and decided she did want him there, where no man had attempted to take her. He was large, so they'd have to go slow, but Noah would know that. Knew her. Biting her lip, she nodded.

He groaned, palms spreading her thighs wider. "Not tonight, baby. Soon."

Shifting, he eased next to her on the bed and encouraged her to turn on her side away from him. He pulled her back to his front, and the binding around her wrist tightened. Taking stock, she realized it wasn't painful and relaxed.

Nuzzling her hair, he ran his hand up her waist, her arm, to her bound wrists. His erection pressed between her cheeks, rocking into her. She pressed back, the desire for him so high that frustration mounted. As if sensing her need, he splayed his hand over her belly and moved south.

"Yes." She spread her legs.

He positioned his thigh between hers and opened her folds with his fingers. "This what you like, baby?"

She nodded. He removed his fingers. But the whimper died in her throat. He aligned himself with her opening, wetting the soft crown before plunging all the way inside. Her walls clamped around him, trying to draw him deeper.

He thrust from behind, his pelvis slapping against her ass. She choked out a gasp, arching her back. Cradling her to him, he pumped in a steady rhythm that drove her insane. Unhurried, so that every glide of his shaft filled her more and more. It wasn't the frantic pace he'd set before. It was a slow build. Tension knotted her muscles, seeking release.

Just as she was about to beg, to cry for mercy, he pressed a finger to her clit and she exploded. Lights burst behind her lids. The binds on her wrists cinched as she shuddered. Air trapped in her lungs. Tucking her chin, she screamed his name as wave after wave unfurled through her. He soon followed, pumping twice more before going rigid. Mouth wide on her shoulder, he roared through his orgasm.

She was still trembling when his shallow thrusts ceased. He moved behind her, stretching. A hand came down over her wrists and released the tie, freeing her. He lifted the other from her eyes.

Then, without a word, he drew his arms around her and hauled her closer, as if wanting to crawl inside her. He wrapped his leg around hers, caging her in. He didn't seem to breathe for several moments, until finally, he relaxed his vise and nuzzled his face in her hair.

■■■

By the time Monday rolled around, Noah seemed to have a tangible hold on his rioting emotions and could at least look at Raven without remembering Max shoving her to the floor. Most of the time. They'd stayed the weekend and hung out with Aubrey, decompressing.

Raven's gallery was still in lockdown until the forensics team was through, so Noah did some work from his laptop at home to keep her company. They'd called the hospital to check on Max about fifty times per Raven's request, and their bodyguard was recuperating nicely. McCannon thought it unwise to visit the hospital until they could get more on Soreno. Max was set to be released today anyway.

From the kitchen alcove, Noah eyed Raven pushing her dinner around her plate, having barely eaten any of the baked chicken she'd made. She'd been quiet most of the day, too, only speaking when asked a direct question.

After they'd made love at the castle, she appeared to relax, but now he was worried about her depression. For years, she'd fought it, winning. She was the strongest damn person he knew. But that didn't mean he couldn't be concerned. It was like she'd crawled inside him, where every action, thought, or mood resounded through him, so that he was right there with her. Stupid as it sounded, they felt like one damn person. As her best friend, he'd known how to reach her when she'd gone dark, but as her lover, he had no idea if he was holding on too tight.

He set his fork down, losing his appetite. "What's on your mind, Raven?"

Her lips twisted in thought. She picked up her wine and took a sip before answering. "Do you want to get married?"

Forcing the wine past his throat, he set the glass down before he dropped it. "Was that a proposal?"

Smiling, she closed her eyes and shook her head. "I mean in the general sense. You never struck me as a forever guy." Her gaze leveled on him. "We haven't discussed...the future. You said you wanted us to stick, but..."

"But you don't know what that entails." He nodded, the clamp around his chest easing. Raven was a planner by nature, always needing to know what came next. The organizational side of her, the one that needed control in all things, had to be going batshit inside her skull. Neither of them had been in a long term relationship. She didn't know what to do, and it was obviously making her crazy.

Leaning forward, he took her hand, linking their fingers. "I'm not against the idea. I love you, and I can't stand the thought of this ending, so marriage seems like the next logical step. But we don't need to rush things." Hell, she hadn't even said she loved him back yet.

Staring at their linked fingers, she sighed. "What about kids? Do you...want them?" This particular question had her the most worried, because she wouldn't look him in the eye and she didn't seem to be breathing.

He thought hard over his answer because this wasn't a conversation to have in passing. Aubrey had been his whole world. He loved her as a father might, putting her needs before his own. The situation may have been forced on him, yet he wouldn't take back the decision.

But to have his own children? He'd never entertained the idea. At once, an image of Raven came to mind, belly swollen with his child. Fraternal desire kicked him hard in the ribs as he imagined a little boy or girl, with her dark hair and chocolate eyes.

He swiped a hand down his face. "Yeah," he grated. "I think I do." He met her gaze. "Again, not something we need to decide right now. After the trial, we'll have to get Aubrey settled and we can discuss it more." He couldn't read her reaction, but when she opened her mouth to speak, he instinctively cut her off. "Here's the thing, Raven. All I want, all I really want, is you. Whether that's as my wife, mother of my child, or just a life partner, I don't care."

Her eyes widened a fraction. "Noah, you can't give up on what you want, even if those plans don't include me—"

"I don't make plans that don't include you."

She seemed stressed over his remark as she pulled her hand away, her brows wrinkling and gaze darting away.

"Let me ask you this. Do you want marriage and kids?" Because something made her think about it enough to bring it up.

"I don't know." She pressed her hand to her forehead. "Three months ago, I would've said no. It's just..."

"Just what, baby?"

"I guess I..." She slapped a hand down on the table and huffed. "This is going to sound so stupid, but I don't feel like I have anything that's mine." Her gaze met his, shining with unshed tears. "Everything is up in the air. My apartment is gone, and this is your home. There are people who want you dead. Want me dead. I can't go to the gallery."

Hell. This he could handle. Relief had him expelling a breath. Her freak out had nothing to do with them. The circumstances around them weren't giving her any power.

He dipped his head, forcing her to look at him. "Closing arguments in the Rizzoli trial are this week. It's almost over. McCannon will find Soreno and we won't need so many guards. The police should be done with Elements by tomorrow. And…" As he trailed off, he took her hand in his again. "We'll go house hunting this week. Find us something that's ours."

They'd need to anyway after the trial because of Aubrey. They'd still have the castle, but his condo was no place for her. She needed a home. So did Raven. A place to start over.

Raven stared at him so long his heart stopped beating with worry. Her face was an unreadable mask, until eventually something clicked and her eyes rounded. A myriad of flickering emotions hit her expression, there and gone too fast for him to keep up. Pain. Joy. Fear. Nerves. Concern. Happy. Resolution.

He involuntarily squeezed her fingers and forced himself to relax. "What, Raven? Just tell me and we'll deal—"

"I wouldn't say no if you asked." Her tone was confident, if not a little distant, as if she was still trying to wrap her mind around something.

He shook his head, not connecting the dots.

Gaze steady, she swallowed. "In the future, if you asked me to marry you, I wouldn't say no."

He froze. In fact, everything seemed to freeze. Time. His pulse.

Staring into her eyes to search for the loophole, he found none. She was serious. *His.* Hell, she hadn't even said she loved him yet, but she would. Soon. She was almost there. Finally, after ten years and too many lies, he had her.

"I don't want a McMansion." She tilted her head, studying the table. Clearly avoiding the previous holy shit moment, she babbled about what kind of house they should tell a realtor to search. "No more than three or four bedrooms. There would have to be a room we could convert into an office for you. A yard for Aubrey. Also, a—"

"Raven."

She glanced at him. "What?"

"Shut up." Hauling her out of her chair, he kissed her hard, cutting off any argument. She softened against him, moaning into his mouth.

Then he took her to bed, where they made love with her on top. Because never let it be said he couldn't let his woman boss him around. He enjoyed every second.

Chapter Twenty

"What about that guy?" Nicole jerked her chin, indicating another prospect.

Raven glanced across the crowded bar to a man sitting alone, nursing a beer. "No."

Flipping her blonde hair over her shoulder, Nicole huffed. "Why? That's been no for about every guy I found."

Raven sipped her fruity cocktail, wincing at the sweetness. "If you can't pick a decent drink, you sure can't pick out a date."

Nicole narrowed her eyes. "What's wrong with him? He's cute."

They'd been at the bar for thirty minutes, fresh off another successful show at the gallery, and Raven wanted to relax. She hadn't been out for fun in ages, and this week had been a mad dash to pull their scheduled exhibit together after the forensics team was through.

Playing along, Raven glanced at the man in question. "He's in the right age bracket, probably early thirties, so he's mature enough. But he's in a swanky bar and ordered a beer on tap. He also hasn't made any attempt to take in his surroundings. He's fresh off a broken heart or too shy to go after what he wants."

Nicole shook her head, awe in her eyes. "You got all that after looking for five seconds?"

"Yep."

Before Noah, she'd made it a point to notice the details. The club where she'd found her dates was just down the street. Her pattern was to watch, catalogue, and approach only if they met her criteria—willing to be submissive, not into hard kink, and not the type to cling. It had only been two months since she and Noah started seeing each other, and already they were discussing marriage, buying a house. Granted, she'd brought up the subject, but still. She was sunk so deep she couldn't contemplate life without him. Part of her warned it was too soon.

"Who would you pick then?" Nicole turned her head to regard Raven.

She forced another swallow of diabetic shock and skimmed the bar from her stool. Her gaze bypassed Noah, sitting with his guard Hintz in the corner, watching every blink she made, and fell onto a man near the back, playing darts. He had two women watching him and a male standing near waiting his turn. Worn jeans, ripped at the knee, and a white shirt. He had muscles, but not overstated. His dark hair was this side of too long, but it was clean and he was freshly shaven.

Raven nodded. "Him."

Nicole followed her gaze. "Really? Why?"

"He's got a bad boy edge, but cares about his appearance. He also doesn't have a preference for easy women. He probably won't be boring in bed and won't cling the next day, yet there's the potential for more."

Nicole's jaw dropped. She slowly shook her head. "You need to work for Homeland Security. How do you know all that?"

She set her drink aside, as it made her teeth ache. "His clothes are worn, but clean, so he's comfortable in his own skin and doesn't care what people think. That type of man is confident in the bedroom. Plus, he's good-looking, so he's been around the block. He hasn't paid any attention to the skanks eyeing him. He tipped the waitress handsomely, so he has a job and respect for those who do. That means he can commit to something, once he finds what he likes. The distracted look in his eyes says he hasn't found that yet, but he's looking."

As Nicole gawked, Raven turned on her stool and called for the bartender. "Send the man playing darts a whiskey neat, compliments of my friend here."

The bartender nodded and filled the order. Nicole's cheeks flushed as she watched from the corner of her eye.

Raven cleared her throat. "Look right at him and give him your shy smile."

Nicole spoke out of the corner of her mouth. "Shy shouldn't be hard. Oh crap. He's looking at me."

Raven laughed.

"Why a whiskey neat? Hurry, he's coming."

"He looks like he has Irish roots and he wasn't drinking beer." Raven turned just as he approached. "My job is done." She slid off the stool and spoke to Nicole. "Call me in the morning. Or don't."

Raven left them chatting and made her way over to a scowling Noah. Wondering what the drawn brows and irritation in his eyes was about, she reached for her coat on the back of her chair. "Problem?"

He rose and shrugged into his jacket. Silent, as if measuring his words, he shook his head and led her outside to the awaiting car. Side by side in the backseat, tension radiated off him. Just as she was about to demand an answer for his mood, he turned toward her.

"You bought that guy a drink." Shadows cut across his face, only relieved by the occasional streetlight.

Jealousy? After everything? "I bought him the drink on behalf of Nicole. The purpose for tonight was to get her laid. What's the deal?"

His shoulders slumped, but his jaw tensed as he turned his head toward the window. After a beat, he shook his head, but wouldn't meet her gaze. "I guess it made me think of your tactics from before we started seeing each other. You going to clubs, watching." His jaw clenched more. "The men you might've picked to go home with."

Was this a safety thing or jealousy? She couldn't change anything about her time before him, and didn't want to. Those experiences led her here, made her appreciate what she and Noah had even more. "In case you hadn't noticed, I'm going home with you."

Without warning, he reached out and clasped her hand, squeezing. Still, his gaze trained away as they wove through the dark, snowy streets. They'd laid all their secrets bare, had nothing between them anymore. She didn't understand his mood.

When he finally turned to look at her, her heart pounded at the raw intensity in his eyes. His gaze roamed her face, taking all of her in as he decided something. He opened his mouth twice before he actually spoke.

"Your preferences, have they changed? Is this relationship... enough for you?" His voice was hoarse and riddled with regret. His eyes were a scary mix of determination, hope, and pleading.

Where was this coming from? Noah was the furthest thing from insecure. Their friendship had laid the groundwork for the steady foundation they had together. Hadn't she opened herself to him? Given him everything?

His fingers tightened around hers. "You let me do anything with your body, but your heart's not completely engaged. Something's holding you back."

He wasn't wrong in that observation. He was so very right. It shamed her, because he was giving his all and she was holding a piece of herself back. She trusted him, wanted what came next in their path, was trying to get them there, but just couldn't bring herself over that last threshold. She didn't even know what to do to breach the small gap, as she couldn't put her finger on what was off.

Maybe they'd jumped too fast. Perhaps the outside danger was clouding her reasoning. But she had a sinking suspicion it was a default on her end. No rationale or excuse would fit, because she was just...wrong. She'd formed attachments in her life, loved a precious few people like Nicole and her mom, yet something always seemed missing. Not right inside her, like she'd been constructed incorrectly.

Honestly, she loved with her head, not her heart. And she didn't think something like that could be fixed.

Noah inhaled sharply and closed his eyes, drawing her gaze back to him. "Stay, Raven." He slowly opened his eyes and worked a swallow. "Stay with me."

"I...am." Guilt tore at her stomach. He deserved so much better than she could offer. After everything he'd endured, dammit, he deserved everything. But for some reason, he wanted her. "I'm here. And you're enough. More than enough."

The half lie tasted sour in her mouth. At some point, he'd have to move on when he realized she was lacking the one thing he desired most—love. Everything he'd ever loved had been taken from him. He deserved the chance to build a family.

Back at the condo, he headed straight for the bedroom, still holding her hand. Without a word, he stripped her out of her clothes, then shed his and pulled the blankets down on the bed. He sat on the edge of the mattress and motioned for her.

She stepped over to him. He took her by the waist, turned her so her back was to him, and eased her down to sit on his thighs. The light dusting of hair on his chest brushed her back when she leaned into him.

His arms came around her instantly, pulling her closer as his chin dropped to her shoulder. The solid feel of him around her comforted, shoving aside her earlier thoughts, so all that remained was them.

He kissed her neck. "I bought something for you." He reached into the bedside drawer and pulled out a black pouch, handing it to her.

The last time he'd bought her something in a small package it had been the vibrating panties. Her skin heated as the apex of her thighs throbbed. She swallowed hard and loosened the cinch on the pouch, pulling out… "A butt plug."

His hands landed on her thighs, stroking. "Do you still want to try anal play?"

She turned her head to look at him, then returned her gaze to the small pink plug. The silicone was soft and pliable in her hand, no larger than her finger, and wide at the base. She'd used ones similar on previous lovers when they'd desired, but had never used one herself. The idea didn't trip her heartbeat. Instead, heat coursed through her core, making her even more wet.

She handed him the plug and nodded.

He nuzzled her hair, his hand drifting up from her thigh to cup between her legs. He groaned. "So wet, baby. You like the idea." He nipped her ear, and she shuddered. "You'll feel incredibly full with me and the plug inside you. It will prepare your body for me, so that later, I can take you there, too."

With every word, her breath caught. Fire licked her skin. She bucked against his hand, urging more, thrusting her backside against his thick erection.

He spread her thighs, so that her legs were caging his. Reaching into the drawer, he removed a small bottle of lube and set it next to his hip. He wrapped an arm around her waist and, with a hand between her shoulder blades, urged her to bend over.

With her ass in the air, he secured her in place with his arm. She grabbed his calves to hold onto something. Blood rushed to her head. Cool air hit her damp skin between her folds. Dizzy with desire, she gasped.

The flick of the lube cap sounded behind her. She tensed, not knowing what to expect.

His warm hand cupped her nape and slid down the column of her spine. "This might feel uncomfortable at first. A burning sensation accompanies the stretching."

"Okay," she breathed. Her chest was tight with anxiety, but the rest of her body wanted the push for more. She held her breath as he shifted behind her.

He worked the cold, wet lube around her hole, rubbing circles with the head of the plug. She swallowed hard as her stomach jumped. After a moment, the sensation was no longer scary, but good, lighting nerves and heat to the area. She grew even more wet, drenched now, for him.

"Take a deep breath, baby."

Before she could, he pressed the plug past her ring of muscle and inserted the tip. Her channel stretched at the invasion, burning just like he'd said. He worked it deeper, slowly, until she was writhing over him. For more? To stop? She didn't know. It was a pain and pleasure mix, both overwhelming.

"I'm at the base, baby. This part's wider. Almost there."

She yelped when her body was forced to stretch around the broad base, her nails digging into his calves. But then the minor amount of pain stopped when the plug was fully rooted, leaving her with a sense of being full. Panting, she held still.

After a moment to adjust, he eased her up, until her back was against his chest. The plug shifted inside her, gliding along her sensitive walls.

He palmed her aching, heavy breasts. "How does it feel?"

"I...don't know." Her channel was hot, muscles clenching around the plug. Nerves she'd never before used seemed to splinter apart, firing on all cylinders. Though she did feel full, her body ached for him to fill her even more. Her clit throbbed and she was all but dripping for him. "Please, Noah."

He cupped her between her legs, moaning at how slick her folds were for him. "Are you ready for me?"

"Yes." She threw her head back onto his shoulder, bringing her arm up to wrap around his neck from behind. Her ass pressed against his shaft, shifting the plug and ripping a cry of desperation from her lips. "Want you inside me."

The next thing she knew, she was flat on the bed. Before she'd even stopped bouncing he was between her thighs, pressing his way inside and thrusting deep. Fully rooted, he paused, holding himself above her with his arms. His muscles shook with tension, his expression fierce.

"You okay?" he ground out, jaw clenched.

His shaft throbbed inside her wet heat, and when she clenched her walls around him, the pressure in her backside intensified, so that she didn't think there was room for anything else. She was on the cusp of orgasm, trembling with the need to release.

She cupped his head and brought his mouth down to hers, kissing him. Their tongues mated, danced. Wrapping her legs around his waist, she urged him as deep as possible and used her heels against his ass as leverage to grind over his shaft. His pelvis rocked against her swollen clit.

And just like that, she exploded. A scream wrenched from her throat. Her body locked in a tormented, beautiful release that touched every part of her body, stronger than anything she'd ever experienced.

As she was still panting breathy cries, helpless to the delirium, he continued his thrusts, circling his hips and wrenching more from her. Her back bowed as another orgasm loomed. She didn't think she could take it. Such intensity. So powerful.

"Come on, baby. One…more time," he rasped against her ear. He grunted with every thrust, his face twisted in wonder and torment. "Let me see you come again."

As his words sank in, her body responded. Her walls clenched as she perched on the edge. Putting more weight on his knees, he slid his hands under her ass and spread her cheeks, lifting her hips. When he drove into her, deeper yet, he bumped the plug, so that it, too, shallowly thrust inside her. Over and over, he rocked over her clit, bucked against the plug, plunged inside her heat.

She came in a flood of desperation, arms banding around his back. He stilled over her, jerked, and roared through his own release.

Chapter Twenty-One

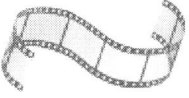

"Get us the fuck out of here." Noah slammed the car door and faced the front seat, too riled to attempt consoling Raven next to him. She hadn't looked upset by the time they walked out of the police station, but she had to be rattled.

When McCannon had called them into the station, Noah figured they finally had something on Soreno. They had something all right. They had a handwritten note that had been shoved in the mailbox.

If I wanted her dead so soon, she'd be dead. Consider the other night a warning. Revenge is best served cold. She'll be cold soon. She won't die quickly and there won't be mercy.

All Soreno wanted in the end was to crank her fear so she'd make a mistake. Or maybe Rizzoli had orchestrated the words himself. People didn't think clearly when scared out of their mind or worked into a rage.

And Noah was in a rage. The note implied they'd torture her first. Noah had no doubt she'd beg for death by the time Soreno was through with her.

"Fuck," he muttered, scrubbing his hands over his face to erase the implanted image of that bastard holding her down… "Fuck," he roared again.

Raven leaned forward in the seat. "Take us to Gallivanting Adventures."

Hintz nodded. "Yes, ma'am."

Noah forced himself to box the past hour and looked at her. "Why?" What could she possibly want to do at his company today?

She closed the partition and turned to him. "You're scaring me."

Pinching his eyes closed, he turned his head away as his body still thrummed with residual anger. He needed to pound the shit out of something. He was no good to anyone like this. "I'm sorry."

Her hand settled on his arm. He flinched and drew back. The motion frightened her even more and she lurched backward, landing against the door.

"Hell, Raven." He needed to get away from her for a couple of hours until he was in a better mind frame. "I'm not...I'd never hurt you." Surely she knew that. He held out his hand for her to come closer.

Her jaw was set, but her eyes were round in shock. Good. He hadn't scared her, just surprised her with the sudden move. Pride surged in his chest. His Raven rarely backed down from anything. She'd stood in that dingy police station and squared her shoulders, chin up. Shit. She'd handled herself better than he had.

After a moment, she took his hand. Instead of scooting across the seat, she straddled his lap, studying him with a blank expression he'd kill to read. The past two months with her had been heaven. Everything he'd ever dreamed. The steady friendship had grown into an unbreakable bond. The lovemaking never lacked emotion or power. But he didn't know what more to do to...make her love him.

His hands dove under her coat to grip her waist. "What's going on in that head of yours?"

She leaned forward, brushing her lips over his ear. "We're going to take one of the small charter boats out on The Sound. We'll get some wind in your hair and speed under you to ride out this anger."

Her sultry voice and hot breath skated across his skin. The scent of rain he'd forever attribute to her enclosed him. His hands tightened on her tiny waist as his cock thickened under her.

She worked her hand between them and slid it under his coat, down his chest to cup his erection. Stroked. "And when we're in the middle of nowhere, with the mountains in the distance and surrounded by absolutely nothing, you're going to..." She stroked him again.

His head slammed back onto the seat as he sucked in a breath. She was ridding him of his rage so fast he shook from the crash. Desire and need shoved to the surface, making him blind with how badly he wanted her. "I'm going to what, baby?" he rasped.

Her lips skimmed over his in the barest of whispers. "You're going to rip my clothes off, bend me over the closest surface, and fuck...me...senseless."

Growling, he thrust up toward her heat, bringing her down onto him to rub against his painful cock. He never hated clothing so fucking much. "Want you now."

It wasn't like her to use dirty talk in foreplay. She'd gotten off on it when he'd done it, and she was open in her sexuality, but something about her like this made his blood roar and reason take a backseat.

"You want that, Noah?" She rocked her hips. "I'll scream for you to take me harder, faster. I'll moan your name until you can feel the vibration right here." The heel of her palm stroked the underside of his shaft.

He gripped the back of her neck and crushed his mouth to hers. Her lips parted instantly to greet him. She swirled her tongue against his, teasing it like she did the crown of his cock when she'd gone down on him. Lost to her, he kissed her for all he was worth, until they had to come apart for air or die.

"Hell, baby. I might come now."

Easing back, she smiled. "We're here. Take me out on the boat?"

He jerked his gaze toward the window, not realizing the car had stopped. Out the side window, his company's main office stood. Pride swelled in his chest. The float planes, the charter boats, the bobsleds…he'd made a fortune doing what he loved. Next to photography and having Raven under him, there was nothing better than flying over the rough Alaskan landscape or jutting across the water. The wind scouring his face, the scent of salt and pine, all balms to his soul.

Just like Raven. Not since he'd first started his company had he taken her out on The Sound. Just her and him on the water? All the things she wanted to do? He may never bring them back to shore. Plus, the location where "Hoan" always craved to take her photograph was only accessible by boat. He'd wanted to show it to her weeks ago, on the night her and Max had been followed, but they'd wound up at Aubrey's Castle instead.

She cupped his cheek and offered a quick kiss. "You ready?"

He nodded and opened the door, letting her slide off his lap to exit first. He had Hintz pop the trunk so he could grab one of his extra camera bags and then took Raven's hand to lead her up the walk to the main building. Turning his head to look at her, he tried to gauge her reaction. She hadn't been here in awhile.

Her gaze swept over the log cabin design, accented by forest green shutters and trim. It looked more like a lodge than a business. Farther down the harbor were two warehouses where they stored equipment and the bobsleds. Only one of the two float planes were in the water, and both of the large charter boats were out. The small one they rarely used bobbed in the choppy waves at the dock.

His assistant, Veronica, met them at the front desk when they strode in. "Thought you were working from home today."

"Change of plans. Do we have the small charter booked today?"

She shook her head, but rounded the desk to check the logs in verification. "Nope. Are you taking it out?" Her gaze swept over Raven and slid back to him. She smiled as if an afterthought.

"Yes. Hold all calls, will you?"

"You got it."

He turned to Raven, who was ignoring them in lieu of checking out the hardwood floors and then the hallway where their offices were tucked away. A sly grin split her face when she looked at him.

He squeezed her hand. "What?" The same saucy expression she'd had in the car was on her face, and he suddenly became grateful for the long coat to hide his reaction.

"Nothing. An idea."

Sensing this idea shouldn't be discussed in front of Veronica, he directed her to grab the charter keys and a small cooler of snacks. When his assistant strode away, he eyed Raven. "What's this idea of yours? Do tell."

Stepping into his space, she pressed against him and tilted her face up to his. "Later."

He narrowed his eyes, but said nothing. Whatever she had up her sleeve, he'd willingly play along.

After getting the keys and cooler, he told Hintz to stay on the mainland. He and Raven walked down the dock to the twenty foot boat and climbed aboard. Leaving Raven inside the aft cabin in the steering station above the rear room to stay warm, Noah checked the gas tank, back up containers, battery, and gauges before untying the boat from the dock.

He climbed the steps into the cabin and started the motor. "Ready, baby?"

Grinning, she nodded.

Easing them from shore, he made sure to get past the harbor and inlet islands without creating a wake before letting loose. Once in the open water, he glanced at her. She leaned over the seat to take in the scenery, her eyes bright and a faint smile tracing her lips. Stunned by her beauty, he found it hard to take his eyes off her. Even in the dusky lowlight that passed for day this time of year, she shone like a beacon.

Chest aching, he tore his gaze away to round a bend to get closer to the island where he wanted to go. He reduced their speed when he caught sight of a fin. It surfaced again, so he cut the motor.

He jerked his chin starboard. "Check it out. Whales."

She glanced to their right and her grin widened. "Can we go on deck?"

Nodding, he held the door and descended the steps after her. She walked to the chest-high railing and leaned into it. He came up behind her and caged her in his arms, kissing her temple.

The Chugach Mountains to the east and Mount Spurr far off to the west, they were pocketed in immense beauty. Saw-tooth ridges and hanging valleys were clouded in a fine mist fog that gave the impression of solitude. Birch and spruce dotted the landscape, scenting the air with pine and mingling with salt and ice off the water.

As the boat rocked, he tugged her closer. "Really something, isn't it?"

"Yeah," she breathed, leaning her head back on his shoulder. "I forget how beautiful it is sometimes."

Because the view couldn't hold a match to her, he nuzzled her ear. "Really beautiful."

"Oh, look."

She straightened and pointed just as another fin broke the surface about forty feet from the boat. The V shape indicated whale, which was surprising as they were typically spotted farther out. He was glad he'd stopped. The fin came down with a splash and disappeared. Another twenty feet from the fin a few seals were playing on a small ice glacier.

"Seals, too, baby." He pointed. The tourists who booked their fishing charters always got a kick out of them and the whale sightings. More than half signed up just for the wildlife.

"Aw. When I was little and my mom first brought us to Alaska, there were a bunch of seals on shore sun-bathing. I wanted one for a pet."

He chuckled and, finally, all the knots loosened in his shoulders. Somehow she'd managed to expel his anger from earlier, turn him on to the point of pain, and leave him in happy bliss. And without the need to punch or fuck his way through the emotions. He didn't think he'd ever loved her more. His chest swelled, rocking him back a step.

She sighed contentedly. "We got distracted from my mission. You seem calmer now." She turned her face up to him, regarding him over her shoulder. Her cheeks were pink from the chill. "Feel better?"

Her mission meaning him bending her over the nearest surface and—how had she put it?--fucking her senseless. He wasn't in the mood to fuck her. He wanted to make love to her with this backdrop. Slide in and out of her wet heat slowly, driving them both to the point of insanity. Savor every inch of her skin and make that perfect red mouth part in gasp after gasp. Watch her eyes cloud with passion until she was blind to anything but the two of them.

Looking in her dark eyes, he carefully swallowed. "There's still time." He tried to grin, but failed. "And I've never felt better." Closing his eyes, he sucked in a breath. "Come on. There's a place I want to show you." And once they were anchored, he'd make good on that fantasy.

They wove around a few glaciers and into open water before he sliced a harsh right and reduced speed near the cove he'd found by accident years ago. A tiny inlet island, probably once a glacier like many of the land embankments, was no more than two miles in circumference. Near the northern tip was a cluster of rock formation that resembled a cave, but other than trees, there was nothing.

The shore was rocky and made docking difficult, so he pulled off to the east where there was more of an immediate drop off. Raven would be able to step right from the boat to land. He dropped anchor and tied the boat to a boulder just in case.

Then he studied her profile, wondering how open she would be to making love outside. The temperature had hit twenty but, on the water ,the windchill felt like ten degrees. The boat cabin had thermo blankets and sleeping bags, plus the cave would block the wind and he could start a fire for warmth. His dick swelled as he imagined her underneath him, hair fanned around her head, while they created their own heat.

She glanced at him and did a double-take. "I know that look. What naughty things are you thinking about?"

His throat tightened as he took a step closer, pulled her into his arms and said the first thing that came to mind. "I don't know what I'd do without you."

Her smile fell. She cupped his jaw, brushing her thumbs over his stubble. "You don't have to, and the feeling is mutual."

Maybe so, but she still hadn't reached the point of no return yet. Not like he had. He was pretty damn sure his heart would stop dead if anything happened to her.

He kissed her forehead and stepped away. "How adventurous are you feeling today?"

Her mouth opened and closed as her eyes narrowed. "Why?"

Unable to help it, he grinned. "I know you hate surprises, but this is a good one. I promise."

Before she could argue, he grabbed a sleeping bag, two blankets, and gestured for her to carry the small cooler. He slung his camera bag over his shoulder. "Ready?"

She eyed the items and shrugged. "Sure."

As they climbed off the boat, she took stock of the private property signs and raised her brows in question.

The wind whipped his hair over his brow as he contemplated his response. He'd bought the island four months after spotting it six years ago. It had taken a lot of legal maneuvering to even find out if it was buyable, followed by land surveys to investigate whether it was stable property or if it would eventually sink or drift away. Turned out, plates below the ocean surface connected it to the mainland. It had cost him a mint, but he never regretted it. As he watched Raven, he knew why.

"You own this island, don't you?" She stared at him like he had three heads.

"Yeah." Intuition said this might not go over as he'd intended. He shifted his weight to the other foot. Silence stretched. "Say something."

She didn't, not for the longest time. "You own an island."

Shit. She wasn't going to start freaking out about money again, was she? He'd give it all to charity if it—

She tilted her head back and laughed. Rich and throaty, the sound drifted over to him on the wind and warmed his gut. "You own an island." Throwing her hand up as if to say, *of course you do,* she laughed harder.

Shifting the sleeping bag in his arms, he frowned.

She sighed, sobering a fraction. "What did you name it?"

"What?"

"This place. What did you name it? I mean, you can't buy an island and not name it."

Well, hell. She was giddy, why not burst that bubble? "I call it Raven Crest. That's what the official tax documents say. It has it's own decree, being an island." He paused. "And it's in your name."

Her grin fell entirely. "Are you serious?"

He nodded slowly, awaiting her panic attack. "We could, you know, build our house here." That was why he hadn't contacted a realtor this week, as planned. He'd wanted to bring her out here first, see if she minded the location.

She reared back as if he'd slapped her. Blinked twice.

He forced air into his lungs. "There's plenty of land for a house and room for Aubrey to play. And…more kids, if you want them." He cleared his throat. "We could build a cabin for your mom, if you want. It would take months, but a bridge could be constructed from the east side of the island to the mainland. The stretch is only three city blocks of distance. We went the long way coming in. We'd have to use a boat until then." If his heart pounded any harder he'd stroke out. Fuck. He should just shut the hell up. "This place would give you the solitude you crave." Shutting up now. "Christ, Raven. Talk to me. Yell. Do something."

Looking so fragile the next gust would topple her, she closed her gaping mouth, shook her head slowly, turned abruptly, and started walking toward a clearing deeper on the island.

Chapter Twenty-Two

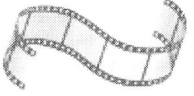

Their feet crunched over snow and pine needles as they made their way silently across the island. They headed deeper into a forest-like cluster of trees, where Noah stopped every now and again to gather fallen branches. She'd glanced over her shoulder once to check on him, but looking at his handsome face just made the panic edge closer, so she didn't do it again.

He'd taken any semblance of control away from her. He, of all people, knew how much she needed that. She'd conceded a lot since they've been together, and now she didn't even have an apartment to go back to. Not that she'd want to live anywhere Soreno had touched, but still.

Everything was moving so fast. Their relationship, her feelings. He'd had years to pick this apart, examine the angles, accept how he felt. She'd had two months, and that was after he'd plowed her down with the truth.

Things weren't bad between them. Not at all. She'd finally started feeling like a woman and not a shell. Noah had opened her sexually and emotionally. They compromised and talked and respected one another. She'd even begun to think she was capable of long term without freaking. But today? This surprise? It felt like backpedaling. A retreat.

Sucking in crisp, cold air, she pushed her legs to walk faster, enjoying the burn in her muscles. Luckily not much snow covered the small island because Raven had only been wearing sneakers, having only planned to visit the police station, not trek across an island. That he bought in her name. Where he wanted to build a house and have kids. Maybe even a place for her mom, because he'd known Raven worried about her mother's financial security and hasty decisions, so having her close would give Raven peace of mind.

God. Just…God. What in the hell was going on?

Two months ago, she had been sitting alone in her apartment, idly passing time, bored delirious with her sex life and her only satisfaction being with her gallery. Now her best friend was declaring love, a hitman was after them, and…Noah bought her *an island.*

She stopped. "When did you make the purchase?"

His footsteps behind her halted, too, but she didn't turn around. They hadn't said one syllable since his tangent and she'd stalked off in a daze. His clothing rustled as he shifted, but he didn't respond.

"How long ago, Noah?" Her pinched voice echoed off the water and the rock ledge where she'd blindly led them.

"I bought it six years ago."

Six years. When he'd started writing the letters. He'd named the damn island after her. He'd never had any intention of their relationship being temporary. This was all a ruse to his endgame. Every move a chess piece to manipulate.

She dropped the cooler she'd been carrying and grabbed her chest. A vise banded her lungs and squeezed. Her airway collapsed. Her eyes welled as she struggled for breath. Her vision grayed, black dots spotting her peripheral. She teetered on her feet.

And then Noah was in front of her, shoving her to her knees and pressing her head between them. "Breathe, baby. Just breathe." He rubbed circles over her back. The hand in her hair massaged her scalp.

Closing her eyes, she sucked in much needed air. Tears welled behind her lids, but she fought them back and focused on slow, deep breaths.

"That's it, baby." He lifted her head and pushed her hair from her face to cup her cheeks. His blue eyes scanned her face, worry and remorse etched in the icy depths. After a moment, his lids fell closed and he shook his head, pulling her to him. "We'll sell the island. Anything you want. Just…don't be upset." His arms tightened around her back, a desperate quality emanating from the gesture.

She burrowed into his embrace, even though her emotions were rioting. Breathing in his cinnamon scent, she clutched the lapels of his coat and rested her cheek on his chest. "Why'd you do it? Why did you buy this place?" *And name it after me? Put it in my name?* Deep down, she knew the answer. It was obvious, really. But she needed him to spell it out.

His sigh ruffled her hair. "I guess, subconsciously, I knew we'd end up here. That I loved you on a much deeper level than I'd believed." He ran his fingers through her hair. "At the time, I told myself I put it in your name just in case, as added protection from Rizzoli. The truth is, Raven, everything about this place reminded me of you."

She was beginning to feel like an ungrateful bitch, but why couldn't he have just talked to her, instead of springing this all at once? She didn't need diamonds and islands. She just needed him…and a little time. "How does it remind you of me?"

He rested his chin on the top of her head. "The quiet strength. After all the elements, the island's still here. The landscape reminds me of your gallery and how you designed it with nature in mind. It's isolated from everyone, but close enough to the mainland to observe the melee."

Was that really how he viewed her? Quiet and strong? Isolated? She closed her eyes, suddenly drained.

"There's a spot just on the other side of this rock wall. The first time I stumbled upon it, Hoan wanted to capture you there on film." He swallowed. "I still do, if you'll let me. It's an image that haunts me, never abating." His voice deepened, his chest rumbling against her cheek. "I don't care if anyone else sees it, or if you don't want it sold. I need that photo for me, baby. Let me show you how I see you."

She'd encouraged him to take pictures at Aubrey's Castle, and it had given her insight to the sexual need in him. But this was different. Hoan Dwell captured women, in various stages of undress, in nature settings. He peeked right into their soul and exposed it to the world. Whether anyone saw them or not, she didn't think she could handle what he'd uncover.

Yet his words, and the deep emotional timbre with which he spoke them, called to her. Something inside him was always searching for her, for everything she could give. One day, she was going to disappoint him to the point they'd never recover. A man like Noah, who had so much honor and strength and love to offer, should never settle for someone who was incapable of returning half as much. She was trying. Damn it, so hard she was trying.

Bowing down as his muse she could do. She lifted her head and looked at him, at the raw emotion in his eyes. "Yes."

His jaw unclenched as he grabbed her nape. "Yes?" he rasped, unbelieving.

"Show me this mysterious location." She smiled, her heart hammering at his happiness. "I'm not exactly dressed for this. I'm not even wearing makeup."

"I want you raw, natural. I would've asked you to remove any cosmetics anyway." He kissed her forehead and drew back to look at her. "Are you sure?"

Standing, she brushed the snow off her knees. "Very. I've been dying to meet Hoan for years." Back at Aubrey's Castle, it had been Noah, her lover and best friend, who'd taken those pictures of her. She suspected Hoan was an entirely different person.

He rose slowly, his hands flexing as if itching for the camera in his bag slung over his shoulder. After a beat, he picked up the blankets and sleeping bag, and headed toward the rock wall. She grabbed the cooler and followed.

They rounded an eight foot wall, where a small cave, no deeper than ten feet or wider than six feet, cut into the rock. Just on the other side was a slope that descended into a shallow valley. Boulders and snow covered the hill. Birch trees sprinkled the small area. In the distance, misty fog from the mountains set a backdrop like that in a fairy tale.

"Noah, it's beautiful."

He set their things down just inside the mouth of the cave. "Wait here a minute. I need to start a fire first to keep you warm afterward."

She nodded, more mesmerized by the view. She wondered where he'd have her pose or…what she'd be wearing. Glancing down at her jeans, she frowned. Under her coat was a black sweater. At least she'd worn her sexy red lace panty set, which was more up Hoan's alley.

Noah returned and made quick work of a campfire just outside the cave opening. Kneeling, he unfolded the sleeping bag inside the cave and pulled the camera from its bag. Task at hand, he muttered over his shoulder, "We'll need to do this fast, or in stages. It's too cold to leave you exposed for long." He fidgeted with the camera. "When in position, just do as I say right away. I'll give you verbal cues when I start. You'll need to hold your breath for a few seconds, so I don't catch your exhalation in the shot."

She walked up next to him, startling him from his focus. "You're so bossy."

His gaze slid down the length of her as if he hadn't heard. "Take off your clothes. All except your shoes and undergarments."

She paused. "Why not shoes?"

"To walk across the snow. You can take them off when in position."

"Right." Since he was all business, she didn't joke around. She stripped her clothes and set them in a pile close to the fire to keep them warm. Crossing her arms, she shivered. "Ready."

He grabbed the red fleece blanket and turned to hand it to her. He froze, gaze skimming over her once more, this time with heat and interest, not with an artistic eye. "You're wearing the red lace. Holy fuck. Perfect."

She almost didn't need a fire with the way he looked at her. Taking the blanket from him, she wrapped it around her shoulders. "Where to, master?"

One corner of his mouth quirked. "Follow me."

He instructed her to sit on the edge of a boulder halfway down the incline, with her back to him and head turned toward the camera. She hurried into position, teeth chattering, and kicked her shoes off out of the way.

"Hold your breath." *Click, click, click.* "Let the blanket slide off one shoulder. Good." *Click, click.* "Give me that look when you're up to no good."

She raised her eyebrows in question.

He pulled the camera from his face. "Tell me what you said in the car on the way back from the station."

She grinned, knowing she looked a little impish. "You mean the part where I said you'd bend me over the nearest surface?"

He was holding his breath, camera at his face. "Yes," he grated. "Say it all. Again."

"I'd like you to bend me over the nearest surface, Noah, and fuck me senseless. I'll beg for you to do it harder—"

Click, click, click.

"—faster. I'll scream your name until you'll feel—"

Click, click.

"—the vibration straight to your cock." She held her breath, cheeks flaming both from the cold and heat.

Click, click, click, click, click, click.

She must've had the "up to no good" expression perfect, because he pulled the camera from his face and adjusted his erection through his jeans.

"Over here now." He pointed to her right. "This needs to be fast. Lay on your stomach, keeping the blanket under you. I'll direct you from there."

Teeth chattering again, she shivered and did as instructed. Cold wind skated over the bare skin of her back, causing goosebumps.

"Fold your arms in front of you. Rest your chin on them." *Click.* "Not right," he muttered. "Shove one hand into your hair." *Click, click.* He growled, actually growled, and looked over the lens at her as if trying to puzzle out the problem.

Freezing, she sat up and wrapped the blanket around her lower arms and torso, then flopped sideways with her back to a boulder to block the wind. She probably looked like a naughty nymph asleep in the snow from his angle.

Click, click, click, click, click, click.

"Fuck me. That's perfect." *Click, click.* "Stay just as you are, but look up at me." *Click, click, click.* "Look sated, baby. I just screwed your brains out and now you want to sleep."

Recalling the feeling well, she fainted a smile in memory and did her best to do what he wanted. Holding her breath, she looked at the lens.

Click, click, click—"Fucking perfect"—*Click, click.*

He edged closer and squat down in front of her. "Two more minutes. Forgive me for this." He scooped up a handful of snow and sprinkled it over the blanket and her exposed shoulder. "Close your eyes."

She shivered and closed them. Cold, wet flakes fell on her face, clinging to her lashes.

Snow crunched as he stepped back. "Keep 'em closed, baby. One more minute. Look asleep. You're dreaming of sweet nothings, sexy romps. Fun."

Holding her breath, she imagined his expression when they saw the whale fin from the boat, how happy he'd seemed. Picturing what she'd like to do to him inside the sleeping bag by the fire, she held as still as possible.

Click, click, click, click, click, click, click...

"Let out a very gentle exhale, baby." *Click, click, click, click.* "Got it. Hold this." He set the camera on her belly and scooped her into his arms. Trudging up the hill, he pulled her tight to his body to keep her warm. "You did so great."

Setting her down in the sleeping bag inside the cave, he reached for her discarded socks and slid them on her feet. Too cold to do much more than watch, she shivered violently when he stripped off his clothes and lay over her, zipping them inside a cocoon.

Brushing his nose with hers, he whispered against her mouth. "That was better than my fantasy, baby. That position, you lying as if in a nocturnal state, was damn brilliant. If you let me, people will look at that photo and wonder what made you so sleepy, wonder what you're dreaming about. Or whom."

Between the fire, the thermo sleeping bag, and Noah's body heat, she was warming up nicely. She relaxed as desire kicked in. But first, she needed to clear the air.

She wrapped her arms around his back, holding his gaze. "You can display the pictures you took today to the public, if you like. Maybe at your opening in a couple weeks." She relented because the photos obviously meant a lot to him. He was proud, why deny him? "And..."

He kissed the corner of her mouth. "And what, baby?"

"I'm sorry about freaking out. Don't sell the island. Let's get through the trial and then we can build a house." *Our house.* She waited for her heart to pound or the air to constrict, but it never came.

God. He'd bought her an island. On a whim and a prayer, he'd purchased a dream for a future together.

He swallowed, gazing down at her through tender eyes and with wonder. "I love you." Leaning in, he kissed her before she could respond, coaxing her to open for him.

There was no frenzy or rush in the kiss, just sweet, deliberate torment. He made love to her mouth, unhurried. Sliding his arms under her back, he crisscrossed them to pull her closer, one hand cupping the back of her head, the other splaying between her shoulder blades. Her hard, sensitive nipples grazed his chest before they crushed between their bodies. He urged her legs apart and nestled his hips between her thighs.

Breaking the kiss, he gazed down at her, breath fanning her cheek. "I love you." Without breaking the gaze, he shifted his hips and aligned himself at her opening.

When she closed her eyes at the blissful contact, he demanded she open them. Rocking his hips forward, he entered her with such slow, measured intensity that her throat tightened.

"Feel me." When rooted to the hilt, he shuddered out an uneven breath, pupils nearly swallowing his irises. "I love you with everything in me, Raven. See me, feel me, let me in."

Her breath caught in her throat as he rolled his hips. There wasn't an inch where they didn't touch, where they weren't connected. He held her to him tightly, rocked between her thighs with gentle strokes, and stared at her as if searching for all the dark corners where her fear was trapped. In and out, he thrust. Unhurried.

"I love you," he rasped again, as if she didn't know, as if she didn't believe him. "I'm not going anywhere. I'm not going to let you down. I love you."

Helpless to do anything but feel, she sank deeper. Her chest swelled. Her eyes misted. It was as if he intended their joining to be a contradiction and a negotiation. Not a battle of wills or rush to the finish line, but…a mating. An assault of her senses.

The thickness of his shaft gliding in and out of her pulled a tremor from deep within. The way his hips pinned her own was possessive and certain. His rough, callused hand against the soft skin of her back was a delicious contrast. He held the back of her head in place, not allowing her to look anywhere but at him, forcing her to see the raw emotion she seemed to rip out of him.

"Come out of the dark, baby. I love you."

Pain pinched behind her ribs. Had it been her depression holding her back all this time? Years, for so many years, she'd fought. Only with Noah had hope seemed possible. Happiness not so out of reach. Could he sense that? Did he know she may never get there?

Tension coiled inside her, dangling her over the edge of orgasm, but he pulled her back by stilling. Just as she was about to break, to beg for him to let her plunge, he moved inside her again, rebuilding. A slow climb that drove her past reason.

When her walls clenched him a second time, her body and mind needing the release only he could give, he stilled again. She cried out in frustration, fought against his adoring, tender hold. This was torture. Mean.

With patience, he grit his teeth and kept that maddening, affectionate stare locked on her. "I love you."

Why did he keep saying that? She knew he did. It was evident in every touch and embrace and glance. And she could try until there was no breath left in her lungs to give it back, but she wasn't there. He was the perfect man—alpha with a deep fraternal nature, selfless in everything he did, protective, devoted, kind, and trustworthy—but she was broken. In time, she'd break him, too.

"Shh," he cooed, as if she'd said something aloud or he could read her thoughts. "You just don't get it, baby. I fucking love you."

"I know!" She couldn't take it anymore. Her chest restricted. She tried to roll away and get up, but he tightened his hold, keeping her under him. "Let me go."

"Not happening."

She shoved at his shoulders. He didn't budge. "Noah, I'm trying. Stop pushing me. I'm trying."

He dropped his forehead to hers, ceasing her frenzy. "I know you are, and I'll keep waiting as long as it takes." He lifted his head, studying her. "I'm not telling you I love you to upset you. I'm telling you because you don't know. I think you're hearing me, but you're not listening." As his gaze narrowed, his mouth opened like something had clicked into place.

Instead of voicing whatever was on his mind, he moved inside her and kissed her again with the same measured, fevered pitch from before. "Last time for now, baby." He punctuated each word with a deliberate thrust. "I—love—you."

Her body responded, inching toward the explosion only he could give. She tried to lift her hips and meet his thrusts, but he kept her pinned beneath him as he did all the work. Giving her all the attention she usually fought against. With single-minded focus, he pushed inside her body, her head, her heart.

And this time, he didn't leave her dangling over the edge. He shoved her. Then, he followed.

Chapter Twenty-Three

By the time they made it back to the mainland, it was late afternoon and pitch black. Stars fought for purchase with the Northern Lights in a mesmeric display over the inky water. A bitter wind swept down the mountains and across the ocean, but the brisk cold revived him.

Noah pocketed the keys and offered his hand to help Raven out of the boat. His chest still ached from the tender love-making, and from the way she'd fought him. He was starting to think she might never get to the place where he was, that place where he couldn't live without her, where love hurt so good he couldn't breathe. After everything, she was still holding back. Time might fix that, but he wasn't so sure anymore. Every time he touched her, he wondered if it would be the last time.

When her feet hit the dock, she gasped and took off for the end of the pier.

Max waited on shore and caught her with a grunt. "Easy, Miss Crowne."

"I'm sorry." She patted his chest. "I didn't mean to hurt you. How are you feeling?"

Max met Noah's gaze as he made his way toward their bodyguard. "A little sore, but I'm cleared to return."

Noah held out his hand to shake Max's. "Glad to hear that."

Max nodded, sweeping his gaze over Raven as if searching for injury, then stared out at the water. He cleared his throat. "The Rizzoli verdict's in."

Every muscle tensed in Noah's body. His stomach revolted. He hadn't heard they'd gone in for deliberation. Last he checked, the defense was doing closing arguments. "And?"

"It's after business hours, but because of the publicity, they're bringing everyone back into court. Should be live in an hour, at least." Max offered Raven a smile that didn't reach his eyes. "McCannon and

Hintz are meeting us back at the condo. I said I'd wait for you and drive you home."

Noah nodded. "Let's go."

He had no concept of the drive home or of any conversation along the way. The deafening roar through his ears was stronger than the tide and he couldn't unwind the tension from his shoulders or gut. Ten years. Ten long years. Most of his family was dead, he'd been forced to put Aubrey in hiding, they'd come after Raven, he had no damn life of his own, and his future now depended on what twelve people would say.

In autopilot, he unlocked the condo door and ushered Raven inside. Hintz stood behind the sofa, eyes glued to the flat screen mounted to the wall. McCannon paced in front of the balcony doors, his FBI badge and service revolver clipped to his belt, reminding Noah just how fucked up his life had been. His living room had two body guards, a federal agent, and Raven. No family, friends, or displays of life on the walls. Because he hadn't had a life.

"Anything yet?" Raven asked, looking at the news channel footage of a quiet courtroom. Updates scrolled along the bottom of the screen, replaying the same loop that the verdict was in after six hours of deliberation.

Six hours. He'd been in hell a decade and they'd taken six hours to render a verdict.

"Not yet." McCannon stopped pacing. "They're reconvening now. It's been over an hour."

Raven sighed and met Noah's gaze. Frenetic worry looked back at him through wide chocolate eyes. She shook her head and went into the kitchen.

Noah took a seat on the couch and dropped his head in his hands.

Some time later, Raven set a plate of sandwiches and a bowl of pretzels on the coffee table. She handed everyone a beer and sat next to him, hand on his thigh. His other knee bounced incessantly.

"Sit down, guys." Raven held her beer up to punctuate her point. "No one's on the clock tonight. Drink your beer and try to relax."

As if unable to deny her, they each took a spot. No one, however, relaxed. Including her.

Noah looked at Max. "Did someone notify the team at Aubrey Castle?"

His bodyguard nodded, his thumb picking the label on his beer. "Called while I was waiting for you at the dock. They're keeping it from Miss Aubrey until you say otherwise."

McCannon leaned forward. "It's on." He turned up the volume and tossed the remote aside.

The TV flashed images of spectators in the courtroom as a voice-over recounted a summary of the proceedings. They zeroed in on Rizzoli at the defendant table, along with his attorneys. Rizzoli's mouth twisted as if put out to be there, and his glassy eyes seemed more than a little confused. He'd dropped weight and his skin was pale, sagging. If Noah didn't know the prick and what he was capable of, he might feel sorry for him.

"All rise."

"Holy shit," Noah muttered, dropping his head in his hands again. Every hair stood erect on his body.

Raven leaned closer and rubbed circles over his back, which did little to ease the knots of tension.

He clenched his fists, glaring at Rizzoli's craggy face as the judge read off the charges against him. "The jury has reached a verdict?"

"We have, Your Honor," a male voice said off screen.

Noah released a shallow breath and froze.

Mutters filled the courtroom until the judge banged her gavel.

Raven's soothing ministrations over his back stilled as the judge called for the verdict.

"What say you?"

Everyone in the room leaned forward. Raven clutched Noah's forearm in a death grip. Noah's lungs refused to draw in air.

"We find the defendant, guilty."

A gale force wind expelled from Noah's chest. He shook from the inside out. Tears burned in his throat, behind his lids. He pulled Raven sideways into his lap and buried his face in her neck. "Thank Christ. Thank fucking Christ."

Her arms banded around his neck. "It's over," she whispered for his ears only. "It's going to be okay."

He yanked her closer, unable to let her go with the deluge of a shitstorm pounding him inside, needing her solid warmth and the feel of her to ground him. Hell, he might be leaving bruises.

McCannon shot to his feet and cheered. The agent looked at Noah and nodded, relief as evident as his own. "I told you we'd get justice for her. I'm just sorry it took so damn long." He glanced back at the television and swallowed. "They might appeal, but they won't win."

Noah returned his gaze to the TV, adjusting Raven in his arms so she could see. "What are they doing?"

Max set his untouched beer on the table. "The judge asked if either side objected to issuing sentencing now. Neither did."

McCannon sat back down. "He'd better get life, so help me."

After a half hour of legal crap, Rizzoli got life in prison with the possibility of parole after twenty years. He was in his seventies, so the bastard would never breathe free fucking air again.

McCannon stood and slapped Noah on the shoulder. "We just need Soreno now. We'll get him."

Noah nodded, unable to speak.

After the FBI agent left, Hintz turned to Noah. "We should beef up security until he's in custody."

Max nodded. "I agree."

Raven climbed off Noah's lap and resumed the seat next to him, grabbing his hand to lace their fingers. "Do I need to worry about my mom or Nicole?"

Max met Noah's gaze briefly before focusing on Raven. "We've had security on them since the gallery shooting. They don't know they're there. Just a precaution, but they'll be safe."

Awhile later, Raven saw the bodyguards out while Noah booted up the laptop to Skype Aubrey. His hands were still shaking when his precious niece's face filled the screen. He almost broke down, but reined the tears back.

"Hey, my love. I've got some news."

Raven leaned over his shoulder and waved to Aubrey. Then she pressed a kiss to Noah's temple and left him to relay the verdict to Aubrey, as if knowing he needed to do this alone.

Through the years, he hadn't hidden the truth from his niece or sugarcoated the danger. In doing that, she wouldn't understand why

Noah had done what he'd done and she wouldn't grasp the magnitude of the threat. She had a right to mourn and remember her parents, even if only by pictures or stories.

He forced a smile of reassurance and gave Aubrey the update. Then he logged off, poured two fingers of whiskey, and stood by the balcony doors overlooking the mountains. The burn felt good going down, heating his gut and spreading.

But the drink couldn't warm him the way Raven could. He set the glass aside and strode into their bedroom with the intention of having her naked and under him in three seconds. He needed release, to lose himself inside her, and remember there was something good waiting for him at the end of this nightmare.

He stopped short in the doorway. Raven must've had the same thought, because there she sat, on the end of his bed, firelight dancing over her pale skin from the corner hearth and not a stitch of clothing. Her hands were folded neatly in her lap, reminding him of a sub awaiting pleasure. Dark hair spilled over her shoulders and brushed the swell of her breasts. Her rose-colored nipples pebbled, begging to be sucked.

Reaching down, he stroked his length through his pants before shoving off the wall and shedding his clothes. Slowly, he strode over and stood before her.

She met his gaze, biting her lip. "What do you need tonight? Tell me."

His heart punched against his ribs. She wanted to take care of him, his needs, before her own. But what he needed tonight was to focus on her, on her pleasure, so he could eradicate the other shit in his head. "You. Just need you, baby."

She rose and set her palms on his chest, raking her nails down his belly. Rising to her toes, she kissed his neck. "You have me. Fill me completely, Noah, like only you can."

His hands tangled in her hair. Fill her completely? He had an idea for how, wanted to take her there so badly he shook. She didn't mean anal play in her request, but she never denied him. They sought pleasure together through many means, and she'd been open to every one. The last time they'd used the plug during sex he'd moved up a size to prepare her body for his. And she came hard. But was she ready for *him* yet?

Holding her nape with one hand, he skimmed his other down the length of her spine and between the cleft of her cheeks, watching her eyes the whole time. He stopped at her tight ring of muscle and kept the pad of his finger there.

Her dark eyes clouded with desire as she breathed out a rasp. "You want me there?"

"Only if you're comfortable with the idea." He leaned forward, kissing the shell of her ear. "You said to fill you completely. I want to show you what that means." He used more pressure against her hole, not penetrating, but massaging.

She whimpered deep in her throat like he'd grown accustomed to her doing when she was too revved to speak. She pushed back against his finger. Her hands grabbed his ass, nails digging into his skin. His baby wanted him to fill her there.

"I'll take that as a yes."

He picked her up and set her in the middle of the bed, then grabbed what he needed from the nightstand and joined her. Leaving the items next to her hip, he rose over her and kissed her. It took restraint not to plunder and seize. What he was about to do, where he was going to take her, required time and patience. If done right, the reward would be worth it, for both of them.

She met him, deepening the kiss and arching her back so that the rosy peaks of her nipples grazed his chest. Her fingers clutched his hair, tugging in desperation. One of many reasons why he loved her was her response to him, his touch. No man before him had been allowed, and it left him humbled. Honored.

Kissing his way down her throat, he stopped to suck her nipples on his descent. With every lash of his tongue her breathing grew more shallow, needy. He settled between her thighs and stared at her plump folds.

"Already so wet for me." He met her gaze and flicked his tongue over her opening.

She bore down, thrusting toward him for more. Her arms flew up over her head as her back bowed.

He barely resisted grinding his shaft against the mattress. Instead, he reached for the generous-sized vibrator he set next to her hip. "Spread your legs wider for me."

She did without hesitation and watched his movements as he rubbed the tip of the toy over her clit. She arched up off the mattress, her cheeks flushing.

So beautiful she was in her response that he couldn't wait. He pressed the vibrator to her opening, letting her wetness coat the tip before inserting it deeper. Her breathing soughed the farther inside he pushed, until it was fully rooted.

"Beautiful, baby." He kissed her thigh. "Does it feel good?" He twisted the toy inside her, earning a gasp. Her perfect breasts rose and fell.

"Yes, but..." Her eyelids fell closed when he twisted the toy again. She moaned.

"But what?" He leaned forward and took her clit into his mouth, sucking hard.

She cried out until he released her. "I want you inside me," she panted, cheeks crimson with desire.

He traced his thumb from the wetness around her opening to the other entrance he intended to take soon. His cock throbbed. "I will be. You said fill you completely, remember?"

She pressed her palms to the headboard. "Yes. Do it."

Reaching for the lube, he unsnapped the cap and poured a generous amount onto his fingers. He coated her crease and massaged the muscle with the pad of his fingertip, then gently inserted a finger. She clenched it greedily, causing his lungs to empty in response. So willing, so open to him. Withdrawing, he inserted two this time and let her adjust for a moment before spreading his fingers in a scissor.

Her breathing rasped in and out, her chest rising and falling. He used his other hand to work her clit, running circles around the hard little bud. Her eyes pinched tighter and her lips parted.

"You like that?"

She ground her hips. "Yes. More."

He shook his head in awe and rose to his knees. Grabbing his pillow, he slid it under her hips for a better angle. She watched him through heavy eyes, not a trace of fear in them. He swallowed hard and coated his shaft with lube, gaze holding hers.

After he was positive he was slick enough not to hurt her with penetration, he grabbed the underside of her thighs and brought her knees to her chest. "Okay?" When she nodded, his fisted his cock and rubbed it along her hole. He swallowed and met her eyes. "You tell me to stop if it's too much."

She nodded.

Using his other hand, he swirled a finger around her clit and then used the little button to turn on the vibrator.

Her eyes widened in surprise before they hazed with lust. The flush on her cheeks spread to her throat and chest as she undulated against the pulsing.

While she was in the throes, he pressed the crown of his cock inside her body until the head disappeared. He wanted to close his eyes at the tight, hot sensation, but he needed to watch her for signs of pain. After a moment, assured she was fine, he pushed a little deeper until she'd taken half his shaft. He paused, letting her adjust, shaking with the restraint.

Her eyes closed hard as her head flew back, exposing the column of her throat. Her mouth open, she rasped in air. She slowly rocked her hips with shallow ministrations, as if seeking more. "I'm okay, Noah."

Nodding, he eased further. A bead of sweat broke out on his forehead and dropped onto her belly. His chest hurt with his held breath. When he was almost rooted inside, her body offered resistance and he stopped.

"Reach up and fondle your breasts, baby."

She did, palming them in her hands and kneading the flesh. While she increased the pressure and pinched her nipples, he used his thumb to circle her clit and bring her pleasure with the discomfort. After seconds, her walls clenched around his shaft and she started rocking her hips anew.

"Just a little more, baby. Can you take it?"

"Yes," she moaned, swirling the peaks of her breasts with faster strokes.

Slowly, he slid home and ground his teeth against the urge to thrust hard. *So tight and hot.* It was different than being inside the soft, giving flesh of her wet heat. Like a band of compression, firm and searing. Not unpleasant in the least, just different.

Needing to touch more of her, to feel her petal-like skin against his, he leaned forward and kissed her. She moaned into his mouth and jerked her hips, causing him to shift inside her channel. He realized his pelvis was nudging the vibrator and pulled away to look down at her.

"You okay, baby?" He forced himself not to move. By his guestimation, using the vibrator to stimulate pleasure would ease the initial uncomfortable stretching and burning until her body grew accustomed.

Slowly, her eyes opened to reveal…hooded lust. "It hurts a little, but it's good, too. You were right. I'm so…full."

His chest ached as he cupped her cheek. He kissed her again and withdrew from her body a fraction to come back in a shallow thrust. When her moans and parted lips told him she enjoyed that, he put his weight on his hands on either side of her shoulders and offered another thrust. The position allowed him to brush her clit and bump the vibrator all in one move.

The thin membrane separating her walls was so slight he could feel the pulsing of the vibrator with every glide. His balls tightened, drawing up. Pressure in his lower back spread, and he knew he wouldn't last much longer. Just as he was about to warn her, beg her to come, her inner muscles squeezed, clamping around his aching shaft.

"Noah…" A cry wrenched from her throat. "I'm coming." She grasped his shoulders and trembled under him, hips bucking and breath seizing.

He gave her two more gentle thrusts before he stilled, dropping his forehead to her collarbone and roaring through jet after jet of his release.

Breathing heavy, he withdrew as gently as possible, removed the vibrator, and fell on top of her. He wrapped his arms around her and rolled them to the side, cradling her to him.

She curled into him, like she always did afterward, but he sensed no difference in her. He suspected all along he'd actually *see* the change, *feel* the exact moment she cracked and realized she loved him, too.

Tonight was not that night.

Every time they came together he lost more of his soul to her. She was perfection, beautiful inside and out, and the only woman he ever desired an eternity with. But if he didn't tip her emotions in his favor, if he couldn't get her to feel the same way after everything they'd done, then one day she was going to shut down for good. And his heart would stop.

The pleasure cooled and reality slammed in. Maybe she'd been right when he'd first proposed the idea of more and outed himself months ago. It was entirely possible she was too broken to love, and too stubborn to want to change. For her, safety was in routine, in what she knew. Unless she got past that and out of the dark, she'd never fully be his.

Perhaps he was holding on too tight, wishing for what could never be. He'd told her time and time again he'd wait, wouldn't push. Yet if his past taught him anything, it was that people could be ripped away in a blink. That mangled, brutal life he'd been living the past decade was finally drawing to a close, opening possibilities and promise.

But the cold sensation of numbness settled in his gut and spread like a virus. An inevitable defense. Because there was no future without Raven, and he knew she wouldn't keep him.

Chapter Twenty-Four

Raven closed her computer program and flagged Max outside her office door. "Ready for lunch with my mom?"

Her bodyguard's eyes narrowed a fraction, but his lips curved in what passed as a smile. "I'll sit off to the side, Miss Crowne, if it's all the same to you."

She patted his shoulder as she passed him. "Smart man."

He chuckled as they descended the steps. At the bottom, he held the door for her and scanned the sidewalk before falling into step with her.

The restaurant was only a couple of blocks away and she needed the air. By the tension in Max's gait, he didn't like her out in the open, but she wanted a clear head for lunch with her mom. Plus, her recent troubles with Noah were bothering her, so best to walk it off.

After they'd made love last weekend and he'd taken her to incredible new heights, Noah had…shut down. There was no other word for it. He'd mentally vacated and hadn't come back. She had no idea what had spurned the shift, and when she'd hinted at the freeze, he'd retreated more. For three nights straight, he'd worked late, claiming paperwork or an overbooked fishing charter, and crawled into bed long after he'd assumed she'd fallen asleep. He hadn't even held her. She'd felt like a trophy wife as she'd sat alone at their kitchen table with dinner cooling. Eventually, she'd thrown the meals in the garbage, unable to eat herself.

And two days ago, he'd flown to Mexico for a photo shoot by the Mayan ruins. He hadn't offered to take her along. Not that she could've broken away from the gallery this week, but an offer would've been nice. She supposed with everything going on as of late, he needed to get out of dodge for awhile. He hadn't left Alaska in at least four months. When they'd been friends and nothing more, he'd take little trips every couple of months. She'd always figured it was business, but now she knew it was Hoan's work, not Noah's. All she could do was wonder what model Hoan was using this time and if he was sleeping with her.

Corralling the thought, she shook her head. Noah would never cheat on her. Yet something was off. He was like a cold, remote version of himself.

A car backfired on the street, the loud crack splintering and echoing off the buildings. Before she knew what happened, Max had her back against a storefront and his body molded to hers.

Heart pounding, she tried to force down the nervous laugh bubbling. "Max, I'm flattered, but what would Noah say?"

He frowned at her and turned his head to scan the street. "Just a car."

"Raven? Who is that man?"

Car horns blared as Raven peeked around Max's shoulder.

Her mom. Lovely. Willow Crowne, dressed to the nines, as usual, leaned across the passenger seat of her vintage Bronco and shouted out the window. "Is that your new boyfriend?" Cars lined up behind her mother, honking. Mom was oblivious.

Max must've assumed her mother was a non-deadly threat because he stepped to Raven's side and shoved his hands in his pockets.

"Go park, Mom. I'll be right in." When the car pulled into a lot two buildings down, she eyed Max. "She might hit on you. Sure you don't want to sit with us, pretend to be my boy toy?"

He regarded her with no emotion she could decipher. "Miss Crowne, what would Noah say?" he mumbled, repeating her words back to her.

She blinked in surprise. "Ha! You made a joke."

He sighed and warily glanced around. There were more guards posted where she couldn't see, and their route had been secured long before they'd ventured out, but her guard was still nervous. Ever observant. "Come on. Let's get you inside."

The Greek diner was nearly empty when they stepped out of the wind. Fried food scented the air and made her stomach churn. Max jerked his chin to the counter, indicating he'd be right there. She nodded, spied her mother at a corner booth, and headed that way.

"He's not my boyfriend," Raven said right away to block any questions. Unwinding her scarf, she slid into the booth. Her mother was wearing a strand of pearls as artificial as her fingernails and a blue pantsuit that was older than Raven. Her short blonde hair was wild around her shoulders, her makeup painted thick. Same ole Mom. "You look nice."

She grabbed Raven's hand and pressed a kiss to her palm, something she'd been doing since Raven was a girl. "So do you, honey. How's work?"

"It's work. We're building quite the cred, though, so that's nice. You should come to one of the showings. Hoan Dwell is doing an exhibit with us next weekend." If her mom recognized the photographer's name, it didn't show on her face. And Raven was preaching to an empty room by asking her to attend a function. Her mom loved her, but she didn't get art.

"We'll see," she said with a wave, dismissing the subject. "So tell me, who is that man if not your boyfriend?" Her gaze sized up Max's body in one fell swoop.

Poor Max pretended not to notice.

"He's my bodyguard."

Mom's eyes widened. "What? Why do you need--?"

Raven held up her hand. "Calm down. He comes courtesy of Noah. Just a precaution, with him being so rich and all."

The waitress came and took their order, setting down two glasses of water and striding away.

Deciding to get the conversation out of the way, Raven rubbed her forehead. "Noah and I have been seeing each other."

Mom's hand slapped the table, her momentary dropped jaw closing in a grin. "I knew it. I knew it. Haven't I said a thousand times how perfect you two would be together?" She patted Raven's arm. "When did it start? Give me all the details."

Raven bit back a sigh. The relationship with her mom had always been more of a friendship, at least from her mother's perspective. Now that she was grown, it wasn't so bad but, as a child, Raven had never known boundaries or rules like other kids. She always assumed her mom had adopted her out of loneliness, to forever have someone to love.

She traced the condensation on her water glass with her finger. "He asked me out on a date a couple of months ago, said he always thought about it."

"Oh." Mom clapped both hands to her chest. "How romantic."

Raven guessed it was kind of romantic, if she thought about it that way. Friends to lovers and falling for what was in front of her all along. Raven had never been a particularly swoony female, preferring logic to dreams. Noah was changing that, though. She'd found herself smiling at sweet little gestures or just thinking about him for no reason and her heart would flip in her chest.

"It got pretty heavy right from the start. I've...been living with him."

Her mom squealed. The few patrons in the restaurant looked at them.

Raven tucked her head. "It's not that exciting."

"Yes, it is. Honey, you've never talked about a man with me before. Heck, I don't think you've ever had a boyfriend. This is worth celebrating."

God. She closed her eyes. "You make me sound pathetic. I have dated, you know."

"You've never been in love, though. And Noah is so dreamy and handsome and rich."

Yeah. None of that mattered to Raven. His character was his most honorable trait. As for love, she still didn't know. Something was still...off. "I think we had a fight. He's been distant."

"Have you told him you love him?"

Unlike her mother, who cracked her chest to expose her heart to any willing male, Raven was more cautious. So cautious, in fact, she couldn't even trust Noah with her heart. Again, she wondered what was wrong with her. Before she could take it back, she told her mother as much.

"Honey," Mom said, gripping Raven's hand, a placating twist to her mouth. Always with the touching, her mom. "You've been like that since you were a girl. A little distant, aloof. You keep others outside your protective bubble. I figured it was because of, you know, how you grew up before *we* became a family."

Raven stilled, the hairs on her arms raising in warning. "What do you mean?"

Mom shrugged and sipped her water. "Well, being raised by that group during your impressionable age had to leave marks. They weren't allowed to show any public displays of affection. Can you imagine? And once the children were old enough to be potty trained, they were put in different housing with other kids. That kind of separation, with no love? No wonder you're the way you are."

With every sentence, Raven's heart pounded louder and louder. She hadn't been abused. She'd had clothes on her back and food in her belly. But she'd never been shown any sign of love until her mom adopted her, and by then she'd grown to hate touch or attention. It made a lot of sense, really.

Except, even with this knowledge, how did she change for Noah to give him all of herself? Already, she'd sensed him backing off, pushing away. As if he'd done all he could and there was nothing left in him to give.

God. She didn't know how to…love.

Her throat closed, but she picked up her glass and forced a sip of water to cool it.

Mom blathered through the rest of the meal about her current boyfriend, and by the time Raven got back to the gallery, she'd been so shaken she didn't even say hello to Nicole. Walking past her assistant, she climbed the steps to her office and sank behind her desk, shaking. She had no idea how long she'd been staring at her blank monitor when Nicole strode in later.

"You have a lot of explaining to do, missy."

Raven looked up, taking in Nicole's blonde locks and green eyes. Now that was the kind of woman Noah deserved. Nicole was kind and gave her all in everything she set about doing. She loved hard and often, was pretty and sweet. And she was talking to Raven, but she hadn't heard a thing.

"I'm sorry. What were you saying?"

Nicole sighed. "I said Michael Hawthorn dropped off Hoan Dwell's photos for next week's exhibit. You never mentioned you were one of his models. You little skank." She grinned wide. "What was it like posing for him? Is he as intense as everyone claims?" She gasped. "Did you sleep with him?"

Max coughed from just outside her office door where he stood sentry, and she swore his shoulders moved in a laugh.

Raven eyed Nicole. "I didn't tell you because I wasn't positive we'd use my pictures, and the rest is private. Even from you," she added with a smile to soften the words. She tapped her fingers on the desk. "How do they look?" She hadn't seen the final product after posing. Now she was curious.

Nicole's grin turned sly. "You look hot. I mean, it's Hoan Dwell, of course they're good. But yeah. You look hot."

Raven rose. "Thanks. I'll check them out in a minute." Or as soon as her assistant left her office. They kept all pieces in a storage room off the back of the gallery, so Raven wouldn't be fooling anyone. She'd have to walk right by Nicole to get to the hallway.

Max followed her down the stairs and to storage, where she entered a key code for access. Fluorescent lights buzzed overhead, kicking in from the sensor.

This room was the only one without direct heat. She rubbed the chill from her arms and took stock of the shelves lining two walls, floor to ceiling. Some held pieces they never sold and others stored props for exhibits. Several tables lined the back wall next to the emergency exit, as well as easels and extra lighting. Noah's photos were on the matting table in the center of the space, having not been framed by Nicole yet.

Raven picked up the first shot, an eleven-by-nine of her from behind while she sat on the boulder halfway down the valley on their island. The mist in the background gave the mountains a mysterious quality. It was the pop of color that was most intriguing. Her black hair falling down her back, white snow dusting the ground, the red blanket—all mesmerizing.

She set it down and picked up another, the one where she lay in the snow. From the top of the hill, Noah captured her looking at the lens as if begging for a companion. The next shot was a close up of her with her eyes closed, snow clinging to her lashes as if asleep. Again, the photos were brilliant and catching and…real.

There was something different about these from his earlier work. She couldn't put her finger on what. She looked at the other photos on the table. His agent had also sent over two previous shoots.

In one, a woman with cocoa skin and huge brown eyes gaily ran along a deserted beach. The sand was littered with debris, the housing in the background crumbling to shambles. Yet she had a wide, infectious smile and wore nothing but a colorful sarong. A couple other shots showed her leaning against one of the graffiti laden walls or kneeling next to refuse. As intended, the ugliness of the backdrop was muted by the cheery woman offering hope among chaos.

Picking up the other shots, her gaze took in a woman with tats from neck to toe. Her blonde hair was short, spiking at odd angles, and the tips dyed pink. One of her legs was amputated above the knee and the only thing she wore was military dog tags around her neck. She was laying in a field of dandelions, arms widespread and eyes haunted by her past.

"He's good, isn't he?"

Raven turned to Max behind her and then back to the photos. "He sure is. No one captures contrast, light, or color like him. He can turn anything into beauty." Such raw, amazing talent. A direct path into the soul.

With one finger, Max pushed the photos around the table, the muscles of his forearm flexing, until he got to the one of her supposedly asleep. "That's my favorite."

She faced him, this big bear of a man who'd put himself in front of a bullet for her, and tilted her head. Max had been Noah's quiet protector since before he'd met Raven. He probably knew things about Noah that no one else did. He didn't talk much, but when he did, it typically knocked her back a step.

Studying the photo again, she bit her lip in thought. "Why's that?"

His gaze never left the table. "I've been with him at nearly every shoot, sometimes in locations at the corner of the world, and with hundreds of models." He tapped the photo again. "That's the first time he ever saw the woman and not the shot."

Yeah. Forget knocking her back a step. He'd knocked her on her ass.

Later that evening, Raven sat on the edge of the bed and stared at her cell. Since Noah had left town, he'd had Max staying in the guest room, just in case, but the company did little for her loneliness. And Noah hadn't called. Not once. He'd sent a few texts updating her on his location and to check in, but damn it, she missed his voice. Missed *him*.

Swallowing hard, she connected and waited as the other line rang.

Just as it was about to go to voicemail, Noah answered with a curt, "Everything okay?"

"Yes. I just..." She sighed. "I wanted to hear your voice."

He paused. "Did something happen?"

"No, no," she assured. "How's the shoot going? What's your model like?" She stilled. Did that make her sound like a crazy girlfriend?

"Fine. I'm at the ruins now. We're doing a night session I wanted to attempt."

He didn't answer the question about the model. Rubbing her forehead, she glanced at the ceiling. "I didn't mean to disturb you. But while you're on the line, I saw the photos for the exhibit. They look great. It was worth freezing my butt off." She laughed nervously. *Really, Raven? Nervous with Noah?*

He took so long to respond she checked to make sure they hadn't been disconnected. Finally, he answered in a low, rough voice. "I should be back on Friday."

"But your show is Friday night."

"I'll be back in time. See you then."

She opened her mouth to say she missed him, but he'd hung up. No, *I love you, Miss you*, or anything resembling affection. Even before they were lovers, he'd been warm and endearing in their friendship. What had changed? Why was he suddenly so distant?

Tears burned her eyes. Had he concluded she was a hopeless cause after all?

She froze as realization struck. He was going to leave her. He was going to leave her because she wasn't what he needed. The pain in her chest expanded, cracking ribs.

Laying sideways on the bed, she thought about the conversation with her mom at lunch. After learning weeks ago about how her parents had died, with her father right beside her, she'd been able to rationalize her fear of intimacy and make love in the missionary position. It had merely taken her knowing what the problem was and taking steps to move past it.

But an incapacity to love wasn't an easy fix. Her mom had summarized her early childhood years and puzzle pieces were snapping into place. Yet how did she get from then to now, from there to here? God. How would she even recognize if she was in love?

Maybe Noah's distance was for the best. Perhaps a clean break, before he got in any deeper and she hurt him beyond repair, was the least likely path for pain. Except the hollow, aching void inside her without him was cultivating. Consuming.

Air trapped in her lungs, refusing to expel. The room blurred in a haze of tears. Hot tracks traced down her temple, absorbing into the sheets. Her insides shredded, torn apart organ by organ. She wanted to dig her nails into her chest, claw this restless, gutting sensation out of her body. It was terrible. So damn terrible, the torture. Burying her face in a blanket, she inhaled his familiar scent of cinnamon and safety. The agony only intensified.

A wayward thought struck her through the melee of emotion. A hammer at her brain.

If this was love after all, why was she fighting to fall?

Chapter Twenty-Five

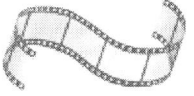

Jet-lagged, Noah folded himself into the chair behind his desk and glared at all the messages. When he'd started his business, it had been out of love for the outdoors and being in the elements. Nature soothed. Took no prisoners. Never pretended it was something it wasn't. Since all the success, he'd spent more time behind a desk than out doing what he wanted. Being Hoan on occasion allowed for reprieve, but it wasn't the same. Maybe it was time to sell.

He scrubbed his hands over his face and leaned his head back. Ten days away from Raven on his recent photo shoot had done nothing to alleviate his need for her. He thought some distance would clear his head or offer up some direction. It hadn't. He still didn't know what the fuck to do.

For a decade, he'd lived in fear, had his life whittled down to a skeleton and doing little more than going through the motions of existence. The women, the cameras, his company—nothing filled the void.

And then he'd had Raven. In his bed, his home, his heart. The pain with her absence almost made him think they could just carry on as they were. Having her, in any capacity, was better than not having her at all. Except, shit. He didn't want to be a skeleton anymore.

The past ten days had felt like the reoccurring ten years of holding back. Hot beaches, hotter women, and all he wanted was Raven and home. He shook his head. His baby was his home.

It had been cowardly to leave the way he had, not calling or telling her how badly he'd missed her. As in, the whole shoot was a wash he'd missed her that fucking much. He wondered what the absence had done to her. Did she miss him even half the amount? Was she as wrecked as him?

Probably not. In the back of his mind, this had been his last ditch attempt to push her over the edge. Selfish and perhaps conniving, but it had to be done. If he didn't see something in her eyes to note a change, they had to end the relationship. He might never breathe normally again, but he couldn't keep doing this.

Dropping his forehead on the desk, he fisted his hands. When Veronica knocked on the office door, he issued his assistant away as politely as possible without moving. Whatever it was, he'd deal with it later.

"It's...me."

His head jerked up, greedy gaze landing on Raven.

If possible, her skin seemed even more pale. Or perhaps it was the shadows under her eyes playing tricks on him. Had she lost weight? He knew every curve and dip of her body, would recognize it was her under his hands even if he were blindfolded. She *had* dropped a few pounds. Hell, she'd been thin to begin with. She had her midnight hair up in a high ponytail, wore not a stitch of makeup, and she was biting that pouty lower lip. She wasn't dressed for work—not in her skinny jeans, purple sweater and peacoat.

Not that he'd moved, but his body froze just the same. She looked like hell, which meant she'd been in hell. Just as he had. Christ. Was that hope sparking after all?

His cock swelled and, damn it to fucking hell, so did his heart.

She took a tentative step forward and blinked the wary question in her eyes away, skillfully rendering her expression blank. "How was your trip? Did the shoot go well?"

Ten days and she asked about his travels. Hope withered and died.

He straightened in his chair. "I scrapped the shoot. Got nothing useful."

"Why?"

Because I couldn't stop thinking about you. "Wasn't feeling it."

She made her way around the desk and leaned against it to stand in front of him. "I wanted to talk to you about a few things."

His hands itched to touch, to stop the longing. Somehow, he resisted. "I've got a lot to catch up on before the show tonight."

Her mouth trembled open. Hurt flashed in her eyes. "It's important."

Closing his eyes to the soft, tormented tone of her voice, he drew in air. "Then I'll try to be home early enough before we have to leave."

She bowed her head. Nodded. "Remember that day you took me out on the island?"

As if he could forget. "What about it?"

"We stopped here to pick up the boat keys and I got an idea." She looked into his eyes, and he swore it took her a lot of effort to do so. Her gaze, for the first time in memory, was wide open. Haunting and troubled. Seeking. "I pictured you swiping the items off your desk, like you made me do to mine, and taking me right here."

Her words belied her expression. She was resorting to sex instead of whatever conclusion she'd reached in his absence. She may have missed him, but she was diverting. As usual.

When he said nothing, she glanced over his shoulder. "How did you know?" Her soft voice hit him right in the chest. Twisted. "How did you know you were in love with me?"

Raven had this uncanny way of dissecting information. If she didn't have all the facts, she didn't invest. If she was asking, then something had sparked the need to know. His heart flipped and exposed its underbelly. "It's just something I know. I can't explain it."

Slowly, her gaze slid to his. "Try."

His hands fisted the chair arms. "I look at you and my heart pounds, when for years, I don't think it beat at all. You fill the cracks and crevices, take away the emptiness. When I think about the future, five years, twenty-five years down the road, you're there. And when you're not by my side, the loss is unimaginable."

Shit. He swallowed and looked away. He had no idea where that had come from, but there it was. His truth.

"Noah—"

He shook his head. And because she was trying in her own messed up way, he rose and placed his hands on her hips. Leaning in, he kissed her forehead. "We do need to talk. You're right. Let me get a few things out of the way and then I'll be home."

Her eyebrows pinched together. She stared at him for long moments, wavering on a cliff somewhere he didn't think he'd reach, and then she flicked her gaze away. Finally, she nodded and walked to the door.

"I missed you," she said over her shoulder before she was gone.

He dropped to his chair. "Me, too, baby."

Pinching the bridge of his nose, he dove into work to keep his mind off. He returned some calls, dicked with the advertising budget, and scheduled a maintenance crew to come out to inspect the equipment before delegating the rest to Veronica. By the time he sat back in his chair, he had an hour before needing to be at Elements for Hoan's exhibit.

Which left no time for the talk with Raven. Not that he knew what in the hell to say.

The condo was quiet when he returned. Too quiet. He strode into the bedroom and found his suit laid out on the bed, a note set on top.

You told me not to give up. I haven't, so don't you dare. I'll see you soon. I'll be the one wearing red. Raven, xoxo

Unsure what to make of the note, regret settled like stone in his gut. He should've carved out more time to get here before the show. Now he'd be forced to make nice until he could have her alone again. He'd swear on his life she'd meant this as an olive branch.

Hope resuscitated and held on for dear life.

He showered, shaved, and dressed to arrive at Elements in the knick of time. Hintz opened the door to let him out of the backseat, and Noah caught McCannon's unmarked car right outside. His security team manned the front door and were spread around the gallery keeping watch. Soreno wasn't getting to her tonight.

He handed his coat to an attendant and scanned the room for Raven. Though early, several patrons were already teeming about, sipping champagne and checking out Hoan's photos along the display wall to his left.

She'd used the ones he'd taken of her for the exhibit. Though she'd said she would, he still had an inkling of doubt. Raven hated being the center of attention. For her to even allow him to photograph her, never mind display them, meant she cared an awful lot. She trusted him.

Stepping closer, he bypassed his other shots and focused on the one of her reclining in the snow, looking up at the camera. He drank in her soulful expression, her pleading eyes, the trace of her smile, and bit back one of his own.

That was his baby right there. The woman who fought her way through depression with quiet strength, who faced her fears with her shoulders squared, and who gave him all of herself, piece by piece.

If he hadn't seen it before, he did now. She wasn't looking at a lens, she was looking at him. With adoration, honesty. Raven hadn't fallen for him in one crushing blow as he'd done with her. Like everything else, she'd fallen in measures, making it damn near impossible to know for certain until it slapped him in the face.

And to think, he almost let her go.

On the spot, he decided to sell Gallivanting Adventures. He'd take Raven and Aubrey all over the world. That would be his next thrill. Family. No more desks, no more schedules. He loved the outdoors, had started something solid with his company, but it was time to pass the torch. If he wanted to fish or hike or climb, he damn well would. Either Raven would come with him, or he'd hurry home to find her waiting.

He turned, searching for her, and found her in conversation with a customer. From across the room, her gaze lifted to his and held. The breath seeped out of his lungs. The red dress was new. It clung to her slight curves, accentuating the swell of her breasts and stopped at her knees. Her hair was pinned up off her nape, some tendrils loose and brushing her shoulders.

Lifting her hand, she patted her chest, then pressed her palm there and nodded at him. She'd been trying to tell him earlier, but he wouldn't listen.

She loved him.

Fuck it all to hell. Screw Hoan's show or the fans or anything else. He was going to take her home and make love to her. For hours. Days. And then they'd plan their life together, the one he never thought he'd have. The darkness? Gone.

As he took a step toward her, an elderly man sidled up next to him and started blathering about the exhibit. With great regret, he remembered how much time and effort it took for Raven to put one of these shows together, and what Hoan's prestige could mean for Elements.

Biting back a sigh, he turned to the gentleman. What was a few more hours compared to the next fifty years?

∎∎∎

Raven had finally broken free of a few customers and was determined to rescue Noah from his conversation when Nicole stepped in her way. Raven fisted her phone in her hand, banking down the irritation.

"Two things." Nicole flipped her hair over her shoulder. "First, the caterer is asking for more small serving plates. Which I'll go get from storage in a moment."

When she paused, Raven lifted her brows, unable to hide her amusement. Nicole's cheeks were flushed and she had an uncanny twinkle in her eye. Which had nothing to do with caterers or plates. "And second?"

"I find it interesting that Hoan is Noah spelled backwards. Or almost. Nice anagram." Her eyes narrowed playfully.

Briefly closing her eyes, Raven fought a grin and failed. "I'll get the plates from storage. I need a break from the crowd anyway." An hour into the showing, and they were back to back with people. "As for the other thing, do keep it mum. He has a pen name for a reason."

"I knew it," Nicole ground out, eyes alight. "So it was the best friend all along? How romantic."

"Jeez. You sound like my mom." Raven looked for Max, but couldn't find him in the throng. She'd only be gone a second anyway. "Do me a favor and find one of the security members. Let them know I'll be in the storage room so they don't freak out."

Leaving Nicole to it, Raven made her way through the crowd and down the private hallway. Punching in the code, she halted in the doorway to discover the lights already on. Since they were on a timer, she shrugged and figured Nicole had just been back here. Her assistant must've tripped the sensor.

Spotting the plates, she moved to the shelf along the wall. Nicole had already washed the dishes and set them out of their container. Raven went to put her phone down and stopped, an idea forming. Unlocking the screen, she pulled up Noah's contact and began thumbing a text.

While he'd been gone, she'd missed him terribly. The ache, the void, was immense. As if she hadn't suspected, her conversation with him today in his office confirmed it. She was in love with him. Insanely, desperately in love. The talented artist, the dedicated uncle, the smart businessman, and her best friend. She loved him. Crazy, the giddiness inside, especially because, for so many years, she didn't think she had it in her.

After the realization had hit, she'd wanted to shout it to the rafters, but this wasn't something to tell him in a note, with a room full of people, or in a text. So for now, she'd just send him a hint. Tonight, when they were alone, she'd finally give him the words he needed to hear.

Something cold and hard pressed against her temple, followed by a slow... resounding... click.

She froze. Oh God. *A gun.*

"I'll take that." A gravelly, tight voice filled her left ear. The stench of stale smoke clung to him. A hand covered with a black glove took her phone and set it on the matting table. "Move and you die."

"O-okay," she breathed. She started shaking and couldn't stop, violent tremors that wracked her whole body.

He pressed the barrel into her temple with more force and came into her line of sight. She'd recognize that massive body, cold eyes, and bald head anywhere.

Soreno. He'd found her. Worse, she was alone with no help in sight. If he got her out of the building, she was as good as dead. She was shocked he hadn't pulled the trigger to be done with it already.

She pinched her eyes closed and tried to keep her stomach contents down.

A quick *thwap* had her eyes flying open. On the matting table, he'd pinned a picture of her to the surface. With a knife. Right between her eyes.

Oh God, oh God, oh God. *Think, damn it.*

Running was not an option. Neither was screaming. He'd have a bullet in her brain before anyone even got past the access code. It would also put everyone in the building in danger.

He grabbed her arm and shoved her toward the emergency exit. "Walk."

With no other choice, she walked to the door on legs that barely held her upright. Going with him would keep Noah, Nicole, and everyone else safe. If she could buy enough time after she was gone, maybe McCannon or the bodyguards could find her before...

He pressed the gun to the back of her head. "Open the door and get in the truck. Make one sound and I'll paint the snow red with your blood."

The building's alarm code was turned off or else a siren would announce their exit. He'd planned this well to do it on a night of a showing. The FBI and Noah's security were all over the place. Someone had to see her leaving. Right?

She pushed open the door to an icy blast of wind. Her bare arms prickled with cold, bumps immediately raising her skin. Just outside, in the back alley, was a black pickup. The same one that had followed her and Max weeks ago. One of Noah's bodyguards was unconscious and bleeding in the snow. A man who'd never been on her detail, but she recognized him. He'd been watching the back of the building when she'd arrived.

"Behind the wheel." He opened the passenger door and pushed her in, forcing her to slide across the seat. The truck was idling with the heat blasting, but it did little to warm her. "Drive."

Setting her shaking hand on the gear shift, she slid it into position and eased the truck forward through the alley. When she got to the road behind the building, she warily glanced at him for direction.

"Left. Head toward The Sound."

As she drove, her mind clicked a mile a minute. She'd read somewhere once that talking to your captor and having them get to know you could make them connect, thus less likely to hurt you. Glancing at the man in the passenger seat, his jaw clenched and face hardened to steel, she didn't think that theory had a snowball's chance. Rizzoli had killed Noah's whole family. Had tried to burn Aubrey alive when she'd been just a baby. Still, it was worth a shot.

Shot. God.

At a red light, she went for broke. "Where are you from? I hinted an east coast accent. I'm originally from California."

His fist cracked across her cheek, knocking her head into the window with an additional blow. Pain and heat spread over her face where the punch landed, and in the side of her head where she connected with the window. Blood filled her mouth, metallic and warm. Black dots hovered in her peripheral.

"The light's green, bitch. Shut up and drive."

Choking back a sob, she eased her foot onto the pedal. The gallery wasn't far from Prince William Sound. She had mere minutes to come up with a plan.

Soreno wasn't wearing a seatbelt. If she floored the gas and could accelerate fast enough, he might fly through the windshield if she ran the truck into a light pole. But that was a crapshoot. He could get a shot off before reaching a decent speed. Plus, she couldn't run very far or fast in these heels and no coat.

"Turn left. Go all the way to the end."

They were at the fisherman's port. There was nothing down this way. Her heart tripped in her chest wondering if he planned to take her somewhere by boat. Her head was throbbing and her cheek smarting with an impending bruise. Dizziness threatened to swamp her. The shudders wracking her body morphed into convulsions. Her hands slipped from the wheel twice before she somehow righted them.

"Park here."

Her gaze darted around, but they were miles past the docks and in an isolated corner of the bluff. The only thing in sight was an old crab shack that had been closed for a decade. Not even a street light. On two sides of the building was the ocean, the other an endless stretch of uninhabitable woods and rock. Just…nothing.

He grabbed a fistful of her hair and pulled her out of the truck, taking strands out by the root. She bit her tongue to avoid crying out. With her hair wrapped around his fist, he leaned into the driver's side, put the truck in neutral, and watched it roll down the embankment into the ocean. It stalled for minutes before sinking into the inky black water.

He pressed the gun to her ear. "Inside."

They trudged up a hill to the shack, her heels getting trapped in the snow several times before they made it to the door. Her feet were frozen solid, needles of agony digging into her flesh. Her face hurt and her eye must be swelling shut because she could only see out of one.

With a shove between her shoulder blades, she stumbled into the shack. The floor was little more than wood planks, rotting through, and the walls didn't fare much better. Through the slats, the wind off the mountains sliced, offering little protection from the elements. Along the back wall was a soiled mattress and, in the center of the room, a pine table. A single chair was nailed to the floor beside it. Filet knives lined the table with precision.

The place smelled like rotten fish guts and year old refuse. She wretched, dry heaving until her belly cramped. Because everything had been unsettled with Noah, she hadn't the stomach to eat before the exhibit. Grateful for that now, she sucked in a deep breath to calm herself as Soreno strode to the table and flicked on a battery-powered lantern.

"The chair. Now."

Her mild relief of the chair over the soiled mattress was short-lived when she glanced at the knives again. Raped or tortured. Was there a lesser of two evils there? Her teeth chattered with enough volition to make a cracking sound over the ocean swells.

The chair was freezing, sending even more chills through her body. He used zip ties to secure her wrists to the chair arms and her ankles to the legs. Then, he straightened to full height and raked a gaze over her, making her shudder. The violation from his gaze alone left a slime-coated film over her skin.

Using the barrel of the gun, he traced a path from her collarbone to her throat. He slid the gun under her necklace and yanked it off. The ruby heart Noah had given her for Valentine's Day pinged to the floor. Soreno's free hand dropped to her wrist and unclasped her watch.

Her heart rate sped and she bit back a gasp. She'd totally forgotten about the watch. Noah had a tracking device planted inside. He had a way to find her, if she could just hold out long enough.

Fighting to control her reaction so she didn't tip off Soreno, she stared at the collar of his sweatshirt above his black coat while he removed the watch, glared at it, and shoved it in his pocket.

That's right, prick. Keep it on you so Noah can find your sorry ass.

He strode behind her, his boots thunking along the floorboards.

She closed her eyes and grit her teeth against the fear. That's exactly what he wanted, and damn if she would give him that much.

Without warning, he grabbed one of her dangling earrings and yanked.

She cried out at the searing rip of her right lobe. Tears burned her eyes as blood dripped onto her shoulders, so hot compared to her skin. She pinched her eyes closed and sucked in a breath when he reached for the other one. When he tore that one from her ear, her teeth sank into her tongue to keep from screaming.

Breaths rasping, she opened her eyes and pulled Noah's face from memory, imagined her and him playing with Aubrey on their island once their house was built. Pictured their wedding. Something small, perhaps at the Castle, and shortly after, her own belly swollen with Noah's baby. The expression he'd wield when holding their child for the first time.

Soreno's footsteps rounded the chair until he stood in front of her once more. Each thunk on the planks matched her pounding heart. Reaching for a filet knife on the table, he fisted it in his gloved hand. He brought it to her throat, the metal tip nipping her skin. Hot blood trickled down between her breasts.

She sucked in a harsh breath through her nostrils, taking in more stench from him and the room. Dead fish, stale nicotine, musty wood. The ocean roared around them, but it couldn't compare to the roaring in her ears.

Struggling not to move, to tremble, she clenched her tongue between her teeth to keep quiet. But the cold was turning her to ice, and the fear wouldn't relinquish the vise around her throat. Tears slipped from her eyes and she whimpered.

"You won't be able to cry by the time I'm done with you. I was paid extra to do more than just shoot you, or else you'd be dead already."

Oh God. Her stomach rolled.

When he brought the knife to the dip between her breasts and cut her dress in one long slice, she didn't bother to hide her reaction. A sob ripped from her chest. And when he parted the material with the blade, exposing her body to him, she gave up any hope of surviving.

The worst regret was not being able to tell Noah how much she loved him before she died.

Chapter Twenty-Six

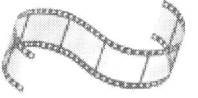

"That's how I knew it was you." Nicole grinned and sipped her champagne. "Raven would never let anyone but you see her that vulnerable." She pointed with her flute to the displayed photo in front of them. "I won't tell anyone."

Noah shoved his hands deep in his pockets. "I appreciate that." He wasn't adverse to coming out as Hoan now that the trial was over, but he'd rather things settle down first and allow the feds time to catch Soreno.

She sighed wistfully. "Such a shame, though. I harbored a secret crush on you. We would've had such beautiful babies."

He couldn't help but laugh. Just in case, he skimmed his gaze over her to avoid insult or hurt feelings. "You are quite lovely, Nicole. But I'm taken." Completely and without bounds. Would this night never end?

"I was only kidding…" She trailed off, eyes rounding.

He tracked her gaze. Two FBI agents followed McCannon through the front door. One stayed there while McCannon and the other strode across the room to Max near the rear of the gallery.

Noah's heart stopped dead. He scanned the room for Raven, but couldn't find her. Panic clutched his chest. "Where's Raven?"

"She went into the storage room a few minutes ago to get more—"

Elbowing his way through the now quiet crowd, he made his way down the hallway to the storage room. Something was wrong. Very wrong. One of the guards was holding open the door, his face grim. Max and McCannon stood at a table in the middle of the room, Hintz and another guard off to the side.

"Where's Raven?" But he knew. The cold claw of fear gripped his heart to squeeze, and he knew.

All heads turned to him.

McCannon spoke first. "She's gone. Your team searched the building. She's…gone."

No. *No, no, no.*

Soreno. The sick fuck had his Raven, doing God only knew what.

"Mr. Caldwell, you need to look at this." Max jerked his chin to the table. "Miss Crowne's assistant told me she came back here. It couldn't have been more than fifteen minutes ago."

Closing the distance, he glared at the photo of Raven, a knife pinning the picture to the table. He scrubbed a shaking hand over his mouth, too many emotions rioting against his skull.

Max handed him a cell phone. Raven's. He swiped the screen to have an unsent text pop up. She'd been texting him?

To Noah: I have something important to tell you tonite...

That was it. She must've been cut off while typing. And he knew what she'd planned to say. But now she might never get the chance. He might never hear her voice again.

He growled, throwing the phone against the wall to shove his fingers in his hair. Crawling out of his skin. He was fucking crawling out of his skin. Panic rammed his temples, seized the air in his lungs. He paced, fingers clenching into fists to yank his strands.

"Local police are on their way. As soon as we have an idea on her whereabouts—"

Noah clutched the lapels of McCannon's jacket and slammed the agent against a shelf. Items toppled around them. "Where the fuck is she? How did that bastard get in here?"

"Sir?" Hintz was at the emergency exit. "Downer is dead. He was guarding this door."

Noah's gut twisted. He shoved off of McCannon and paced the room. "Where would he take her? Did you get any leads?"

McCannon rolled his shoulders. "Not a damn thing."

They couldn't just stand around while she was being tortured, raped, killed… Noah swiveled to Hintz. "Ready the helicopter. Get in the air."

Hintz was already halfway to the door.

"They couldn't have gotten far. Watch for—" Cutting himself off, Noah straightened. "Watch. *Her watch.*" He pulled his cell out of his breast pocket with a shaking hand and fumbled with the screen to get to the app. "I had a tracking device planted in her watch months ago."

Hintz nodded. "I'll ready the heli to search by air. Text me if you get coordinates."

McCannon barked orders to his agent to pull the car up so they'd be prepared. Max commanded their guards to do the same, telling one man to hang back at the gallery and manage the confused patrons.

The fucking coordinates were still loading. "Come the fuck on," he roared just as a map pulled up. A little red dot appeared near...The Sound? The pocket by that area of the bluff was deserted. Why the hell would Soreno take her there? With the rocks and shoreline, he couldn't even dock a boat in the vicinity. Noah held the screen out to show McCannon. "Let's go."

While they amassed out the emergency exit, Noah texted the directions to Hintz and ran for the SUVs. Climbing in the passenger seat, he yelled for Max to go before his door shut.

He stared at the little ret dot on the screen, clinging to hope it meant she was still alive. He tried to recall what was out that way, not having been near that area in years. The king crab fisherman typically launched farther down if on this side of the sea. Closing his eyes, he pulled the location to mind, struggling to remember.

Shoreline. Trees. Boulders. The winding road past the port. Didn't that road stop at...?

"There's an old crab shack." His knee bounced. "Abandoned. There's only one access by car. It's surrounded by water, too rough to dock."

Max pushed the button to activate Bluetooth. When McCannon picked up, Max repeated what Noah had just said.

"He'll know we're coming then." The FBI agent cursed under his breath. "All right. We'll park as far down and out of sight as possible. Go in by foot." He paused. "If we tip him off, he'll kill her before we have a chance to bring him down. No one does a damn thing without my order."

Noah texted Hintz the update and pulled up the app again. The red dot hadn't moved. Why the hell hadn't Soreno taken her out of town? Why hole up in the shack unless...?

Unless she was already dead.

"Soreno never planned to get out." He pounded his fist on the console, frustration pummeling, his head about to explode from pressure. "He planned to hurt her to get back at me, then lure me there." Cursing, he shook his head. Ground his jaw. Fisted one hand in his hair. This waiting was killing him, eating the lining of his gut. "Christ, Max. He... Fucking Christ."

Max's fingers tightened on the wheel. "We'll get her back, Mr. Caldwell."

Tension knotted his shoulders, his spine. He looked out the window, not seeing anything but her perfect face, hoping to hell fate could bestow him just one request. He hadn't asked for any of this. Raven sure hadn't either. Throwing fairness around mattered not. Little in his life had been fair but, damn it, Soreno and Rizzoli couldn't take her away from him. Not when he'd finally had a chance with her.

"Be alive, baby."

Max cut through the southern strip of town and onto the port access. The SUV screeched to a halt several yards before the bend where the road ended. Noah got out and met McCannon at his car behind theirs. The rest of his security team followed.

McCannon's gaze swept the perimeter. "It's up that hill?"

Noah nodded. "If you follow the curve, the shack should be visible."

They ran in silence to the dead end and crouched at the base of the hill. Lowlight peeked through the slats of the shack, but he couldn't make out any sound or movement.

McCannon looked at his agent. "You go in from that end," he said, jerking his chin toward the open expanse just left of the location. Trees and boulders would offer them some cover. He pointed at one of Noah's guards. "Take him. Stay low. No shots, no one moves, unless I command."

The two men, veering left, climbed the hill in a low crouch and ran for the cover of rock.

McCannon pulled out his cell. "Cops and medics are on the way." He shoved the phone in his pocket. "How steep is the drop-off on the other side?"

Noah tried to recall. "The far end? Maybe four feet down. Not far. The other side slopes right to the water. No drop-off." The fall wasn't the problem. The temperature of the water and the currents were.

"All right," McCannon sighed. "You stay here. We're going up."

"Fuck that. No." He held out his hand to Max. "Give me a gun."

Ignoring McCannon's balking, Max pulled a 9 mm from an ankle holster and passed it over to Noah, then removed a 22 from under his coat to arm himself. His bodyguard glared at the agent. "He won't stay here. And we're wasting time."

McCannon ground his jaw and rose to check the building before ducking back down. "You two take the front. We'll come in from the right. On three. One…"

Raven's scream pierced the air, stopping Noah's heart for the third time tonight. An uneven breath frosted before his face.

He didn't wait for orders. He climbed the hill, kicking up snow in his wake. As he secured his footing atop, wood splintered. The crack echoed off the water and bounced back. The door to the shack burst wide, catching in the wind.

Soreno appeared from the opening with…*Raven.*

Noah's relief was short-lived. The bastard had wrapped her hair around his fist and had a gun to her side. But hell, she was alive. Noah stopped in his tracks, barely resisting the urge to run to her.

"FBI. Freeze!" McCannon stepped forward, gun trained.

The two men they'd sent ahead emerged from the left, weapons ready.

Soreno pulled Raven in front of him and pressed the barrel to her temple. Easing backward, he stopped at the edge of the clearing with her as a shield and the black ocean behind them. "She's dead if you come any closer."

Noah fisted his hand around the handle of his gun. Sirens wailed in the distance.

"You're surrounded," McCannon shouted. "Let her go."

They crept forward, Noah following their lead, until Soreno jerked Raven's head back and she whimpered.

"I repeat, hand her over. You have nowhere to go."

Stopping twenty feet or less from them, Noah got a good look at her for the first time. The entire right side of her face was swollen to the point her eye wouldn't open. Her wrists and ankles were red, as if Soreno had her restrained. A trail of blood dripped down her throat and stopped between her breasts. She was holding a hand to her left side, favoring the ribs. Her dress was…slashed right down the middle, flapping in the wind and exposing her pale, trembling body.

Noah's blood pressure soared, the rage raking in his chest uncontainable. Blood surged through his veins, pounded his head. He lifted his gun. "You fucking son of a bitch! What did you do to her?"

Max stepped behind him and wrapped a beefy arm around Noah, caging his arms. "Wait. Think. We move and his gun goes off."

Breaths soughing, Noah nodded. Max released him and moved back into position.

The sirens were right behind them, at the base of the hill. Red and blue lights swirled against the snow. Car doors slammed. Feet crunched and, in his peripheral, Noah caught several flashes of black as officers joined them.

"No one moves unless I say," McCannon barked, never taking his eyes from Soreno.

Noah lifted his gaze to Raven's. Behind the fear, resolve filled her eyes. A tear slipped from her open eye and traced a path through the mascara smudges.

Her throat worked a swallow. *I love you*, she mouthed.

Tears clogged his throat. The gun in his hand wavered. He sucked in a breath and mouthed the words back to her.

The whirring blades of a helicopter rent the air, kicking up wind and snow. A spotlight shown down on Raven and Soreno, so close to the water.

"Give it up," McCannon yelled over the noise of the propellers.

Soreno…grinned. "We both know how this ends, Caldwell." He shrugged. "How do you want her to die? Bullet to the brain? Or…" The fucking bastard lowered the gun to her chest. "How about the heart? Poetic, don't you think?"

Noah couldn't suck in any air. "She has nothing to do with you. Come take me. I'm who you really want. I'm the one who gave the feds evidence to lock Rizzoli away, not her."

"You think I give a shit about Rizzoli? This was a job." Soreno dragged her by the hair to his side, and for a fleeting moment, Noah thought the asshole would take him up on his offer. But he pressed the barrel to her chest, his soulless eyes narrowing on Noah. "I always preferred poetry myself."

No. *Christ, no.*

At the last second, Raven cried out and twisted her body.

Noah lunged forward just as the gun went off. The *boom* from the discharge cracked the air, so powerful the reverberation rattled his teeth. He froze mid-step. The wind punched from his chest.

Raven's eyes widened, locking on Noah. Mouth open, she stumbled back. She pressed a hand to the right side of her chest, just over her breast, and looked down. Blood seeped from between her fingers. Confusion wrinkled her forehead. And then...she stumbled off the edge.

"*Noooo...*"

Gunfire rang out, muting the helicopter blades, the roar of the ocean, his own screaming.

Soreno jerked, fell to his knees, and flopped face-first in the snow.

Noah dropped his gun and ran forward, hindered by the deep drifts of snow. Tears burned his eyes, blinding him. Losing his footing, he went down. Crawling, he reached the edge and peered over. Raven was within reach, not yet carried out by the current. Her motionless body floated between the rocks, face up. Her eyes were closed.

Max sank down by his side. "Get the medics," he yelled over his shoulder.

Noah wasn't waiting. Every second she was in the water brought her farther from him, closer to death. Except...Fucking hell. She wasn't moving.

Vaulting over the drop off, he jumped in the waist-deep water and snagged a boulder with one arm so the current couldn't pull him. Needles spiked his skin, the freezing temperature already stealing his breath and numbing his limbs. He reached out for Raven, grabbing her around the waist.

"Drag her closer," Max called. "I'll haul her up."

Fighting the violent shudders, he braced his feet between two boulders. He slid his arms under hers and yanked her up, her back against his chest.

Max lifted Raven from his arms, disappeared from view, and came back to offer both hands. Noah couldn't move. His breaths rasped in his lungs. Ice weighed down on him, the cold stabbing and biting as if he was being filleted alive.

Hands grabbed his shoulders, fisting his suit coat. And then he was back on solid ground, staring up at the stars fighting the Northern Lights for beauty. With the little strength he had left in reserve, he rolled to his side to get to Raven.

Medics had swarmed her, were taking her away.

He got up on his hands and knees, his extremities so heavy, just as more EMTs sank next to him. He couldn't take his eyes from the direction Raven had gone. They tried getting him on a gurney, but he shoved them away. *Need her.*

"Mr. Caldwell." Max set a hand on his shoulder. "Let them take care of you. We'll be in an ambulance right behind Miss Crowne."

Shuddering, eyes wet with tears, he looked at his bodyguard. "Was she…alive?" His voice broke.

Max's lips thinned, his eyes regret-laden. "I don't know."

Chapter Twenty-Seven

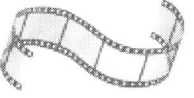

"Sir, you came in hypothermic. You need to lay back."

Noah withdrew his arm from the nurse's clutches with barely restrained homicidal impatience. "Someone fucking tell me something! Is Raven okay?"

Sighing, the nurse relented. "Let me cap off the IV and I'll go find out."

Gnashing his teeth, he jerked a nod.

She removed the tubing from his arm, flushed the part still inserted in his vein, then taped the exposed portion. "All set. I'll go hunt up a doctor for you."

As she stepped out of the cubicle, Hintz strode in and tossed some clothes and shoes on the foot of the bed. "They don't know anything yet, sir."

Now that he was detached from the IV and heart monitors, Noah rose from the bed. Pain shot up his stiff legs, but he managed to keep upright. Shoving into the sweatpants Hintz brought, Noah shucked the hospital gown and pulled the tee over his head.

"It's been two hours." Noah fisted his still damp hair. He couldn't focus on anything but getting to Raven, seeing her with his own eyes. Remembering all her injuries, her fragile body and how it had been beaten, he slammed his eyes closed and tried to swallow past the lump in his throat.

McCannon walked in, assessed Noah with a once-over, and nodded. "You're looking better. Any news on Raven?"

He growled. "No." Plopping back on the bed, he fought the urge to trash the room in frustration. This was fucking torture. He reached for his shoes and put them on.

McCannon sat in a corner chair. "Soreno's dead."

Noah wanted to bring the bastard back to life just to kill him again. Slowly. He shook his head. Scratched his jaw. "Did you see her out there? What he did to her?" His voice came out more like a whisper.

The sight of her hurt and broken haunted him, probably would until his dying day. "Christ, she has to pull through. She has to."

He didn't even know if she was alive. Figuring no news had to be good, he rubbed the back of his neck.

Hintz crossed his arms. "She's a strong lady, sir. She'll be okay."

Except his bodyguard didn't look any more confident than Noah felt. Pressing his palms to his eyes, he rocked forward.

"Mr. Caldwell?"

Jerking his gaze up, he launched off the bed to face the doctor. "Is she okay?"

In his late forties and wearing blue scrubs, the doctor looked around the room and back to him. He removed a cap to reveal dark brown waves. "Is it all right to speak in front of everyone?"

His gut twisted. Sank. *Don't be dead, baby. Don't be dead.*

Noah cleared his raw throat. "Yes."

"Let's start with the most serious first. The bullet went through her chest, below the shoulder. It just missed her lung and anything vital. It didn't require surgery. Because of her hypothermia, there was minimal blood loss. But..." The doctor tensed. "Her heart stopped once."

No. *No, no, no.*

The doctor raised his hand. "We were able to revive her in a short time, so that's a good sign. Her body temperature was very low, but through a warm IV and heating blankets, it's normal now." He sighed and looked down. "She has two broken ribs on the left side. They should heal in time on their own. The right side of her face was badly swollen, but there's no broken facial bones."

Noah breathed for the first time in hours. "I want to see her."

"They're getting her situated in ICU right now. I need to warn you. She's not out of the woods. She's hasn't gained consciousness yet and there's no telling if there will be any brain damage from her hypothermia or her heart stopping."

Noah was at the end of his rope. Clenching his fists, he met the doc's gaze. "I'm not leaving this hospital without her. Get this IV out. I want to see her."

"I'll send a nurse in with instructions."

Five minutes later, the same nurse finally returned. Biting back a string of curses, he vibrated with tension as she removed the capped IV. When she started blathering about discharge orders, he cut her off.

"Raven Crowne. What room is she in?"

The nurse looked up, startled. "Um…" She grabbed a tablet and swiped the screen, pushed a few icons. "Four-seventeen—"

He shot off the bed and strode from the room. At the end of the hall, he searched for an elevator, made his way over, and punched the button for the fourth floor. Inside, Hintz and McCannon calmly stared at the numbers while Noah paced.

Taking fucking forever…

With a ding, the doors opened. He surveyed the sign to find her room and turned right.

Max sat outside one of the rooms and stood when he saw them. "They just brought her in a few minutes ago. She's still asleep."

There were no words to match the gratefulness for what his bodyguard had done for Noah or Raven. One day, Noah would find a way to properly thank him but, for now, he just needed to see her or he'd split apart at the seams.

He laid a hand on Max's shoulder, squeezed and let go. "Can you get in touch with Raven's mother? Let her know what's going on. Nicole, too."

"Consider it done."

He turned toward the room when McCannon called his name. Noah glanced over his shoulder. "Thank you for everything. But seriously, just go the hell away until morning, McCannon."

The agent laughed as Noah entered Raven's room.

The drapes were drawn, the room dark save for the dim light above her bed. Murmurs from McCannon and the bodyguards in the hall faded with the beep of her monitor. She had an IV in one arm and a blood pressure cuff on the other.

She was so damn pale. Her face was disfigured from the swelling, the bruises stark against her skin. His eyes welled and he had to choke back a sob.

"Ah, God, baby. Look what he did to you."

Shaking, he gingerly sat on the bed by her hip and took her delicate hand in his. The solid weight of it, of being able to touch her warm, soft skin, cracked his chest wide open. Gutted. And, fuck it all. He let the tears free and reached up to brush the hair off her cheek.

"I thought you were dead." Bringing her palm to his lips, he kissed it. Held it there. "I thought I'd never see you again. Shaved twenty years off my life, baby. Swear to God."

As if he needed more confirmation, he looked at the monitors again and let the relief swallow him whole. He swiped a hand over his face and blew out an uneven breath.

He stared at the ligature marks on her wrists and fought a wave of nausea at what she might've gone through before he'd gotten to her. When they'd first begun their relationship, she couldn't even handle sex without him in restraints. They'd come so far since then. He could only hope this one terrible night didn't set back all their progress.

None of that mattered if she didn't wake up. He couldn't do this without her. For as far back as he could remember, it seemed as if every breath he took was for her. As her friend, then her lover. He wanted to be her everything. She already was his.

Rubbing his thumb across her knuckles, he thought about the ring he'd bought her before leaving for the photo shoot in Mexico. He didn't know if it was hope or idealistic stupidity that sparked the purchase, but the ring had called to him. Immediately upon seeing it, he'd known it would be perfect. The unique band had silver and gold winding together to form a knot that held a princess cut diamond. Like them, tangled in chaos.

He reluctantly let go of her hand and strode to the doorway to find Hintz. "See if you can figure out what they did with my clothes. There was something inside my coat pocket…"

He trailed off when Max held up the black box. "Thought you might ask for it."

McCannon grinned and bowed his head. Hintz stared at the ceiling, fighting a smile.

"I'm giving you a raise." Noah took the box from Max's outstretched palm.

Max shrugged. "How about tomorrow off and we'll call it even?"

There would never be an "even" here. Max had been with him, a silent protector, since before his move to Alaska. He'd watched over Raven, had taken a bullet for her, and there was no way to repay someone for that kind of dedication. "You can have the whole week off. Hell, take the month. And a raise."

Before Max could protest, Noah strode back into Raven's room, pulled a chair over to the bed, and sat. Taking her hand in his, he slipped the ring from the box and slid it onto her finger. Tightness pulled at his chest seeing it in place. Tears burned again.

"You have to wake up so I can ask you properly, baby. I'm not living a day without you, so open your eyes. Please."

The thick, black lashes fanning her cheeks didn't flutter, but he talked to her for another hour before exhaustion claimed him. Setting his head down on the mattress, he kept her hand in his and reveled in the beautiful sound of her breathing.

"No!"

He jerked awake and lifted his head.

Raven tried to pull her hand from his. Her eyes were pinched closed, her heart monitor going crazy. "No. Get away from me!"

Rising, he leaned over the bed and cupped her uninjured cheek. "Shh, baby. It's Noah. You're safe." When she relaxed a margin, he continued. "You're in the hospital, but you're okay. You're safe."

"Noah?" Her breathy whimper nearly brought him to his knees.

"Yes, baby. I'm here."

A nurse strode in and narrowed her eyes. Glancing at the monitor, she frowned. "Sir, you're upsetting her. Please—"

He glanced over his shoulder. "Back the hell off for a minute, would you?"

"Noah?"

When he turned back, Raven's eyes were open. The swelling in her face was gone, leaving only purple and blue bruises in its place. "You're okay, baby."

Her wide, confused gaze found his. "Wh-what happened?"

"Sir, you need to leave the room—"

He stroked Raven's cheek with his thumb and ignored the nurse. "You were hurt. You're in the hospital, but you're fine. You almost died, so please, just calm down."

She nodded frantically and winced. Recognition dawned in her eyes. "Soreno—"

"Is dead," he assured. "He can't hurt you anymore. Take a deep breath, baby. Calm down."

She did as he instructed and winced again, but her monitors ceased the frenzy. "He took me from the storage room."

"That's right." He didn't want her upset again and didn't want her reliving this now, so he changed the subject. "Hoan's show sold out."

A waning smile tilted the corners of her mouth and she drifted back to sleep.

The nurse huffed and stormed out, only to come back moments later with a doctor. Not the same one who'd given Noah the update last night. This one was a younger woman in her thirties with blonde hair tied back in a tight bun.

"I heard she woke up." The doctor leaned over and lifted Raven's eyelids to shine a light in each one.

Raven grimaced and swatted her hand away.

Good girl. "Yes. She was lucid."

The doctor straightened. "That's excellent. Her vitals look great, too. If she keeps this up, we can move her out of ICU." She set a hand on Raven's shoulder. "Raven, can you open your eyes for me?"

Her lashes fluttered and lifted.

After a series of questions, to which Raven responded, the doctor left.

"How are you feeling, baby?"

She seemed to take stock. "A little sore, but I'm okay." She rubbed her eyes and drew her hand back to stare unblinking at the ring. Not one muscle so much as twitched.

"I love you."

Her gaze darted to his and softened. "I love you, too." Her lower lip trembled and her eyes filled with tears. "I didn't think I'd get a chance to tell you."

Scooting closer, he took her hand and kissed her knuckles over the ring. "You're safe." He swiped her tears with his thumb. "Scared me half to death." He looked in her eyes, heart pounding. He wanted to pull her into his arms and squeeze, but they had time for that, after she healed. "I wouldn't mind hearing it again, though."

"I love you, Noah." She didn't hesitate, not even a second.

The band around his heart loosened and he had to clear his throat twice before responding. "Then marry me."

∎∎∎

Raven closed her eyes and lifted her face to the sun, basking in the glow of summer that was too short-lived for Alaska. Brine and cut grass blended with the lingering scent of rain to remind her how much life was around her. Letting the warmth consume her, she tugged Aubrey closer to her side and fought the small wave of insecurity that sometimes still rose.

It had been four months since she'd almost died, but she'd come a long way. The nightmares from her kidnapping had become infrequent. Noah was always there when she woke with a soothing voice or his solid arms enveloping her to quash the fear. Fear didn't belong in happily ever after, and today was an ever after day.

The ceremony had been short, with her and Noah reciting their own vows. Only about twenty people had been invited, and they were currently lingering on the other side of the island. It had turned out to be such a great day, but it wasn't about the wedding. Not to her. No, it was about all the wonderful things that would come afterward.

"I love the house." Aubrey rested her head on Raven's shoulder.

She opened her eyes and looked at the modern two-story log cabin before them. Stone and wood and windows, with a wraparound porch and balcony off the master bedroom. Not enormous by any standard, but it was spacious with a wide open floor plan. It was pretty perfect. Noah had been determined to have the house on their island finished by today. It had actually been completed last week, but they wouldn't move in until tonight. As a family.

Along with their new home, a modest one bedroom cabin for her mother was just down the path and within a two-minute walking distance to the Brisbins' caretaker cabin. They still needed to use a boat to get on and off the island, but the bridge would be finished by winter.

"I love it, too." She kissed Aubrey's temple and spoke against her hair. "I love you more, though, niece of mine."

Aubrey's arms banded around Raven's waist. In the distance, over the hum of music and the chatter of guests, the click of a camera sounded.

Raven shook her head and smiled. "Your uncle's up to it again. I swore I took the camera away from him today." She wouldn't mind a minute alone with him, so she gazed down at Aubrey. "Why don't you head back and eat another piece of cake?"

"Don't have to ask me twice."

The girl ran off, blonde curls bouncing, and Raven swallowed hard at the sudden emotion in her throat. Everything was so wonderful, so happy, she didn't know what to do with it all. Even Hoan had cut back on traveling, and Noah selling Gallivanting Adventures to spend more time at home had bonded them as a family even more.

Noah stepped beside her, bringing his scent of cinnamon, and kissed her neck. He looked so sexy in a tux her knees almost gave out.

"I think I like you in white more than I do in red." His heated gaze slid down the length of her simple satin-slip wedding dress. He wrapped an arm around her waist and tugged her to his hard chest, making her girly parts zing. "Though I like you in nothing best of all."

She brushed away a few strands of his blond hair that had blown over his forehead and cupped his jaw. Delight and adoration lit his blue eyes, more cerulean in the sunlight than glacier. Never knowing love could be like this, her chest swelled for the hundredth time today. "I promise to wear nothing all night long but, for now, we have guests."

His eyes narrowed. "Not soon enough."

She eyed the camera in his free hand. "I thought we agreed you wouldn't take pictures today. What's the point in hiring a photographer if you're going to sneak your camera anyway?" Even as she chided, her grin remained. God, did she love him. So much.

He didn't even try to look guilty. "Nobody captures my baby like I do. Besides, you'll only wear this dress once."

"True." She rose on her toes to kiss him.

He dropped his forehead to hers. "So tell me, bride, why are you over here all by yourself?"

She'd needed a minute to herself, to take everything in, but didn't want to tell him that because he'd worry. Besides, it wasn't as if anything was wrong. Just the opposite. "Well, husband, I was looking at our amazing new house and found two things wrong with it."

His brows knit and he turned to glance over his shoulder. "What?" He looked back at her. "Tell me."

"First, I'm afraid not all the rooms have been…christened."

A slow grin spread over his face and her heart tripped. His hands slid from her lower back to her ass. "That's a problem we'll have fixed by morning. Next?"

She bit her lip and held his gaze, even as nerves pinged in her belly. "The extra bedroom next to Aubrey's is going to need renovation." She paused. "To accommodate a crib." At the widening of his eyes, she carried on. "A rocking chair, too, for late night feedings and snuggling."

The look on his face...Oh, mercy. His expression was priceless and erased any fleeting doubt. A small wrinkle formed between his brows as his breath hitched. His lips parted in awe, his eyes tender as they searched hers. Like she'd just handed him the moon.

He shook his head as if to clear it. "Are you..." He cleared his throat. "Ah, God, baby. Really? You're pregnant?"

She nodded. Between the hospital stay and recovery afterward, it seemed she'd forgotten to take her birth control. And once her body had healed, she and Noah had made up for lost time. Hourly.

A strangled sound escaped him and he cupped her nape to draw her into his kiss. Soft and giving, his mouth slanted over hers. Mutual regret and pain were forgotten when he deepened the kiss, telling her, like he'd always tried to do, that she mattered, that he couldn't go on without her. She sent her sentiments right back, because she wasn't going anywhere. Not without him.

The past would always be there, haunting and tragic in parts, but they'd worked too hard to move beyond it to let it swallow them again.

Sweet, and not a little desperate, he broke away and dropped to his knees. Clutching her waist, he pressed a kiss to her belly and rested his forehead there. "Ah, baby. It doesn't..." When he looked up, his eyes were wet. "It doesn't seem real."

For a man who'd had his whole family wiped away, all but a little girl he gave up everything to protect, the thought of building a new family, of having that within reach, would be surreal. She'd spend her life showing him it wasn't a dream.

A warm, humid breeze skated across her skin. Dandelion seeds floated in the air, reminding her of that long ago journal entry.

I remain someone of little consequence, as if nothing more than dandelion fluff caught on a breeze.

Thanks to Noah, she wasn't that person anymore. She'd gone from being a no one to being someone's everything.

"I love you." She cupped the back of his head and wove her fingers through his hair.

"I'll never tire of hearing that. I love you." He dropped his forehead to her belly again, his hand just below with his fingers splayed. "And you, too," he whispered.

Check out these other great romances by Kelly Moran!
The Dysfunctional Test
Covington Cove Series
Return to Me
All of Me
Phantoms Trilogy
Ghost of a Promise
Give Up the Ghost
Ghost of You

Kelly Moran is a best-selling & award-winning romance author of enchanting ever-afters. She is a Catherine Award-Winner, Readers' Choice Finalist, and an Award of Excellence Finalist through RWA, plus she earned one of the 10 Best Reads by USA TODAY's HEA. Kelly's been known to say she gets her ideas from everyone and everything around her and there's always a book playing out in her head. No one who knows her bats an eyelash when she talks to herself. Her interests include: sappy movies, MLB, NFL, driving others insane, and sleeping when she can. She is a closet caffeine junkie and chocoholic, but don't tell anyone. She resides in Wisconsin with her husband, three sons, and her black lab. Most of her family lives in the Carolinas, so she spends a lot of time there as well. She loves connecting with her readers.

Website: www.AuthorKellyMoran.com

Made in the USA
Charleston, SC
12 December 2016